The Lamplighter

By

C. Brennan Knight

The Lamplighter

©2017 Caje Brennan Knight

Cover Art by ChrisCold

Cover Design by Brian Fisher

For updates on future projects, follow me on Twitter: @VanitasKnight

Chapter 1

The dream never changed, no matter how many times Pearl had dreamt it. It always began with Pearl laying on her back, prickled by the green, frail blades of fake grass beneath her. She would stare at the large, blue moon dominating the black, star-speckled sky. Music, soothing and melancholy, drifted through the air, familiar beyond the repetition of the dream, but its strange lyrics spoiled any recollection.

Sitting up, she found herself behind the large, square house where she always started the dream. Made of dark stone, the building had no doors, and rusted metal bars closed off each of its windows. But Pearl didn't care about what laid within this house. She wanted to find the music's source and followed it to the front of the house. A strange, empty village awaited her, each house similar in structure, but built of different materials. Paths of gray stone rooted the houses to a road as black as the sky above.

By this point in the dream, Pearl often found she had some lucid control of her actions, a sign of the dream's impending end. She had mentally prepared for this as best she could, and turned to the house sitting to her left. Made of wood and painted in her favorite shade of blue, the building reminded Pearl of her own home, something she had only just noticed. She sprinted to the door, the music growing louder as she reached for the door knob. She only ever made it this far, so she hesitated to touch the door, for fear of ending the dream too soon.

But she reached out again, her hand grasping the door knob and twisting. With a small shove, the door swung open without a sound and the music escaped from the house. Pearl gathered herself, unsure if she should continue into these uncharted territories, and took a step inside. The music came from a room to her left, and she peeked in to find a slender figure standing in the middle of the room, looking away from her. Never in this dream had she encountered another soul, and she recognized it as the intrusion it was. This person wasn't supposed to be here. A choking dread washed over her and seized her voice away.

As if they had sensed her, the person stood up straight, their head touching the ceiling then warping it to make more room for their abnormal height. She prayed to wake up before the person saw her, closing her eyes tight and then opening them again, hoping to find herself back in her room. Yet she remained in the dream, and the slender figure turned towards her like the hands on a watched clock. In her body's only attempt to escape, Pearl fell against the wall behind her and slid down to the floor. The slender person gazed upon her in horrid silence, their face white and blank like untouched parchment. Then came the screaming. Not from the person, but within Pearl's head, shattering her thoughts like glass and drowning out the music.

Pearl awoke screaming and shot up in her bed, only to collapse again under the ache of injuries and bruises a few days old. The collective pain kept her on her back. She tried to rub the sleep from her eyes, but found her arms stiff, heavy, and almost useless.

"Damn it." She had gotten farther in her dream than ever before, but still not far enough. If only that…something..? Her eyes creaked open like the doors of an ancient tomb, slow and encumbered. She had seen something in her dream, but couldn't remember it anymore. The more she tried to remember it, the more she forgot it, until... What was she thinking about? "So close. Maybe next time."

She propped herself up, a challenge with her arms' lack of strength, but after a few attempts, she got onto her elbows. Looking around, she discovered she wasn't in her room, but instead in a room carved into brown stone. Straw littered the center of the room, underneath the lone, hanging lantern, which illuminated all but the corners of the room. The cot Pearl laid upon, one of three in the room, felt like a stone slab, its fabric pulled so taut. The wall opposite Pearl bore the only exit, a plank door on iron hinges.

She struggled to get up, her whole body stiff and weak. Someone had dressed her in a new white shirt and pair of black pants meant for a small man. Not that Pearl minded. She preferred form fitting pants to the cumbersome frivolity of dresses. Beside her cot, a dark blue jacket and a black traveling cloak laid on top of a pair of black shoes. Underneath her shirt, bandages wrapped her entire body, the thickest of which covered her back. The wounds beneath sent jolts of pain through Pearl as she twisted to inspect her body. Where was she and what had happened that left her so wounded?

She thought back. Her fifteenth birthday. The ceremony. Crowley pulling her aside. Mrs. Graham...

The door swung open from the outside and a large man squeezed into the room, his muscles just fitting through the door frame. A sword hung sheathed at his side, and the air cooled in his presence. Pearl grimaced as a shiver traveled her

6

body, stirring pain from every injury. He looked right at Pearl and then a smile cracked across his stoic face.

"Pearl." The man spoke with her father's voice and shared his hair that had more salt than pepper, but looked twice as big as him. Then he seemed to deflate, his body shrinking in all dimensions, until meek, soft spoken George Chaucer remained. "Pearl, you're awake."

"Father?" Pearl asked, unsure and confused. A moment ago, this man towered over her, and now he stood barely an inch taller than her. In the past, her father often appeared to grow taller whenever anyone threatened Pearl, but she had thought it a show of authority and intimidation, rather than an actual transformation. "Father, what's happening? Where am I?"

He hugged her, tight at first, but eased up when Pearl yipped in pain. He held her close without speaking, and Pearl embraced him back, the warmth soothing her body and mind. A smile crept onto her face, and a tear leaked from her eye. "I don't know why, but I'm so happy to see you. It's like when you would hold me after a bad dream."

"I'm happy to see you too, Pearl. My pleasant Pearl." He broke the embrace to look over her body. "How are you feeling? Are you bleeding anywhere?"

"No. No blood," Pearl informed him, lifting her shirt enough to show her white bandages. "But my whole body hurts. What happened to me?"

"What was the last thing you remember?"

"The ceremony. The gifting of the swords. I had just become a Lamplighter, then Crowley pulled me aside to speak to me. Something to do with Mrs. Graham…did something happen to her?"

Her father frowned, his eyes drifting away from Pearl as he processed her words. "The ceremony was four days ago. You've been asleep for past three, and much has transpired in that time." He motioned to the door. "Come. I'll explain on the way."

Pearl followed her father into a hallway carved out of rock and earth, with wooden planks and beams supporting the ceiling and walls. Braziers made of dark metal hung on the earthen parts of the walls, and illuminated the hall with a soft, warm glow, though something unsettling undermined the warmth, hidden in the shadows beyond the light's edge. The hall stretched to the left and the right outside the room. Her father went left and then took the first right, with Pearl close behind him. He knew his way through these halls, despite the lack of any markings.

Pearl paid attention to each turn, creating a map in her head back to the room they started from, but soon found herself lost. Nondescript wooden doors, their frames cut into the earth, led to mysterious rooms beyond. Pearl peeked through those she found ajar, but found most rooms empty, filled with hungering darkness that devoured the light from the hallway. One room had a fire burning in the corner, the light from which shined on the weapons hanging from the walls. Swords, knives, and axes shimmered and flickered in and out of the shadows.

"Father, where are we?"

"Three days ago, you and two other newly anointed Lamplighters escorted Mrs. Graham into the woods while she picked berries. Ordinarily, we wouldn't have sent an escort for something so simple, but with the disappearances of late, Father Alexander and the other leaders didn't want anyone leaving the village alone. When you didn't return after Nightfall, we sent out a search party." An urgency and gravitas Pearl didn't know he possessed filled his voice. "You alone were found."

A mumbling of human voices echoed down the hall towards them, the faint sound filling the silent hallways like the rumbling of thunder. Her father continued, "I had brought you home to allow you to rest, but the town began to fall apart. Once

Frederick threatened to burn our house down just to get to you, I moved you here."

Frederick Crowley, the lesser of the two Crowley brothers. So much so, no one acknowledged Frederick's last name, and referred to his elder brother Michael solely as 'Crowley.' Just hearing the name 'Frederick' made Pearl's heart leap in fear.

"Now, he's on a witch hunt. This was all he needed to get people to openly hate you, and they've formed a mob around him."

"But where is 'here?'"

"The church. We're under the church right now." He raised a finger to his lips as they reached the door from which the voices came. They hushed when he knocked on the door and, after a few seconds of shuffling around on the other side, Brother Gen opened the door.

"Good. She's awake. We're running out of time," Father Alexander exclaimed from within, his calm authority evident in his words, but the compassion of the priest Pearl knew abandoned. He sat at the lone table in the room. His nimble fingers danced on the surface of a small golden orb, sealing it shut. He didn't rise to greet her. His bony body had lost its frailty, its angles now harsh and dangerous. His white beard looked less like soft wool and more like a thistle bush. "Nightfall approaches and the mob outside grows restless. We must send her now."

"Perhaps we could stall them for another evening?" Brother Gen offered, his gentle voice and innate kindness the few things unchanged in the world Pearl had awoken in. He stood a head taller than her, and his brown hair cut like a bowl worn as a hat. "The Khaous grow smarter and more monstrous every night. Let's send Pearl in the morning, then await support from Sanctuary."

"Any reinforcements from Sanctuary would arrive too late. Little holds Frederick's crowd from torching the church after he set George's house ablaze with no opposition or repercussions. And that's assuming we're worth the resources." Father Alexander held out the golden orb towards Pearl. "With our duties here, there is no better choice than Pearl. No one is as prepared as she. Take it."

"Where are we going?" Pearl rolled the walnut sized orb around in her hand. The polished gold glowed in the light of the fire burning in the corner. Seams on the top half marked the small, sealed hatches holding whatever it contained. She slid her finger over the smooth bottom half.

"You alone are making this journey," Father Alexander answered. He pointed at Brother Gen, and ordered, "Prepare the horse."

11

As Brother Gen left, Father Alexander continued. "He will direct you from the village. Listen to his instructions, lest you want to find yourself lost in the forest and easy prey for the Khaous. Your ultimate destination is the house of a man named Theseus Aeker. It is imperative you deliver that orb to him."

"And what about you?" Pearl looked to her father. "Why can you not come with me?"

"Well..." He stared at Pearl and looked for the answer on her face. "The lamps are dark, and I am a Lamplighter. I must stay and protect those under my charge."

"Those under your..." Pearl repeated in confusion. "Those people? The ones you said let our house burn down?!? Frederick, who would have me burned on a stake?!? We should leave all of them to the demons, and go to this Theseus's house together."

"My duty is to protect the living and to serve justice. I do not have to like those I defend, but I must defend them nonetheless. You must learn to put your emotions aside when you serve higher ideals." Pearl couldn't think of a rebuttal, her father's unwavering certainty ending the conversation.

"Pearl, respect our decisions." Father Alexander now sat bent and tired, his body worn by burdens he alone shouldered, the commanding elder replaced by a broken old man. "Every moment of our lives, we find ourselves at a crossroads of seemingly endless decisions. For your father and I, our decisions of the past have made the way forward apparent. But for you, there is no clear path, just a multitude of potential. This journey we're sending you on…it's hypocritical, yes, us choosing your fate for you, but you must survive, and no other path can insure this. Respect our decisions and live."

"But—"

"The journey is long." Pearl's father put a hand on her shoulder and waved her towards the door. "You must leave soon, or Nightfall will descend upon you."

"Pearl," Father Alexander called out to stop her. His eyes watered as he looked at her and his mouth moved without a word, until he found what he wanted to say. "We are at war. And in war, blood shed is inevitable. But we, the soldiers, were supposed to be the only ones to bleed."

"This little experiment of yours would say otherwise," Pearl's father remarked, his voice laced with venom, as he guided Pearl from the room. Again, they entered the maze of earthen halls. Her father led the way, never second guessing his path. Neither of them spoke, and in the silence, the echoes of their footsteps filled the space around them. A hallway to Pearl's left darkened as they passed, the braziers dimming themselves to smoldering embers. Shadows poured into more of the hallways, as if night had seeped underground. They made one last turn and reached a wooden staircase that led into the dirt ceiling. Then Pearl's eyes adjusted and she saw a pair of wooden doors at the top. At last, her father spoke, "This will take you outside the town. No matter what, do not return until we send for you. I...the bags have most of your things in them. I thought they'd make your stay at Lightholme comfortable."

His voice wavered, betraying the sorrow behind his stern face, so when they hugged, it was she who comforted him. For the most part. Not knowing when she would see her father again worried Pearl. They had no one else but each other, and neither knew what it meant to be apart. But she promised, "I'll see you soon."

When her father released her from his spine cracking embrace, he smiled and wiped the single tear falling from his eye before it reached his cheek. "My pleasant Pearl. Travel swift and safe, and with my love."

"Good bye, father." Pearl lingered to watch her father disappear around the corner. Had her farewell been enough? Unanswered, the question sat in her heart like hot lead. She climbed the stairs and pressed against the doors above her. Her first push failed, and loosened dirt sprinkled onto her face. The second and third attempts bore no success, but by the fourth, she found her footing and when she pushed against the doors, amber daylight seeped through the gap between them. With a final shove, Pearl threw open the right door. Brother Gen, waiting in his humble brown robes, caught the door and set it down with a soft thud. She didn't need his help, but when he offered a hand, she accepted it. Pearl had never seen Brother Gen leave Father Alexander's side, so the awkward sight of him alone disturbed Pearl.

"You've said your farewells?" He showed emotion on few occasions, but today he appeared shaken. His wide eyes jumped from side to side, and his body moved in a series of flinches, as though he expected an impending attack at any moment. The soft, warm glow of the setting sun belied the dangers of the impending Nightfall, an hour or so away by the sun's position. "And you have the orb?"

Pearl nodded and revealed the golden ball. He smiled, another oddity, and handed her a sheathed sword, which she recognized as her own. Chosen during the ceremony, its lightness afforded her some speed, yet it had enough weight to do some damage. She pulled the sword out to check its edge, then wrapped the sheath's belt around her waist. A short walk away, tied to a tree, a stallion with a coat as black as the forest's depths waited. Pearl ran her hand over his body. She had ridden before, and knew a horse built for speed when she saw one.

Brother Gen helped her mount up and handed her the reins. The steed considered his rider and made his reluctant approval known with a snort. Brother Gen pointed into the woods and told her, "Ride North. Directly North. The way is clear of trees, for the most part, so you can travel along a straight path. Lightholme is surrounded by a wall of trees, much like the one around New Bethlehem, but tighter and denser. Do not slow as you approach it. It will part for Nocturn. And keep the orb safe."

A fevered commotion arose in town, drawing both of their attentions with a jerk. "Godspeed, Pearl. We will...send for you. When we can."

"Take care of my father," Pearl called out before he disappeared into the hidden stairway. He gave a simple nod in response, then closed the doors. From without, Pearl saw no trace of the doors nor of any way to open them. Pearl rode around the trees, getting a feel for Nocturne, yet her eyes kept finding their way back to the town.

She had to ride out now before Nightfall, but curiosity demanded otherwise. Pearl needed to see what had happened to her town and its people. She needed to know her father would be safe. She returned the ebon steed to the same tree Gen had him tied to, and snuck back to the town, moving from tree to tree to conceal herself. She spied the white of the church's back wall and when she reached it, she found a small cross carving, deep and smooth, as if cut with a burning knife. She had never seen it before.

She peeked around the corner and saw the backs of a mob surrounding the entrance of the church. She joined them without a sound, and acted like part of the crowd, an easy feat with all eyes focused forward. A few eyes drifted towards her, but no one noticed her arrival. Though the church remained sacred in their eyes, the mob waited to trap anyone leaving the building.

A large fire burning in the middle of the square before the church grew in bursts as the Lamplighters in the crowd took turns throwing their lanterns in with unhesitant abandon. If each lantern did burn with the Fire of God, then the Fire of God burned like any other flame. Its crimson light branded the church doors with the twisting shadows of the four grim, wooden crosses awaiting their victims. Then a titanic, crooked shadow grew upon the church, as a man took his place before the crosses and shouted to everyone and himself.

"Lies and liars. That is what we have suffered for years," Frederick barked, his voice as filthy as his unbathed, unshaven face. His pale visage gave the impression of perpetual illness. Though he stood a few inches taller than Pearl, despite being twice her age, he terrified her more than anyone else. Of those townsfolk who hated Pearl and spoke nothing but cruel words to her, Frederick hated her the most and his cruel words stung the worst. His sharp, dark eyes swept the crowd. Pearl felt his gaze passing over her, piercing into her being and judging her for the black sins he suspected her of committing. It took all of Pearl's willpower not to cower. "Supposed men of God poisoning our town with whispers of sin and allowing the demonic spawn of a witch to run amongst our children."

He raised his fist at the church. "Come out, false priests. Bring forth the demon and her father. Judgment awaits."

The crackling of thunder and a shower of splinters answered him as the doors of the church exploded open. From within, armed for battle and without a trace of mercy, three men emerged, looking like knights from a fairy tale. Brother Gen wielded a large cleaver-like sword in each hand, and had traded his robes for chainmail armor beneath black garb. His golden gloves glimmered in the firelight, the embedded gems sparkling in a rainbow of colors. Father Alexander had replaced his white robes with black ones, and Pearl caught the shine of chainmail within his sleeves. In one hand he held a sword with a white hilt, and in the other a tall staff of polished, white wood. George Chaucer held only his Lamplighter's sword, but on his arms and legs had donned black plate armor, decorated with gold floral detail. Each man stood a foot taller and newfound muscles filled their battle attire. Pearl, and the rest of the crowd, stared at the three accused with mouths agape.

Father Alexander's voice shook the earth and the souls of the mob when he spoke. "And who shall be our judge?"

"I, God's eyes on Earth, his hunter of sins." Frederick believed every word he said. "As far as I'm concerned, you have already been judged and are guilty of your sins."

"And what about all of you?" Brother Gen spoke to the crowd, his gaze pressing down on them. The entire crowd shifted in discomfort, but only a few failed to meet his gaze.

"What does your brother Michael say of this, Frederick?" Pearl's father pointed his blade at the man. Frederick motioned to two young Lamplighters, boys Pearl's age, who brought him a brown, burlap sack. He grabbed the bag by its bottom and turned it over. Crowley's head rolled out, hacked off at the neck with fresh, shallow cuts. A pool of blood welled beneath his head when it came to rest. Pearl gasped, but covered her mouth to not draw attention to herself, since the display surprised no one else. Michael Crowley had been the only other friend of Pearl and her father, and had often silenced his brother's hatred. But now his head laid still, hair soaked with blood, mouth gaped, and eyes glossed like marble.

Father Alexander trembled with rage and growled a warning. "Your misguided and ignorant zealotry has lead you down a dark path, and damned those foolish enough to follow you. You hold the swords we gave you not for this town's defense, but shed its blood. Nightfall approaches and you have forsaken the Fire of God, your only ward against the demons. If you are not destroyed this night, you will spend your last, fleeting hours being hunted."

The orange sun had fallen low. With none of the lamps lit, shadows had engulfed the rest of the town. Nothing existed beyond the town square. Yet only Pearl, her father, and the two priests worried about this.

"I am the hunter," Frederick roared so loud, his body shook. Spittle sprayed from his face like dragon's breath. "Demons, sinners, and blasphemers are my prey. For my service, God will protect this town."

"Enough!" Pearl's father reached out to stop Father Alexander, but the elder priest stepped forward and stamped his staff on the church steps. Thunder rolled across the cloudless, starless sky above. "Enough of your madness and your deafening hypocrisy, Frederick Crowley. You seek sinners? One stands before me. A murderer of his only kin."

Father Alexander and Brother Gen shot off the church's steps, two blurs lunging towards Frederick. His hand darted to the sword on his hip, but not fast enough. The priests had covered the distance between them and him, and readied to strike. Yet he had only freed a sliver of his blade. For the first time, Pearl saw fear and doubt in the eyes of the one she feared most.

Then, nothing happened. The priests hung in the air and Frederick froze, caught in a moment of time, like puppets abandoned in the middle of an act. A pillar of light descended from the sky and encompassed them. The hairs on Pearl's body rose and a tingling sensation danced across her skin. The air stilled, then became energized, pungent with a strange, sharp smell.

From on high and all around them, a voice spoke a single unrecognizable, but understandable word. A word of punishment and woe unto the guilty.

A flash of light blinded the entire town and thunder, so loud and close, threw it off its feet. Pearl's ear rung and her vision blurred. As the ringing subsided and her hearing returned, Pearl could hear panicked screaming coming from all around her. When her hearing returned in full, she recognized her own screams amongst the other indistinguishable sounds of terror. Confusion choked the air and the world shrunk until its entirety fit within the square, suffocating and trapping them.

In their blindness, people stumbled and tripped over one another. Those who had regained their senses searched for their family and friends who had stood right next to them only moments ago. Pearl's focus fell upon the scorched earth where the light had caught Father Alexander, Brother Gen, and Frederick. Nothing remained of them. Not a scrap of clothing, char of flesh, or blackened bone.

The mob's panic reached a fever pitch, as people abandoned their searches and ran to the assumed safety of their homes, trampling those too slow to rise to their feet. A roar loud enough to shake the buildings silenced the frenzied crowd. Timber snapped under the weight of a great beast in the outer ring of houses. A stream of fire shot into the sky, lighting the town. As the flames burned away, New Bethlehem returned to darkness.

Over the second town-shaking roar, Pearl heard her father commanding from the church. "Everyone, to the church! Get to holy ground! To me, Lamplighters! TO ME!"

A collective realization washed over the people of New Bethlehem. The lamps were dark, the Lamplighters were scattered, and the demons were upon them. It had come and they were unprepared. The cursed, twilight moment between day and night when God is blind to the world and demons spawn freely upon it.

Nightfall.

Chapter 2

Hushed ignorance filled the church. People sought answers from one another, despite no one knowing what had transpired. Some said they had just witnessed God's wrath, punishment for the dead men's sins. Others suggested Frederick had ascended, rewarded for his righteousness. And some cursed the priests for an extravagant escape.

Pearl suffered the blind speculations running amok from the pew she sat in. Much like the rest of the modest church, the pews were crafted from a light brown wood and left unpainted. The lone remarkable feature, the altar adorned with golden crucifixes on each face and one standing on top, sat in reverence at the front. From there, every Sunday, Father Alexander would deliver his sermons and perform his sacraments. Now it served as a back rest for a mother holding a lifeless boy with twisted legs.

When her father's call to arms went out, those who answered had brought with them any injured during the panic. Few families had managed to stay together during the confusion. Parents worried over missing children, and children cried for absent parents. Neighbors consoled each other as best as they could, but when the demon outside roared, a silent dread washed over the refuge.

Eyes shifted between the burning town outside and Pearl's father, the only one to step up and take command. Lamplighters gathered around him at the church's doors, asking hundreds of questions. Some questioned themselves, doubting their reasons for staying. Yet their mere presence inspired hope in the huddled, fearful masses within the church. That so many Lamplighters had heeded his call pleased her father, but his smile crumbled into a scowl when his eyes met Pearl's.

"Pearl!" His bark startled everyone and his gaze split the crowd around him. The anger he reserved for Frederick now fell upon her. "What the hell are you doing here?"

His outburst at his daughter drew curious looks from everyone else in the church. The tears in Pearl's eyes cooled his fury and he lowered his voice. "Nevermind. It's far too late to leave now."

He stepped up onto the pew next to him and addressed the rest of the refugees. "Our town is under assault, besieged by a singular demon from the southwest. That it is alone is a godsend, but may also speak to a ferocity no other demon wishes to be near. Lamplighters, and those willing to help…go out into the town. Bring every living soul you find here. These sanctified grounds will protect us. Since the lamps are dark and most of you have…discarded your lanterns, be swift and ever-vigilant."

"And what of you?" Pearl asked to her father's annoyance. "What will you be doing?"

"I will confront the demon," he explained, not taking his stern eyes off Pearl. "Defeat it if I can. Otherwise, distract it for as long as possible."

Back to the rest of the group, he raised his sword. "This is our home and we are honor bound to protect it. Draw your blades and go forth."

Those listening gave a short "Rah!" and took off into the night, scattering to the different parts of the town. As Pearl ran out the door with them, her father caught her by the arm and pulled her back inside. "Not you."

"I'm as much a Lamplighter as anyone else," Pearl protested. She whipped her arm free of his grasp and stepped away from him. "Why shouldn't I risk my life while you are?"

"You think sacrifice is a privilege? Living is a privilege. You not taking advantage of it is a spit in the face of those trying to protect you."

"But I—" He grabbed her arm again, and yanked her outside. He pointed at the town ablaze before them.

"Can't you see this is beyond you?!?" Another roar shook the town as the demon, a serpent five houses in length, reared up from among the homes. Its fangs, each as long as a man is tall, shined in the flames streaming out of its mouth. "Don't you understand? No Lamplighter in this town is prepared for a situation like this."

He turned her to face him, and she saw the tears in his eyes. "I... I don't know if I can beat this Khaous. Even if I do... When an alpha Khaous hunts, the swarm lingers back, cautious not to get in its way. So even if I manage to fell that beast, there is only so much I can do when the swarm descends upon us. Even holy ground..."

He dropped his eyes towards the ground and took a deep breath. He pulled Pearl in for a hug, and gave her a smile. "I love you, Pearl. Your duty is to protect the church and its occupants until my return."

"But I could...yes, father," she resigned. He chuckled.

"I never thought I would become a father, you know." He marched down the stairs and charged off towards the demon. Pearl watched him disappear among the houses still standing, then examined those under her charge. Not half an hour ago, these people wanted to see her burning on a cross, their eyes aflame with hate. Now, they cowered, whispering desperate prayers, and looked to Pearl as their guardian. But when Pearl looked at them, all she felt was an apathy that voided any sympathy she had. She wanted to do as her father told her, but these people...They had made her entire life a hell. They didn't deserve her protection. She gave them one last glance, turned her back to them, and sprinted off into the night before anyone could stop her. Lamplighters escorting townsfolk to the church took no notice of her as she passed, their eyes locked on the paths in front of them as they hustled to safety.

When she reached the outer ring of houses, Pearl found herself alone. The demon and her father fought further down the row, and the other Lamplighters scurried about elsewhere. She stepped into the first house she saw, and found it dark and empty. She called out into the house, but no one responded. *I guess someone's already been here,* she assumed. Then she heard the shuffling of feet and the shushing of voices. She shouted out, "Hello? Is there anyone here?"

When no answer came, she shouted again. "If there's anyone here, go to the church. You'll be safe there."

This occurred at the next few houses Pearl checked. Though each house appeared abandoned, soft, careful noises drifted within them, as if the inhabitants hid just out of sight. The wind brought an unseasonal chill, and despite the fires spreading throughout the town, the air grew cold. Pearl shivered, pulling at her jacket for a little warmth, and hurried to the next house.

"Is there anyone in here?" The house answered with the familiar silence and darkness. "It's Pearl Chaucer. I'm here to take you to the church. It's safe there."

"Pearl." A voice, somewhere in the house, repeated her name like an echo.

"Is...Is someone here?" Pearl walked down the hall, listening for the voice.

"Here," a girl's voice echoed from behind the door to her left. The bedroom within looked like Pearl's, with a bed tucked in the corner, a nightstand next to it, and a dresser on the opposite wall. A pale, blonde girl about Pearl's age stood in the middle of the room, waiting. Her eyes swirled and glowed like moonlight on rippling water. "Right here. Always here. At least...from my point of view. You're here too. Now...and then. From my point of view."

"Wha—" Pearl didn't have time for crazed rambling, and offered the girl her hand. "You need to come with me. Right now. Where's your family? Are they here?"

"They'll all be here. The holy and the damned, one in the same, when the layers collapsed into one plane. It's all just layers from the side. At her lover's battle cry, the girl in the sun will abandon her machines. The dragon knight will come to redeem himself for a post abandoned, and a promise broken. He doesn't know it, but the stars will summon him when the cocoon is complete. The mother, the father, the brother…they'll be here. All of them. At least…from my point of view." Her tone, steady and flat, lulled Pearl into a daze, her heavy eyes falling shut. The sound of shattering timber outside snapped her awake. A strong wind raged against the house and room heated like the inside of an oven. The girl had wasted enough time. Pearl grabbed her hand, but released it when the girl shrieked at Pearl's touch.

"What the hell are <u>you</u> doing here?" The girl's father stood in the doorway, his wife behind him with a baby in her arms. "Leave. Now. We want nothing to do with you."

"What? No. You don't understand. The town is under attack."

"We don't care, witchspawn." He spat at her feet. "You and your kind bring nothing but trouble. Leave us be."

The ceiling groaned and caved a little, before a chunk fell to Pearl's feet. Flames flicked over the sides of the hole above them, and the edges glowed with embers. "Your house is burning down on top of you."

The man and his wife took a step closer to one another, and he wrapped his arm around her. "We'd rather burn here than the hell you would lead us to."

Pearl protested, but jumped when a hand grabbed her shoulder. The pale girl embraced Pearl and whispered into her ear. "Leave us. They will not budge. We'll see each other again. Remember? Here. At least, from my point of view."

The girl went to her family, embraced them, and they bowed their heads in prayer. Pearl, determined in her mission, took a step towards them, but a loud crackling from the ceiling gave her pause. Pearl shouted a warning, but too late. A large wooden beam engulfed in flames fell upon the family. A quick, last second jump backwards spared Pearl their fate. Flames leapt from the rubble, ignited the room, and surrounded her. Smoke and showers of burning specks choked the air, and clouded her vision.

Needing an escape, Pearl's eyes went to the fallen, wooden beam ramping out the hole in the ceiling. She balanced atop it, but as she walked up, the fire-chewed beam gave out with a crunch. She jumped, an awkward motion off a falling surface, and crashed to the center of the room. Stuck once again, she searched for another way out, but found none.

"Damn," she swore to the sky. But no one answered. No one would. For all anyone who cared knew, she was still in the church. No one was coming to save her. "God damn it. I...I just wanted to help."

The stars watched, indifferent to her plight, as the fires closed in and ash fell around her. A mote of ash landed on her nose and, to her surprise, melted. She wiped the droplet away, then stared shocked at the snow falling upon her. A sudden, frigid gust blew down upon the house, extinguishing the flames and freezing the ruins. With the way clear, Pearl scrambled over the debris in front of the doorway, not questioning from where her snowy miracle had come. The demon roared outside, close enough to make the house tremble. Pearl drew her sword, but knew trying to fight the demon would get her killed.

She rushed out of the house, making a beeline for the cover of the homes across the road, but the moment her foot hit the ground, it slid out from under her. She reached back to catch herself, but her hand slipped as well, dropping her onto her back, where she stayed as she glided the rest of the way. Ice, inches thick, covered the ground and every building. Reflected fire light set the whole town aglow. The demon, which sounded right on top of her a moment ago, had vanished from sight. Blanketed by ice and snow, the town slumbered in silence.

"Pearl?!" Pearl's father shouted down from a nearby rooftop, blade in one hand and a strange mist wrapped around the other. Cuts covered his body, and heat had warped the armor on his arms and legs. "Damn it all, you're too much like your mother. What did I tel—TAKE COVER!"

An explosive inferno tore the house in front of Pearl asunder, throwing her backwards amidst a storm of splinters. She crashed against the wall of the house behind her. From the epicenter of the blast, the demon emerged with a roar. Its pitch black scales, darker than shadows, absorbed the light of the fire around it. It wore a mask made of black iron bolted onto its face and extending up into three spear points like a trident. Though the mask had no holes for its eyes, Pearl felt its gaze upon her, and her breath escaped her body. Behind rows of sharp serpent's teeth, within jaws large enough to swallow Pearl whole, fire burned red hot and savage. It reared its head back and opened its mouth, the flames within swirling together into a ball. Pearl's mind went through the thoughts of standing up and running away, but her body failed to respond, fear holding her in place.

A bolt of ice struck the side of the demon's face, knocking its aim away from Pearl as it launched the fireball. The orb shot out like a giant cannon ball and blew away a house across the road with a ground-shaking explosion. The demon twisted back towards Pearl, but more ice bolts found their mark on its body. Frost built up over the demon until it trapped the demon within a block of ice. Pearl's eyes followed the ice back to its source. From the rooftop he stood upon, her father held out his mist covered left hand, his palm trained on the demon.

"That will hold it." He pointed his left hand down as he jumped off the roof, and he slid down the ramp formed by the ice pouring from his palm. "But not for long. Get back to the church."

"Let me help you." Pearl pointed to the mist hovering around his hand. "How are you—"

He silenced her with a raised hand, and gestured to the block of ice holding the demon. The ice's core glowed and the surface cracked. The demon fought to free itself. "Go. Quickly. I'll cover you."

They only took a few steps before a large cracking sound struck their ears like a whip. Her father screamed something as ice poured from his hands, forming a curved wall in front of them. The demon's breath crashed against the wall, flames flickering around the edges. Ice and fire met at a standstill, but, inch by inch, the wall melted, revealing more of the demon. Her father redirected his stream of ice towards the serpent's mouth, but still the inferno crept towards them. A tongue of fire licked her father's hand, and he screamed in pain. A wave of cold air erupted from his hands, knocking Pearl and himself off their feet, and throwing the demon into the house behind it. The building collapsed on top of it, burying it beneath a pile of lumber and stone.

"Gods! Gggh my hands!" Hardened, popped blisters cratered the blackened flesh on her father's hands, the mists surrounding them evaporated. He looked to Pearl, his eyes wide with terror. "You-agh- must flee now. My magic...I can't...I can't use it. And this town is as good as cinders."

"But the church?" Pearl stumbled over her words, shaken by the sight of her father so injured and vulnerable. "You said it would protect—"

"A lie, Pearl. A trick Father Alexander used in the town's early days," he growled. He glared at his hands. His fingers twitched, then bent into hook shapes. "Before the Lamplighters...before the candles. If they saw what I could do, they would burn me at the stake. Even when I'm trying to save them."

The demon twisted and shook the ruins of the house off its body. It roared to the forest, and the cries and howls of innumerable demons awaiting beyond the trees surrounding the town answered. So many…Too many… Pearl's fear kept her on the ground next to her father. He shouted at her to run, but she couldn't respond. The demon rose up, its head drawn back. It hesitated, torn between Pearl and her injured father. Its gaze settled on him, then snapped back to her. It opened its jaws, and shot forwards towards Pearl, an arrow burning with hellfire.

Time crawled and sprinted through the next few moments. A strong hand gripped Pearl's shoulder and threw her backwards. Her father stood up between her and the demon, standing straight and with head high. His charred right hand held his lantern out towards the demon. Jaws snapped, bones cracked, and flesh tore. Pearl's father wavered and stumbled, then collapsed backwards into Pearl's lap. The serpent demon shrieked, whipping its head around, coiling its body tight then flailing and tumbling around, as if trying to escape the grasp of some invisible hand. Fire spilled out of its mouth. Flaming jets launched scales off its body. The demon rose and roared one last time before the inferno within it erupted and consumed it. A wave of air so hot Pearl thought it had burned her face and charred her hair crashed over her. As explosive as it raged to life, the firestorm died away with a whisper. Nothing of the demon remained, save the smothering earth where it had stood.

Stunned near speechless, Pearl could only ask, "How?"

"The Fire of God," her father coughed. His body shook in her arms. "An antithesis of the Khaous. Doesn't quite agree with them. But it was a costly gambit. We no longer have the lantern's protective light and…" He stared at the bloody stump of his arm in silence. Then his body shook words from him. "The Khaous, the demons, will be swarming the town any minute now. Killing their leader bought us their hesitation. Hierarchies are new among them, worthy of study. If only…Pearl, find your horse and ride to Theseus. The cross on the church will point the way."

"But father—"

"I cannot be saved. It is too far to carry me and I will only slow the horse. You must live. I do this out of love…as I've done so much else…" He stared into her eyes and smiled. "No father wants to see his child hurt, and will do anything to protect them. But it's pointless because inevitably it is your path to choose. It will be scary. Who you are now will not be the person you are tomorrow. But if you stay true to yourself, the path ahead will make itself known. I'm…sorry I won't be here to see it."

His burnt left hand reached up to touch her hair. He saw his grotesque hand, and lowered it again. "You have your mother's eyes, and her hair."

He grew heavier in her arms. His mouth moved, but no words came out. His eyelids fought to stay open, but the weight of death pulled them shut. Tears fell from Pearl's eyes onto his face, and Pearl wiped them away in hurry. She lifted him from her lap, placed him onto the ground, and covered him with his cloak. "I love you, father. Good...good bye."

A loud shriek from the forest told her to leave. Heart aching and tears blinding her, Pearl ran back to Nocturn. As she ran through the town square, she noticed the townspeople had shut the doors to the church. Had they even waited for Pearl and her father to return? The rustling of the restless demons around the town sped her to the back of the church. She raised her lantern and found the carving of the cross. Back pressed against the wall, she ran straight forward until she found her horse. Despite the demon cries, Nocturn had remained and she thanked him for it. Pearl hopped onto the saddle and cut the horse free with a swing of her sword. A yelp and a strike of her heels sent her steed into a full gallop.

Shadows rushed past them as they rode into the black of the forest. Pearl raised her lantern, illuminating the darkness around her. Demons of various shape and size swarmed into the town, ignoring her in favor of the prey packed together like hens in a coop. Pearl lowered her head and kept her eyes forward. Focusing on the path before her almost kept the victory cries of the demons and the mortified screams of their victims out of her mind.

Almost.

Chapter 3

'When comes the twilight hour, woe onto any soul among those trees." This was the warning the village elders often spoke to discourage children from wandering into the forest. But the children knew to stay in the village. No one escaped childhood without catching a glimpse of a demon stalking just beyond the tree line.

Pearl remembered the woman holding the babe as their house fell upon them and gripped the reins tighter to stop herself from becoming sick. As the horse leapt over yet another fallen tree, Pearl recalled another saying, something her father had told her. 'When they're not hunting, the demons have little concern for subtlety. The destruction left in their wake will always mark their paths.' This deep in the woods, few trees stood unscathed, scarred by tooth and claw if they stood at all. Moonlight through the thinning foliage illuminated the well beaten path she traveled alone.

It had taken an hour of riding before Pearl could no longer hear the screams coming from New Bethlehem. *A matter of distance,* she prayed. The realization she needed those screams frightened her more than the idea of a town with no one left to scream. Undistracted, the demons' focus would shift to the lone rider deep in their territory. Pearl urged Nocturn to run faster, as she drew her sword and scanned the trees around her. The passive and unmoving shadows of the forest now followed her.

A clicking sound coming from the creaking branches above and to her left broke the silence. She raised her lantern towards the sounds and they faded as the demon fled from the light. Despite it all, this reassured Pearl and a smile slipped onto her face. In time, the clicking returned, now accompanied by snorting and growling and the rumbling of a hundred feet. Demons pursued her on either side, but with the lantern too close to her face, Pearl could only make out their vague shapes. They followed as close as they could, the lantern's glow warding them off.

A commotion among the demons to Pearl's left forced her horse to veer right off the path it alone knew. After a minute, she heard nothing on her left side, but felt something watching her from the darkness. The clicking above her grew louder and overtook her. A demon leapt out of the trees ahead of

41

her, a giant lizard with obsidian skin, its tongue whipping out of its mouth as it prepared to strike Pearl with it. She tried to steer the horse out of the way, but it refused to leave the course it had just corrected. The demon's tongue shot out at her like a spear, a burst of wind brushing past her as it missed her. Pearl raised her sword, ready to attack.

A whisper fell on Pearl and sent a shiver down her spine. Pressure wrapped around her head, squeezing so tight, she thought it might collapse in on itself. The whispering continued and bore into her mind as a cacophony of sounds no human could replicate. Pearl's own thoughts scattered, and colors and spikes of anger, despair, and glee replaced them. The world around her changed colors, sometimes shifting into black and white. Something lived in and ruled the in-between. Long, slender fingers dragged through her mind. A storm of strange geometry surrounded her and the immensity threatened to break through the bulwarks of her sanity.

Pearl blinked, then looked around. The horse had traveled further into the forest, and trees now choked the path, forcing the steed to avoid them with subtle turns. She tried to get her bearings. Her hands had a death grip on the reins. Her sword hung sheathed on her waist, her lantern on the opposite side. Something had ripped away the small bags of her possessions her father had packed. Everything had changed, as if she had ridden for several minutes, but mere seconds had passed. Thinking back, the image of a pale scarecrow dressed in black flashed into her mind. Something pressed against the back of her head, and crooked thoughts crept into her head like worms and shook her entire body. The dark, incomprehensible whispers slipped off her like fingers running through her hair, and she realized the shaking came from the ground, powerful tremors in regular intervals, like footsteps.

A scan of the treeline failed to reveal the source. Movement out of the corner of her eye made her look to her right, yet she saw nothing. The ground shook again and a nest of startled birds took flight from a tree behind her. Pearl's eyes followed them up, when she noticed something in the distance above the treetops. It seemed as though a mountain had appeared in the middle of the forest, but as she watched, she saw it sway back and forth in time with the tremors. A terrified prayer escaped her lips as a whisper, then she screamed at her horse. "Faster. We have to go faster."

The demon stood high above the trees, and wielded one in its hands like a club. Its black flesh made it indistinguishable from the night sky, if not for the moon's glow and the bright stars. With its head plopped between its shoulders without a neck in between, it looked more like a mountain. A mouth, filled with jagged, pointed teeth, stretched across its gluttonous belly. The back of the mouth glowed like a dying furnace, and smoke seeped from the corners. Its eyes, two small black dots on its head, were locked on Pearl. She didn't know where it had come from or how it had seen her through the trees, but it followed her, gaining on her with each slow, heavy step, and growing as it drew closer.

At her command, the horse had sped up, but not enough to put distance between them and the demon. She could now hear the trees splintering under the giant's earth-shaking steps and the crunch of the ground beneath its weight. She felt the rush of air around the demon's tree-club as the demon swung it back and forth. The sounds of restless demons brought the forest to life. They waited for the giant to make the kill, so they might fight over the scraps. The hordes surrounded her on every side, forcing her forward and leaving no other avenue of escape.

A speck of light shone through the trees ahead of her, and a faint glow hovered above the trees. So close, she refused to die now. Deafening noise crashed against her from all sides. Demons pushed against one another, growling and snapping at each other in impatience, drawing closer to Pearl, but not so close as to get in the giant's way. Trees snapped like twigs behind her. She kept her eye on the light growing with each gallop, and focused on nothing else. A cleared route before her revealed a wall of trees woven together by their branches and roots, separated at their trunks by a space wide enough to squeeze a reaching arm through. The trees directly in front of her bent out of the way, forming an opening large enough for a horse to jump through. Light from the wall of trees pouring into the forest.

"Good boy," Pearl whispered, before crying out and snapping the reins. The earth trembled with hellish force as the giant's circular foot crashed down a stride away, putting them well within swinging distance of its tree-club. Nocturn let loose whatever reserves of strength he had left, bolting forward so fast, Pearl almost fell backwards out of her saddle. The other demons swarming after her, flowing into the cleared path like a dark flood, realizing their giant brother wouldn't catch the steed and its rider.

The knot in Pearl's stomach erupted as a scream as the horse leapt through the gap and the wave of demons crashed into the wall of trees. The horse's landing threw Pearl from her saddle and she rolled to break her fall, the soft grass making the tumble more forgiving. As she laid on it, exhaustion washed over her body, but she couldn't rest with the demons right behind her. The giant demon reached the tree wall and grabbed the trees to uproot them like weeds.

The sound of a gunshot cracked like a whip, silencing all else, and a beam of light stretched out from behind Pearl to the giant's no-neck. On contact, the light blew off the demon's upper torso and head, leaving behind a circular wound in its chest. Its arms clung to its body on sinew of flesh and the fire in its stomach-mouth went dark, until the giant demon dispersed like a mountain of black dust in the wind. The beam of light continued through the demon and twinkled like a star before fading into the night's abyss.

"Damn it." A growl came from behind Pearl, followed by the sound of wood hitting the ground and snapping. She turned and gaped at the lone house in middle of the forest, shining with gold light from its windows, a beacon in dark nowhere. Two chimneys rose on opposite ends of the roof, with a glass orb, with what looked like a small sun inside it, propped up by a metal pole between them. Besides these differences, and its second floor, the house was designed like a stone and wood house of New Bethlehem. A man stood in the doorway, his features silhouetted by the light behind them, a broken rifle at his feet. "Damn thing always breaks after the first shot."

As Pearl moved up the hill away from the demons, the man drew a pistol from his belt and pointed it into Pearl's face. "And what the hell are you doing here?"

Before Pearl could answer, he leaned forward and took a closer look. "Who the hell are you?"

He was a head-and-a-half taller than her, with broad shoulders and a jaw of chiseled stone. The gray scruff of his unshaven face and the peppering over his trimmed hair hinted at his age..

"Theseus?" she asked, but he didn't hear her. He grabbed her shoulder and whipped her around to look at the forest.

"Eyes forward. They'll be breaching the trees soon," he told her without looking at her.

After the brief panic of the giant demon's death, the swarm of demons had resumed their pursuit of Pearl, surging through the trees and rushing up the hill. The man didn't move to stop them as they drew closer, and his grip on Pearl's shoulder trapped her next to him. A feline-shaped demon bolted to the front of the swarm and leapt high into the air from halfway up the hill. Pearl struggled to escape as the demon descended towards them, a dark blemish growing on the moon, claws the size of sickles pointed at them.

The man's rifle, the only weapon capable of killing the demon before it reached them, laid broken and useless on the ground. Pearl considered throwing her sword, but that would leave her defenseless and she lacked any confidence in making a lethal throw. The man remained statuesque, prepared to die steps from the safety of his house. Then, a stream of light, gold with a red core and wider than the rifle's beam, shot out from the miniature sun on the roof and disintegrated the feline demon on contact. Multiple rays fired out as demons got too close to the house, none coming closer than twenty strides away.

Pearl flinched at the sizzling-cracking sound the demons made when they burst from the beam, and each time she did, the man would laugh. The demons didn't relent in their impossible approach, and soon, both Pearl and the man numbed to the spectacle. With his grip on her shoulder, the man spun her to face the house and pointed inside. "Wait inside while I gather your horse. Thought I saw the beast run round back."

He kept close to the house as he disappeared around the corner. Pearl didn't hesitate to get inside, stepping into a small parlor so warm and comfortable, Pearl forgot she didn't live here. Despite the exterior's similarities to the houses of New Bethlehem, the interior looked like no building Pearl had ever seen. Polished wood planks floored the room, stretched down the hallway to her left, composed the staircase to the second floor, and continued into the room to her right through a wide opening. A forest green, circular rug laid in the middle of the floor, the sole furnishing in the room.

She searched for the source of the abundance of light she had seen from the outside, but saw no candles or fires burning. Instead, she noticed glass tubes glowing with golden light running along the ceiling, down the hallway and through the wall into the room off to her right. The glass tubes in the parlor traced the edges of the ceiling, providing the whole room with illumination. All of the glowing tubes on this floor connected to a thicker tube running up to the second floor and down the center of a metal, spiral staircase in the back corner of the room. What caused the tubes to glow, Pearl couldn't even guess. Like the rest of the house, it seemed magical.

The door clicked shut behind, followed by another click as cold metal pressed against the back of her head. "Don't move, girl. You may not be who I thought you were, but doesn't mean I won't put you down all the same. Who are you and why are you here? Unless another colony sprung up over night, you're from New Bethlehem, right?"

"It's not there anymore," Pearl blurted out. "When I left, it was on fire and overrun with demons. I'm only alive because Father Alexander sent me. I'm supposed to give you this."

She reached for her pocket, but the man stopped her. "Ah ah ah. Stop. No sudden movements. Slowly." She nodded and slid her hand into her pocket. A groan of disappointment escaped her when she felt a disk instead of an orb. The orb's gold plating hadn't protected it from her fall off the horse. Tiny crystals and metal strings poked out of the broken device. The man snatched the orb out of her hand and studied the damage as he lowered his pistol to his side. "Quite a beating this took, but no doubt it came from Alexander. What did you say your name was?"

"Pearl Chaucer." The man stopped fiddling with the orb for a second, then resumed turning it over and over again.

"So you're George's girl. What happened to him?" When Pearl described her father's final battle, the man chuckled. "Just like George. Great man, but not much of a fighter. Relied on magic a bit too much, but that's what happens when you become an exorcist and a warder." The frown on Pearl's face stoned his face. "I'm sorry. I didn't mean to speak poorly of a dead man. Merely reminiscing. And your mother?"

"She died giving birth to my brother when I was young. He didn't survive either," Pearl choked back her sobs, her loneliness overwhelming her. "Please. Just tell me you're Theseus. Tell me I've made it to Lightholme."

"I am, and you have. Theseus Aeker. Welcome to Lightholme, my home." They shook hands, then stood in silence, both unsure of what to do next. Theseus studied her, his eyes jumping around her face. "Sorry about before. You looked like someone else in the dark. Same brown hair and everything...you said your mother was dead?"

"Yes." Pearl bowed her head and mumbled a brief prayer for her mother and brother, a daily practice she had learned from her father. Theseus scoffed in annoyance, but said nothing. "Did you know her?"

"No," he spat in disgust, then saw Pearl's hurt confusion. "Apologies. It's a tad late and looking at this flat orb, I know I'll be up for a few more hours repairing it. Not to mention everything your arrival has brought. My thoughts are scattered, and need time to come to gather, so we'll discuss matters in the morning. No doubt your journey was tiring. Even on the fastest horse, the trip is a long three hours."

A yawn escaped Pearl's mouth at the word 'tiring." Without anything to fight or run from, the energy in her body crashed. Theseus waved Pearl to the stairs and led her to the second floor. He walked her past the shut doors at the top of the stairs and on the left side of the corridor, to the door standing ajar at the end. Someone had prepared the simple room for an anticipated occupant, polishing the wood of the dresser and making the bed with clean linens. The lone window in the room looked out onto the clearing around the house and the forest threatening to swallow them whole. Moonlight alone illuminated the room, until a globe of light on the ceiling came to life when Theseus touched a small white button-like switch on the wall next to the door.

"Take anything you want from the dresser. Most it won't fit. We'll gather what does from the other room in the morning. Did you bring anything with you?"

"I did, but something ripped them off the horse." More things the demons had taken from her. "All I have now is my sword, this lantern, and these clothes."

"I'm sorry to hear that," Theseus assured her. "It hurts, losing that which we care about. One can only take so much…If you need something in the middle of the night, my room is at the end there.

Though, I doubt I'll be in there anytime soon. If that's the case, you saw those stairs going down in the corner downstairs? Just shout for me from the top. Here, let me take that lantern. It will be hard to sleep with the light. Do you need anything?"

Pearl looked around the room given to her. Her intrusion discomforted her, and the events of the day tearing at her soul. She wanted to curl into a ball on the bed and cry her eyes raw. But she told Theseus, "I think I just want to sleep."

Theseus waited for more, but when she said nothing, he bowed his head, said his goodnights, and closed the door behind himself as he left. She listened to his footsteps descending the stairs, and once he left ear-shot, she hit the button-switch as Theseus had done. In the dark, she changed into the clothes she pulled from the dresser, none fitting proper, all tailored for a large man. She laid down in the bed, but sleep would not come. The immensity of the day's event crushed her spirit and she wept into the pillows so Theseus couldn't hear.

When Pearl was younger, and had trouble sleeping, her mother would sing to her. It was the only thing Pearl really remembered of her mother, time having eroded every other memory away. Once her mother passed, Pearl's father would sing the lullaby to her when she needed to hear it. But now she had no one, save herself, to comfort her. So, through her softer sobs, Pearl sang herself asleep.

Good night, sleep tight.
Until the morning's light.
Rest on your head on the pillow.
Your warm, comfy pillow.

*   *   *

Pearl awoke in a bright room, confused when she rolled onto her back and stared at the dark globe on the ceiling. It dawned on her that the light came through the window and, judging by the sun's position, she had slept to late morning. The pants she wore kept falling, forcing her to catch them every time she let go. The shirt dropped to her knees like a white dress. While in the dark, the size of her new clothes hadn't concerned her, but in the light of day, they embarrassed her. Gutting the dresser proved less than useful. Every shirt and undergarment she changed into hung loose on her, but she managed to find a pair of pants that stayed at her waist, so she considered it an improvement.

"Theseus," she called as she left her room. The wooden floor warmed her bare feet as she walked towards his door. An indistinguishable call from Theseus echoed out of the large opening in the foyer below and she followed it into the largest kitchen Pearl had ever seen. Waist high cabinets on the ground lined the walls in front of her and to her right, forming an "L" shape in the corner. Another row of cabinets, suspended above the rest, paralleled them, with a break among them on the far wall for a window looking out the side of the house. An island of counter space filled the center of the room, with two water spigots facing in opposite directions above two metal tubs embedded into the island, though Pearl didn't see any pumps to draw water. Two sets of double doors composed most of the wall to her immediate left, while a large window made from a single sheet of glass comprised the leftmost wall. The light from this wall flooded the room, washing away any trace of shade. Theseus sat at the table in front of the window-wall, his back to her. Their carpenter had used a dark wood for the table, the six chairs surrounding it, and every other wooden structure in the kitchen. Theseus heard her approach and turned towards her, a fresh green apple with a single bite taken out of it in his hand.

"Morning." Theseus waved his apple at the two double doors. "Food's in there, if you're hungry."

The rumble of Pearl's stomach answered him and she turned away with an embarrassed smile. A burst of cold air surprised her when she opened the leftmost set of doors. The cupboard remained chilled within and Pearl shivered as she eyed all of the food inside, shelves of cheese, milk, fruits, meats, and breads. She searched, but couldn't find the ice cooling it all. "How is it so cold?"

Theseus didn't leave his chair and waved his apple at the doors. "On the inside of the door frame. Nordic runes carved into the wood cool the air. Don't touch 'em or you'll freeze your damn fingers off. And just grab something already. There's something we need to discuss."

Apples sat in a wooden bowl on a shelf at eye-level and she took a greedy bite of a green one, its tartness puckering her mouth. She snagged a small block of white cheese on her way out, nudged the doors shut with her foot and took a seat across from Theseus. The sun shining through the window warmed her back like a blanket. The gold orb, once again an orb, albeit dented and cracked in places, rested on the table between them. With a bite of his apple, Theseus tapped the orb and it hummed to life. Pearl opened her mouth to ask a question, but Theseus silenced her with a finger to his lips.

After a few seconds of humming, the top plates of the orb parted, revealing several chipped crystals embedded within. Again, Theseus had to silence Pearl. The crystals glowed and an image of a miniature Father Alexander materialized above the orb. Theseus glared at Pearl, and she kept her questions screaming within her. She reached out and, when Theseus did nothing to stop her, poked the tiny Father Alexander, her finger going right through him. And then it spoke.

"Greetings, Theseus. Greetings, Pearl." Pearl gasped, but forgot to close her mouth afterwards, and stared at the spectre of Father Alexander like a simpleton. "If you're listen-chchzzzzzz-periment a failure. We've been unable to contact London, so relay-bzzzzz"

"What's happening?" Pearl couldn't help but ask. Theseus sighed in resignation.

"I fixed it as best I could, but some of the damage was irreversible," he explained. "The crackling we're hearing is because the orb can't decipher the broken parts of the crystals. The message is clearer further along, but we won't be able to hear any of it if you keep asking questions."

They hadn't missed anything important, as the image of Father Alexander buzzed, hissed, and crackled his way through a recount of the events leading up to Pearl's awakening in the chambers beneath the church and her receiving the orb. Pearl shrunk in her seat at the mention of the deaths of Mrs. Graham and Pearl's Lamplighter peers in the forest, even more so when Father Alexander reported how the town laid blame on Pearl. But Theseus said nothing and didn't even glance at her.

"With my death, you're in command of the Brotherhood's operations in the new world and I charge you with two final tasks. First, if she is willing, Pearl is to be trained and made a member of the Brotherhood. You are the only two people equipped to undertake the second task: traveling to the Black Hill to destroy the Black Heart within. A heavy burden, I know, and a contingency reserved for the worst situations, but it is a threat to the whole of existence and must be eradicated. Understand, were you a lesser man, I would not leave such a task in your hands. You are as fine a Brother as any man or woman I've had the honor of working and fighting beside."

Father Alexander stopped and lowered his head. His shoulders shook once, but then he picked his head up and continued. "There is one more point I need to mention, which I passed over earlier for the sake of the narrative of past events. Based on- cahzzzurrr-"

"This is the last break," Theseus informed Pearl. "Though it seems to have corrupted a large portion of information."

"—raises some alarming possible explanations. One, they are not truly immune to the power of

58

Chaos. Two, some other party has them under their sway. Or three…" Dread burdened his words. "Our weapons have discovered themselves. Gods know what would happen if it turned on London." Father Alexander fell silent again and Pearl could make out a tear smaller than an ant falling down the elder priest's tiny visage. "I know you abandoned your faith long ago, with the losses you have endured, but may any god that favors you bless you and protect you. I've always been proud of you. You and Gen may not have been my flesh and blood, but I took as much pride in you as any father would his sons. Good bye, Theseus Aeker. I…Godspeed."

Theseus tried to turn away and hide them, but Pearl saw the few tears rolling down his face. He wiped them away with a rough brush of his hand, then glared at the small image of Father Alexander with glistening eyes. "Stupid, old man."

Chapter 4

Layers of dust coated the room between Theseus's and Pearl's, and as Theseus opened the door, the freshest layer rolled away from them like smoke in a breeze. Four bunkbeds stood in wait, their sheets flat and long undisturbed.

"Who slept in this room?" Pearl followed Theseus inside, and looked back at the footprints they left behind. In front of each bunk sat a footlocker, all four coated in dust. Theseus knelt in front of the closest footlocker on the left, the cleanest one by the look of it, though it still had gone untouched for years.

"No one." Theseus threw open the footlocker and dug through the piles of clothes within. "The only guests Lightholme has had prior to you, with the exception of Father Alexander and Brother Gen, were seven elders of the Brotherhood and a battalion of the Brotherhood's warriors, all of whom arrived before this level was complete. Here, try these on."

Pearl took the pile of clothes Theseus handed her to her room to change into them. Odd enough, they fit as if tailored for her, from the shoes to the jacket. When Pearl asked about the coincidence, Theseus explained, "The room is stocked for any member, male and female, of any size. Not too strange to find clothes that fit well. Now, head to the foyer. I'll join you shortly to give you a tour."

The hallway opposite the kitchen remained the only part of the first floor unknown to Pearl, so they started there. A narrow hallway, they walked single file with Pearl leading towards a dark brown door at the end. A door partway down the hall led to a small privy, with a metal sink, toilet, and tub inside. The door at the end of the hall refused to budge until Pearl planted her back foot down and pushed with all of her weight.

Warm air escaped through the opened door. The room beyond stretched from the front of the house to the back, much like the kitchen. Shelves covered the walls, each packed with, and some bending under the weight of, more books than Pearl ever thought existed, in a variety of color and size. Theseus stepped in front of her and gestured to the entirety of the room with a sweep of his arms. "Welcome to the study. On these shelves are the records of the Brotherhood's history as well as some of the greatest pieces literature the world has ever seen. Though none of these are the originals. Those the Brotherhood safeguards in London."

"How many books are in here?" A small fire burned in the corner fireplace, though most of the room's light came from the ceiling high windows on the far wall. The green carpeted floor cushioned Pearl's feet like soft grass.

"I'm not sure. When I first built the study, I didn't have enough books to fill one set of shelves. During my travels, I acquired more and more books, and sent them here. Never thought to count them though." Theseus leaned against the ornate, wooden desk in front of the windows and stared at one of the bookshelves, his eyes looking through and beyond it. "There was a time when I didn't think I would return here."

"Why is that?" Theseus didn't hear Pearl's question. He had lost himself in a memory, a smile sneaking onto his face. He returned to the here and now, and the smile disappeared.

"I'm sorry. My past seems to be haunting me." He took a moment to register his surroundings. He tapped his hands on the desk. "I made this. The desk and the chair."

The chair looked more like a throne, larger than the leather chairs in front of the fireplace and as decorated as the desk, both constructed from the same dark wood as the kitchen. Pearl ran her fingers over the polished surface. Though impressive, the desk and chair failed to hold Pearl's interest. "It's...very nice. Didn't you also make the rifle that broke last night?"

"It did break," Theseus growled. Pearl realized what she said and apologized immediately. "I can't deny it. For some reason, the longer the barrel is, the more unstable they become after a shot is fired. Though I haven't tried..." He trailed off, but caught him. "To answer your question, yes, I built the rifle. I built most of what you see."

"That's truly impressive," Pearl admitted as she looked at everything with a new perspective. "Who taught you how to build all of this?"

"I taught myself." Theseus made his way towards the door, beckoning for Pearl to follow. "Most of the years I lived here were spent alone. Beyond my regular training, I had plenty of time to learn a variety of skills. Failures revealed my mistakes, guiding me to success."

Back in the foyer, Pearl asked, "By yourself for years? Wasn't it lonely?"

Theseus glanced at his bedroom door. "No...no. I told you I had guests. Other Brothers of the Flame and the like. Now enough talk. The sublevels are vast and we have much to do."

Pearl had noticed the metal stairs in the corner of the room the night before. A small wooden wall guarded the edge of the opening. The lit tube, connected to the other lights in the house, ran down and through the central pole the stairs circled around, but when Pearl looked down, she saw nothing but darkness. Their clanking descent echoed up from the earthen depths like bells tolling from forgotten antiquity. Bony fingers of cold air crept up Pearl's leg, a haunting shiver shaking her body, and she longed for the sword in her room.

She only knew they had reached their first stop when six torches, hanging next to six doors, illuminated a circular metal landing at Theseus's arrival. Five of the doors he waved off. "More bunks and two additional privies. All of which haven't been used in years. But this room..." He gestured to the remaining door. "This is one of the more impressive rooms within Lightholme."

Sunlight blinded Pearl as it exploded out of the opening door. She held onto Theseus's shirt to follow him outside as her eyes adjusted. When she could see, she found green grass under her and a blue sky decorated with thin, white clouds above her. The sun hid behind a cloud passing on the soft breeze, then returned to warm Pearl and the animals around her. Wooden fencing separated and penned cows, chickens, pigs, sheep, and even a few horses. Grazing on fresh hay and drinking fresh water, they took no notice of Pearl or Theseus. Beyond the pens, a variety of crops grew in a bountiful garden. A small orchard stood on the other side of the garden, the trees forming a lane to a natural incline uniform enough to act as a ramp. All around them, a sea of green grass, dotted with patches of colorful wild flowers, stretched to the horizon and rippled in the breeze. Pearl had never seen so much open space. All her life, trees had surrounded her.

"Trees…" She turned to Theseus. "This isn't real. We're underground and even if we weren't, the house is in the middle of the forest."

"Take a walk." Theseus nodded his head at the fields to Pearl's left. She studied him, suspicious of what might happen, then made her way towards the field, only to run into a wall a few feet from the pens. Theseus bent over laughing as Pearl nursed her face, which had taken the brunt of the collision, now flushed with hot embarrassment. Aware of wall now, she reached out and touched the wall. The scenery appeared painted on, but Pearl couldn't tell how it could move.

"Later," Theseus dismissed her questions, wiping a tear of laughter from his eye. "The walls and the ceiling fool the animals, and some people, into thinking they're outside. The ramp in the back lets them outside for some real fresh air and actual sunlight. I can't stand to see them trapped in here, but they attract the Khaous. So, we built a Farm room."

"Why do you need all of this?" Pearl realized she could see the corners of the wall. "And who did you mean by 'we'? I thought you lived alone."

"I did and do. Brother Gen would visit and help me with most of the house's more...complicated rooms," Theseus explained. He motioned for Pearl to follow him out of the room. "And why else would the house have a farm room? Where do you think the food comes from? Come, time to move on."

Theseus skipped the next landing, saying they would return there in the future. Pearl noted the strange, glowing symbols carved into the lone door. Skipping the next few landings, more storage according to Theseus, they stopped on a landing with a single door. Within, blocks of stone connected into pairs by thin metal rods, horizontal bars elevated on poles and other strange equipment rested on a thin, yet firm mattress-like covering on the floor. It gave under Pearl's weight, though not by much, making it only somewhat softer than the stone beneath. "This is the gymnasium, where you'll undertake most of your physical training and shape your body into a weapon."

The next landing had only three doors, but Theseus showed her that they all led to the same circular room. In the first part of the rooms, wooden crates held stockpiles of various metal near a stone smelter. A forge stood further along the circle, next to an anvil and rack of tools. The path ended at a collection of handmade armor and weapons, sitting next to the crates of raw material waited. "The connected room represent the cycle of blacksmithing. You smelt the raw metal into a more malleable state, then shape it with the forge and anvil, and once it is to your liking, you place it in the armory. Then you start anew at the beginning."

The woodshop and the workshop, rooms identical to the smithing room, took up the next two floors. In the woodshop, large piles of various woods awaited a carpenter to shape them at the work tables, each with their own box of tools. Theseus described the workshop as a place for 'tinkering.' Unlike the woodshop or smithing room, the piles of raw material gave way to drawers of components of varying sizes and shapes, some small enough to fit in Pearl's palm. "This is where you would go to build a clock, for instance. Any mechanism built from smaller pieces."

"Like your rifle?" Pearl asked. "The one that broke—"

"Yes," Theseus grunted to interrupt Pearl. "I would need to bring it to this room for repairs and to find out why I can't get it to work, the stupid piece of junk."

After the workshop, they skipped the last few landings and continued down the staircase, deeper into the earth, where the air grew heavy and cold. The candles lighting the way became seldom, but regular, so Pearl counted them to measure how deep they had gone. Ten…twenty…thirty…She wrapped her arms around her body to fight the chill. A light beneath them grew brighter as they descended, from a pinpoint in the darkness to a soft glow. An eerie calm filled Pearl, relaxing and unsettling at the same time.

No metal landing awaited them at the bottom, only a passage wide enough for two to walk side by side cut into the earth and stone. A layer of moisture on the walls reflected the dim light coming from the dying embers of the torches mounted on the wall. Sand thrown on the floor absorbed the water dripping off the wall and provided traction underfoot. Pearl followed Theseus down the passageway, which grew in size when it reached a set of giant wooden doors. Theseus stopped in front of the doors and looked back at Pearl.

"Once you go through these doors, there is no path back," he warned her. "Step beyond them and you've committed yourself to the Brotherhood. Understand?"

"Open the door," she commanded him. He smiled, then opened the doors with a strained grunt. The hinges groaned, then cried as rust fought against Theseus. From the room beyond, warm air rushed out, drying Pearl's eyes as it flowed over her. Theseus gave each of the doors a final push, making an opening wide enough for the two of them to walk in together.

"Wow," escaped Pearl's lips.

"Wow," echoed the smooth walls and the ceiling of the large cavern they entered. A single fire on the opposite side of the cavern illuminated the entire space, its glow reaching every corner. The walls showed no signs of carving, as though created in a single, uniform scoop. Pearl wanted to ask, but it felt sacrilegious to speak here, so she followed Theseus across the room in silence, until he stopped in front of the fire.

"This is the prize of the Brotherhood," Theseus told her, his voice filled with reverence, as he stared into the fire with her. Pearl noticed nothing extraordinary about it. It burned on top a stone pedestal, surrounded on all sides, except the front, by small, hexagon-shaped metal plates. A series of wires attached to each plate came together as a single, thicker wire behind the pedestal and ran up the wall into the ceiling. A burning sensation grew within her the longer she stared at it, as though the fire was eating her. She looked for what fed it, and discovered it hovered an inch above the pedestal, a singular, smokeless flame burning on its own. Every time it flickered, Pearl saw something more within the flame, a construct strange and in motion, but outside her perception.

"We are the Brotherhood of the Stolen Flame. This is our founding and our legacy. Our past, present, and future. Our namesake and our purpose. The first and last light in the darkness."

"What is it?" Pearl asked, not taking her eyes off it. The burning within her had stopped, replaced by a warm, comforting sensation, like wrapping oneself in blankets on a cold winter day.

"This, Pearl, is the first fire. The Fire of God."

Chapter 5

"I must preface the telling of the Brotherhood's history with some notes on its philosophy and beliefs," Theseus stated as he sat down in the dirt. He cast an expecting look at Pearl, who, after her confusion cleared, joined him while mouthing an apology. "First: every piece of text regarding divine beings and acts, from the scraps of destroyed scrolls to the massive tomes of religion, is part of a larger narrative, the beginning of which predates humanity, Earth, and perhaps all of creation. They're united by their truths, but their fictions divide them and isolate believers. Second: in conjunction with my first point, the Brotherhood fully acknowledges that every 'god' exists and has some influence on the Earth. We do not deny them, but we do not worship them. For the most part, they have removed themselves from the day-to-day affairs of man."

"Do they answer prayers?" Pearl thought of her mother and brother. "What happens when someone dies?"

"We don't know. Communication with the dead is difficult unless one dives into dark magics, and even then their descriptions of the afterlife are vague and conflicting. As for prayers, no definitive proof has been found to support or refute their effectiveness, but the gods' power is derived from belief, so answering prayers would be in their interest." This gave Pearl a small measure of relief. "Those will be the last questions for now. We don't have time to sit around, exchanging questions for answers. Your training is going to be rushed as is, so allow me to begin the admittedly abbreviated history of the Brotherhood."

Theseus cleared his threat. "When the gods created the beasts of the world, they bestowed each a gift, be it tooth, claw, stealth, or what have you. The first man and woman, who had been safe within the Gardens of Paradise until exiled for committing the original sin, entered the world with no such gift. By day, they struggled to survive among the beasts, eating whatever they could hunt and scavenge. By night, they hid, for the creatures of Chaos, the Khaous, roamed undeterred. The gods, their creators, now hated the humans for their lowly state, and turned their divine attention elsewhere. Luckily for mankind, there were those among the gods who pitied the plight of the humans. Three such gods

72

united to steal the Fire of God, a light to break the darkness humanity feared. Loki, trickster god of the Nords, distracted the Flame's Keeper, the Greek thunder god Zeus, with riddles. Crow, trickster of the North, retrieved it for Prometheus, a titan of Greece and humanity's chief sympathizer. Prometheus journeyed to the mortal realm, arriving just as the Khaous were spawning during the twilight when the gods are blind. With the Fire of God, which shines like no other flame, Prometheus showed the first humans how to use it to repel the darkness. He taught them how to make their own fires and how to use them for cooking and heat, before returning to the Divine Spheres, leaving the Fire of God in mankind's hands."

"Time passes differently for gods, so no one can say how long it was before Zeus or the Christian god Yahweh, the Flame's gifter, realized the Flame was missing. The two gods searched the Earth for it, and the humans they met, the first children and grandchildren of man, wielded fire of their own creation. Their search fruitless, the Fire of God hidden per Prometheus's instructions, Yahweh and Zeus returned to the Divine Spheres to find the thief. Prometheus, betrayed by Loki and Crow, suffered for his crime, chained to a rock where a giant eagle would eat his liver, which would grow back at night.

The torment repeated each day, yet he refused to reveal the Flame's location. Passed from one generation to the next, the Fire of God remained hidden from the gods. Only once was it mistakenly shown before the eyes of Yahweh, who flooded the Earth in order to destroy it. Yet the Flame survived, and an order of Keepers was formed to protect it, share its light with the world, and fight the Khaous with its power. The Brotherhood of the Stolen Flame has survived the rise and fall of empires, schisms and civil wars, treachery and zealotry. Now the Flame is here, in the new world, to vanguard the old world's inevitable migration across the oceans." Theseus closed his eyes, sighed, and then look into Pearl's eyes. "Your training begins now."

"Now?" Pearl asked, surprised. Theseus patted the dirt off his pants as he stood. From behind the Flame's pedestal, Theseus retrieved two swords, one he threw to Pearl. Metal flashed in the light and Pearl panicked, her hand shooting out on instinct to catch it and wrapping around the blade. She yelped, but didn't feel the blade's edge. Theseus bent backwards, laughing at the ceiling, as Pearl realized she had caught a scabbarded sword. She drew her sword, a rusty blade with a dull edge, and assumed her stance. Theseus's laughing faded to chuckling, then he shook it away to ready for a fight. He studied Pearl's stance, and grimaced in disappointment.

"We have so much work to do," Theseus grumbled. Pearl didn't worry about his dissent. Since she was young, she had always been faster and stronger than her peers, and could even outrun several adults as a child. What could this old man do that she couldn't match? She gave him a nod and prepared for his attack. Theseus returned the nod and lunged forward with a slash at Pearl's side. Pearl leapt backwards, and brought her sword down at Theseus's sword arm, embarrassed at how slow he moved. But her sword cut through empty air. Theseus had sidestepped the attack with practiced speed, and spun around on his heel like a top, slashing out at Pearl. She raised her sword as fast as she could and managed to parry the attack, but the force of his slash pushed her off balance and she stumbled backwards. She readied her guard for a follow up attack, but Theseus didn't pursue her.

"Try and kill me," he instructed her, lowering himself back into his fighting stance. "I assure you, you won't be able to."

"Just remember your words," Pearl warned. "I was the best among the Lamplighter trainees."

"The best among children? Hardly a boast," Theseus mocked. Pearl stepped towards him and brought her sword down at his head. His blade met hers and knocked it away, back over her head. She stepped back to keep her footing, as Theseus chased after her with a cut to her stomach. Her strength, which could fell a tree in a handful of swings, failed to bring her sword down fast enough. Pearl closed her eyes as the cold metal touched her side. However, instead of cutting her, the blade smacked her side like one of the wooden swords she used training with the Lamplighters. She let out a low, rather masculine "Oof" and staggered away from Theseus.

"Too easy. Were it not for the ward around my sword, you would be dead," Theseus teased. He held up his sword, and Pearl saw the distorted air around the blade, as though a haze hung on it. Pearl's sword had no such distortion around it. "Like I said, you would be hard pressed to try and kill me."

He mocked her, and all she had done so far just encouraged him. The advantages she had enjoyed in New Bethlehem meant nothing here. Her arm shook whenever their blades clashed, and for every attack she managed to block, three more would strike her arms and legs. His continual mocking irritated her, but his evident restraint for her sake made her seethe. Beating him to submission had become impossible, but landing a single blow wouldn't satisfy her.

Her blood boiled, burning her core, but fueling her body with new, wrathful strength. She watched him waiting for her, her vision red and her attention pulled to different parts of his body by some internal voice. He left shoulder exposed, attacking it would cause him to step away in defense. Attacking his left leg would leave him vulnerable to an upward slash. Theseus rushed her, and the internal voice revealed new openings. With his sword in his right hand, he exposed his left side, his neck in particular. *Go for the throat*, the voice growled with hunger. Pearl gave into the sensation, wanting bloodshed as much as it did, and swung her sword as hard as she could at Theseus's jugular. He parried her blade as if he knew its target. He had some counter to this sensation, blocking or avoiding every fatal blow. With every jump, twist, sidestep, slide or subtle shift in his body, the voice within Pearl would shift, revealing his vulnerabilities.

The voice screaming inside of Pearl brought her to her knees and filled her head with undecipherable chatter. Too much movement, too many changing factors. The screaming wouldn't stop. Theseus knelt down next to her, his mouth moving, but the words drowned in shrieks. She looked at him and thought, *Claw his eyes out, rip out his tongue, tear his throat*. She wanted to listen, but she turned away to shut up the voice. Theseus wrapped his arms around her, pulled her close to him, and held her head against his chest. The screaming in Pearl's head faded away, and she could hear Theseus humming and singing in another language, his voice soft as if he didn't want to wake some sleeping child. With every word, Pearl's body relaxed more and her vision cleared. The last of her rage dropped down her cheek as a tear, and she took a deep, calm breath.

"What was that?" she asked as Theseus released her.

"A prayer, though some would think it more of a spell." He leaned forward and looked into each of her eyes. "I learned it during my travels years ago. It calms those that hear it and soothes one's Bloodlust."

"No, I meant..." Pearl pointed to her head. "What happened to me?"

"Oh, your Bloodlust. Much more powerful than I thought it would be." He placed a finger in the middle of her forehead and another on the top of her head. He mumbled a few words with closed eyes, then smiled. "Good. No residual effects."

"What is my 'Bloodlust'?" Pearl asked, as she inspected the spots he had touched with her own fingers.

"The Bloodlust, and its companion the Forewarn, are what remain of ancient instincts humans possessed when we were simple hunters. A way to catch prey faster than us and defend ourselves against beasts deadlier than us. The Bloodlust helped the ancient hunter focus on a prey's vulnerabilities, while the Forewarn alerted him to a predator's proximity and movements. These two instincts may seem like feelings and urges coming from within you, but truly they're physical and rely on external stimuli. Our eyes can detect muscle contractions in another living being, telling us where and how it's going to move, while our bodies can detect subtle changes in our environment, like shifting wind or air temperature. Factors we usually don't notice, but can alert us to danger.

"But how..?"

"The Fire of God is a construct of enlightenment as well as destruction. Being this close to it has awakened your Bloodlust and Forewarn." Pearl stared at the fire and, for a moment, felt it staring back at her. "The one that awakens first is typically the more powerful of the two. Be wary, Pearl. While the Bloodlust will guide you to your enemies' weaknesses, it will also leave you vulnerable, and to rely on it too much will reduce you to nothing more than a feral beast."

"What about my Forewarn?"

"Let's spar again." Theseus raised his sword. "Focus on not getting hit. That should encourage your Forewarn to wake up."

"Should?" The ringing of clashing swords, echoing off the walls of the chamber like the inside of a bell, drowned out Pearl's question, which went unanswered. Pearl's Bloodlust, much more contained now, directed her only to Theseus's most vulnerable openings and didn't scream at her or turn her vision red. But she didn't feel any other sensations or voices guiding her, no matter how many times she blocked Theseus's sword. Save for the occasional grunt, Theseus attacked in silence, his assaults growing more complicated. Pearl struggled to defend herself, as one thrust she parried brushed against her arm and a jolt of pain made her jump backwards. A warmth dripped down her arm and soaked into her shirt. The ward's haze gone from Theseus's sword, blood smeared the blade's edge.

He's trying to hurt me, Pearl realized as Theseus charged at her. Pearl blocked a slash to her side, but as their blades touched, Theseus spun in the other direction and slashed at her other side. Pearl managed to meet his sword in time, but with her sword feeling twice as heavy and her arms exhausted from sparring once already, she doubted she would stop the next attack. Then, she noticed the leg Theseus had spun on tensing up again, the other leg lifting off the ground, and his torso tilting away from her, subtle details she wouldn't have noticed.

A new voice, cautious and calculating, alerted her about an oncoming kick from Theseus. She hesitated and the sensation screamed at her, just as her Bloodlust had, as impact grew imminent. She leapt to the side and Theseus's foot swung out through the empty space. He lunged at her with a roar, and Pearl's Forewarn told her to jump out of the way, while her Bloodlust told her to stab at his exposed chest. Pearl listened to the former, leaping out of the way, and Theseus's sword cut through the air and shattered when it hit the ground. Her Forewarn made her jump straight up and she watched as a large chunk of Theseus's sword shoot right under her.

"And that would be your Forewarn." Theseus tossed his broken sword aside without a second glance.

"You were trying to kill me," Pearl shouted, throwing her sword down. "Your sword didn't have the ward around it."

"Your Forewarn wouldn't have awakened unless you were in danger." He grabbed her arm, examined the cut he had given her, then placed his hand over it.

"Why would you do that?" Pearl asked.

"Because that's how mine awakened," Theseus told her, his voice full of frustration. "That's how Father Alexander trained me. It's the only way I know." He pulled his hand away and walked to the chamber's doors. He had healed her cut, leaving only a blood stain on her sleeve. "We will both have limits to overcome in your training. There's one more thing to determine before your training truly begins."

They climbed the stairs to the landing beneath the Farm room, the one they had skipped on their descent. The lone door here was made of a dark metal, and marked by five unrecognizable runes forming a circle in the center of the door. The runes pulsated like a heartbeat with violet light. Theseus grunted as he strained to pull the door and released it once it was halfway open, its own weight swinging it the rest of the way. Theseus gestured Pearl in and followed after her, pulling the door shut behind them. Layered circles of runes on the floor glowed one at a time in a cycle, from the smallest in the center of the room out to the largest encompassing almost the whole room, their violet light punctuated by the darkness between one circle dimming and the next one shining to life.

"Welcome to the Magic Room, where you will learn the mystic arts." Theseus pointed to each of the room's four corners and four brazier burst into life with green flames that drowned out the light of the runes. Pearl stared at the green flames and walked to the closest brazier. She didn't feel any heat, no matter how close her hand got to it. From behind her, Theseus explained, "It's falsefire. It provides a light like fire without an elemental quality to disrupt the mana in the room. The light strands throughout the rest of the house use mana gathered from the Flame, so they can't..."

Theseus's voice trailed off, and the echoes of Pearl's sobs filled the room. Since her arrival, Pearl had heard the word "magic" spoken so nonchalant, it still seemed the thing of fairytales. Of all the things she had seen and heard, nothing had shaken her as the falsefire, actual magic she could see and touch. The immensity of reality fell on her shoulders. She trembled and cried as she remembered every insult, mean name, and degradation she had suffered at the hands of the New Bethlehem townsfolk. All of these wounds started with the accusations of Pearl's mother being a witch, and now they could be true? She could endure them when they were founded in superstitions, but now felt their full sting.

"Were they true?" Pearl demanded. "Am I a witchspawn?"

"All you have seen, even before coming to Lightholme, and this is what shakes you?" Theseus asked in return. "You have been surrounded by magic your entire life."

"I've been despised my entire life because of magic," Pearl screamed, her tears cooling her heated face. "Hated by those around me. And if magic is real, I am the Witchspawn they cursed me for being."

Pearl could feel her Bloodlust stirring to life, telling her where to lunge at Theseus's body, but she turned from him to cry alone. He approached her, his heavy feet thumping on the stone, and squeezed her shoulder, first too hard, then so soft she thought he had let go. But she bumped into his hand as she turned around. He looked down at her, the sounds of different words trying to leave his mouth combining into a verbal mess as he searched for the right thing to say. "I…when…you have…Damn it."

He paused, then punched the palm of his hand. "This isn't how your training is supposed to go. You're supposed to receive an education to aid in the removal bias you have towards magic. But I don't think even that could help you. Listen. Whether you're a witchspawn or not, doesn't matter. Your mother…Her path is not yours, whichever path that was. Your path, Pearl, is yours and yours alone. It will lead you to strange places and people. There will be times when it will challenge you in any number of ways, and your strength and ideals may not seem like enough. But stay true to yourself, trust your instincts, and remember how strong you are and how much you've endured, and the path forward will always be clear. You shape what happens to you. So you're a Witchspawn and dead men spoke ill of you? Do these thing truly define you? You are no different than when you walked into this room."

A smile crept onto Pearl's face and the tears stopped as an overwhelming desire to hug Theseus filled her. But before she could move, she yelped as something poked and pinched her all over her back, causing her limbs to twitch and her body to go limp, then stiffen like a board. She blacked out at one point, but somehow remained standing. Theseus spun her around with a jerk on her shoulder and struck her arms, chest, and stomach multiple times with the tips of his fingers, his hand shooting out like attacking serpents. He finished with simultaneous palm strikes to her chest and forehead, neither strong enough to knock her down. Then something like lightning blasted her in the same spots and threw her backwards onto the ground.

She grabbed at her chest as a painful, tickling shiver flowed out through her body to her fingers and toes from what felt like a new heart beating next to her real one. It felt weak like a discovered muscle and its weakness made her queasy. Theseus picked her off the ground and held her up, her own legs incapable of doing so. She tried speaking, but could only sputter out, "Wha..?"

"Your ability to use magic relies on your body's ability to circulate mana throughout your body." He placed a hand on the middle of her chest and closed her eyes. Energy, like a wave of warmth, spread from Theseus's palm into Pearl and her fatigue faded as the beat of her new "heart" improved, until she could stand on her own. "Since you've never used magic or mana before, I had to manually start the circulation. Your body, not used to its own mana flow, attempted to compensate for the weak flow, exhausting you. I've supplemented the mana in your body with mine own, which I'll have to do before each magic lesson, until you've naturally strengthen your mana flow."

"How do I do that?"

"With practice, like any other muscle." He pulled out a scroll from the only cabinet in the room, tucked in the corner and made of the same metal as the door. Pests had eaten away at the loose end of the scroll, leaving the paper jagged much to Theseus's agitation. He drew a hidden knife from his sleeve and cut a straight edge onto the paper before cutting off a rectangular piece off. He started to roll the paper back up, but stopped to cut off another rectangular piece. With the scroll back in the cabinet, he presented the two strips of paper to Pearl. "First, however, we need to discover your attunement."

Pearl didn't bother to ask and Theseus didn't wait for her to ask. "Every soul resonates with a specific element, one of the primary four: water, earth, wind, and fire. Depending on which element you're attuned to, certain spells will be easier to learn and use, and we'll know where to start your training." He waved the paper strips. "Watch."

Theseus placed a strip on the ground and knelt beside it. He pricked his thumb on the tip of his knife and dripped three drops of blood onto the paper. The blood drops soaked into the paper, then, to Pearl's surprise, turned into black ink, moved across the paper, and grew three times their size. The three spots stretched out into lines, arching and connecting until they drew the image of a fist grasping a bolt of lightning. The air above the paper crackled and sparked, and a tear ruptured in the middle of the lightning bolt.

"Lightning," Theseus announced, the violet light of the floor's seals casting an eerie glow on his face and shining in his eyes. "The Weapon, the Power, the Sky-Fire, the Cloud-breaker, the Herald, the Judgment, the Punishment, the Guilt."

"Wait, lightning wasn't one of the four elements," Pearl pointed out.

"I said that there were four primary elements." Theseus crumbled up the paper. "A variety of other elements exist. Lightning is one of four impure elements that are combination of adjacent primary elements."

"Adjacent?"

Theseus let out a huff of air. "Discussing alchemy, the study of elements, and the expansive catalog of associated theories would take days we can't waste on subjects you don't need to know. Simply put, lightning is the impurity formed from wind and fire, which lie adjacent to each other on the elemental meta-structure." He placed the other slice of paper in front of Pearl and held out his hand. "Now, let's see your attunement."

Hesitant, Pearl gave Theseus her hand and after a quick poke on her thumb, three drops of blood fell onto the fresh strip of paper. Just as before, blood turned to ink and danced around the paper, before meeting in the center and stretching into an image of a triangle with three progressively smaller flames within it, one inside of another. The paper's edges smoked, then singed, and glowed with a soft heat.

"Fire. The Light, the Warmth, the Youth, the Will, the Summer, the Soul, the Untamed, the Dragon, the Phoenix, the Emperor, the Igniter, the Sun, the Sword, the Purger, the Consuming, the Wrath."

"What does all of that mean?" Pearl asked. The image had her eyes locked to it.

"Titles given to each element, reminders of what they're capable of, both good and bad. It's up to you to decide how you use your magic and which of these titles applies to you." Theseus clapped his hands together, startling Pearl. "Time for your first lesson."

Theseus stretched out his hand, palm up, away from his body, and focused on it, his face strained with concentration. His hand tensed for half a second, and then, hovering above it, an orb of lightning crackled and popped into form. "Summon your attuned element as a simple ball. Nothing more, nothing less. This will teach you the basics of magic: gathering mana and utilizing it."

"You act like it's so simple." But Pearl stood up anyway and focused on her palm. Muscles in her hand, arm, and face clenched, but nothing happened.

"You're mimicking the physical efforts well enough," Theseus chuckled as she exhaled with a puff of breath. "But you couldn't see the inner workings. Focus beneath your muscles, on the mana flow within

and throughout you. Direct it to your hand. The concentrated flow will feel like muscles contracting beneath your real muscles. Concentrate your gathered mana on the space above your palm, which will feel—
"

A small ball of fire whooshed into existence above Pearl's hand. A nervous, shaky laugh tumbled out of her mouth, broken by huffs and puffs as the effort left her breathless, like she had run up the entire spiral staircase. Proud of her work, she turned towards Theseus, sticking out her hand to show him, but the sudden movement launched the fireball at him. The fire burst against the cold stone wall behind Theseus, who had leapt aside before the ball left Pearl's hand, leaving a small sprinkling of red sparks in the aftermath. Breathing became more demanding for Pearl, and she could only manage short, shallow breaths. She fought to remain standing, her shaking legs threatening to bring her down.

"Deep breaths." Theseus inhaled and exhaled with Pearl, giving her a pace to follow. Once Pearl's breathing stabilized, Theseus stared at the scorched spot on the wall and warned, "Like I said, you control what your magic does. You're certainly more capable than I had anticipated..."

"Is that bad?" His trailing off left her somewhat unsettled.

He didn't look at her and continued to study the burnt wall. "No…not bad nor unheard of. Just unusual. Indicative of some natural aptitude for magic among your parents and ancestors."

An image of her father's ice magic clashing against the serpent's fire entered Pearl's mind. "Maybe…"

"But thankfully for us, it means we'll be able to progress through this part of your training faster than I thought. I honestly thought this lesson would take the rest of the day." The falsefire torches dimmed as Theseus helped Pearl to the door. With one arm supporting Pearl, Theseus pushed the metal door with his other arm, grunting as the door inched ajar. He smiled at Pearl, and the swell of pride made her heavy body that much lighter. "You did well today. Tomorrow, your training begins, and let me assure you, it will be grueling. A month from now, you will dream of today."

Theseus sat Pearl down on the stairs so he could use both hands to shut the door. As the door crawled shut, the torches within flickered one last time and died out all at once. The seals on the floor continued to glow and, before the door closed, Pearl imagined some part of her remained inside, and would remain there as she moved forward into the stranger, challenging days ahead.

Chapter 6

Summer's end hung on the horizon of tomorrow, painting the leaves amber, cutting the days shorter, and chilling the nights. The cool breeze felt frigid on Pearl's tears. She pulled her legs into her chest for warmth as she sat and watched the sun setting behind the hills. She enjoyed the solitary quiet, but knew the Khaous would break it once Nightfall came. She appreciated the break from training. Theseus's words rung true. A month of training later, and Pearl longed for the day when the extent of her training included a short sparring match with blunt blades and creating a single ball of fire.

She remembered wishing for death after the first day of real training, her body aching so much as she laid in bed that night. Despite the agony, she had awoken at the crack of dawn the next day to begin her training again. Each day, the process repeated, never getting easier. Sleep passed in the blink of an eye, allowing her to recover just enough strength to get through another day.

Mornings followed the same routine, starting with a breakfast of fruits, breads, and eggs while the sun rose. Then, they would go to the Gymnasium and perform a series of stretches Theseus called 'yoga' to help ease any pains from the previous day and clear their minds and spirits in preparation for the tasks ahead. According to Theseus, "Yoga originates in the Far East, in a land called India, taught by yogis, who practice to achieve total enlightenment." Pearl became fond of yoga after the first few sessions, and found pushing her flexibility and endurance to their limits more rewarding than she expected, though knowing what followed often spoiled the morning session.

After yoga, Theseus led Pearl on a run through the woods. Back in New Bethlehem, Pearl could outrun all of the trainees and most of the adults, but Theseus often left her behind, marking a trail for her. During one run, Pearl took a shortcut back to the house. How Theseus found out, Pearl didn't know, but he waited for her when she got back, and made her run the full path again, the only time he ran with her until she became fast enough to keep pace with him. Sweat-sheened and out of breath, they returned to the Gymnasium for acrobatics and combat training.

"Fighting is movement. Whether it's pressing an advantage or recovering from an attack, you're constantly moving, so you'll need to learn how to move effectively while staying conscious of your enemies' locations." As much as Pearl liked yoga, she loved acrobatics practice. Where Theseus possessed strength, experience, and magical prowess, Pearl excelled at jumping, flipping, diving, cartwheeling, and tumbling around him. Compared to her nimble movements, Theseus appeared to stand still. Pearl would win every time if fighting depended on movement alone. However, as Theseus added, "Fighting is knowledge, precision, and directed power, as well."

He made this clear when teaching her how to fight with and without weapons. He punished her for every opening she presented. In swordplay, this meant a quick thwack. When grappling, it meant being tossed and slammed onto the ground. And in hand-to-hand combat, it led to a strike on her body. Her training clothes, a thin shirt and pair of pants with arms and legs cut short to help her stay cool, provided no protection or padding, so she felt the severity of every blow and learned from every mistake.

After a light lunch break, which consisted of fruits, vegetables, nuts, and cold refreshing glasses of water, they would sit outside and meditate in silence.

"Why are we doing this?" Pearl asked on the first day of training, not long after they started.

"Because…" Theseus grumbled. "Meditation is the best way to increase the amount of mana your body can hold. And to be most effective, it should be done in silence."

"But how do I do it? What do I think about?"

"Sit in silence and think about nothing. Let your mind be free, and your mana flow will become receptive to the mana in the air. Since your body's mana stores are full, the mana entering your body causes them to become more potent, more concentrated. Your body adjusts to this potency over time, and it becomes your natural level, the point you'll recover to when resting."

"Wait, there's mana in the air?" Pearl studied the air around her, looking for any sign of mana.

"There's mana everywhere. That's why you're not still exhausted from throwing that fireball at me yesterday."

"Sorry about that again."

"You can make it up to me by shutting the hell up."

A second, less rigorous session of yoga warmed their bodies in preparation for sparring. Armed with wooden swords, the two fought holding little back and relied on their Forewarn to avoid any grievous injuries. Theseus encouraged Pearl to use what she had learned during training as they sparred, though she suffered for every error and misstep she made. Sparring would end when Pearl struggled to lift her arms, then they'd go to the Magic room to practice her casting until her mana flow weakened. During the first week, this never took long, a single spell pulling her close to fainting, and once she mastered the basic spells, she graduated to more complicated ones that drained her just like the early days. Drained and amazed at the things she could now do.

Magic practice gave her body a break, but not enough for their return to the Gymnasium for another warmup session of yoga and a series of weight exercises. Theseus reveled in strength training, just as Pearl loved doing acrobatics, smiling while throwing around weights heavier than her. She imagined him judging her for using weights so much lighter than him, and her rage burned as she refused to let him win. Pearl pushed her already tired body to exhaustion as she lifted, pressed, pulled, and curled the heavy stones connected by metal bars.

A second wind would come to her just when she wanted to quit, and drive her through the final hour of her physical training. For dinner, a heartier meal, they ate roasted meats and vegetables, cheeses, and stews, though at this point in the day, Pearl craved water the most. As with every meal they consumed dinner in silence.

Pearl's days didn't end at dinner, only the physical training. In the study, Theseus would teach Pearl anything he considered useful for their mission, such as the medical properties of plants and flower and finding the structural weaknesses in caves and tunnels. She never knew what she would learn in the next lesson, but it never failed to intrigue.

On occasion, Theseus would conduct lessons in one of the sublevel rooms he had skipped over in his initial tour. In the dark garden rooms in the lower levels of the house, Pearl learned about the variety of poisonous plants she could mill and coat her weapons with, and in the alchemy room she concocted elixirs capable of bringing a man back from the edge of death and vials of chemicals which would burst into flames when the glass shattered. "Knowledge is your most powerful weapon," Theseus told her. "Strength and speed are nothing if you don't know how to use them. If you know how to make use of the resources around you in any situation, you'll have the advantage every time. But stay sharp. Acting on erroneous information or ignoring obvious truths can be as fatal as any misstep. Ignorance and arrogance are your greatest weapons against yourself, so keep them sheathed."

Pearl's daily training ended there, as Theseus would disappear to some other part of the house, leaving Pearl to do whatever she wanted before bed. She never followed him or asked what he planned to do, because she imagined he enjoyed his time alone at the end of the day as much as she did. Beside the occasional trip to the privy and sleeping at night, she had no other time to herself. More often than not, she chose to read one of the study's many books, grabbing one off the shelves and sitting in one of the big leather chairs next to the fireplace.

Brothers and Sisters of the Flame had authored most of the books in the study. While some recorded the Brotherhood's history and activities over the past thousands of years, a majority covered topics unrelated to the Brotherhood. With these books, she educated herself on the cities of the worlds and their secrets, the recovered, unreplicable ancient technologies from civilizations long dead, and the strange beasts and monsters that lived in the dark corners of the world. Each printed word revealed the truth of mysteries she didn't know existed, unraveling her world one page at a time. She enjoyed this fantastic new information, but it made her old life, the life she had with her father in New Bethlehem, seem more and more unreal.

"Pearl." Light from inside the house broke the dark of night around her, and Theseus's shadow stretched over her own. Pearl didn't want to look at him and stared at the hills glowing with the sun behind them. Her raw, shapeless emotions searched for an outlet, and anger directed at Theseus came easy, but she bottled it up, choosing silence instead. Theseus sat beside her and watched the sunset. "Nightfall is coming."

"As it does every day," she snarled. She cringed on the inside, realizing too late the harshness of her words.

"It's funny," he chuckled, ignoring her tone. "We've spent all this time together, and yet we're as strange to one another as the day we first met. I know little of you, and have told you nothing of myself. And that...that is my fault. We need to train as hard as we have been, but I hoped it would keep you occupied and distracted. I'm trying to help you with the pain, trying to make it better, but I don't think it's working. Problem is, it's the only way I know. It's how I chose...actually how I was forced to deal with it."

"Deal with what?" Pearl asked, still not looking at him. Theseus reminded her of her father, possessing two sides: the stonehearted, educated man who trained her, and the more familiar peer who spoke to her now as an equal. Nostalgia warmed Pearl's heart and loosened another tear from her eye.

"I know what you're going through. Before there was a New Bethlehem, there were three boats full of people, livestock, and supplies. In London, Father Alexander had preached of a new promise land for the faithful where we would welcome the next coming of the Savior. He enlisted any who would join, no matter their degree of faith. Not that it mattered. The whole thing-" He coughed. "Nevermind that part. My parents had died years before, leaving my sister and me in the charge of my father's friend, John Russell."

"I'm...I'm sorry about your parents." Pearl had been curious of Theseus's past, but an appropriate time to ask had never arisen.

"I was only two when they passed and all I remember of them is their love of books, my only inheritance." His parents' deaths didn't seem to disturb Theseus, though his tone sadden. *Is this how I'll see my father's death? A sad note in a long story?* "My sister Beatrice was all I had. When Father Alexander enlisted Russell to be New Bethlehem's quartermaster, we were brought along as apprentices, though that didn't last long. Russell died during the first night, when the Khaous attacked. My sister and I fell into the care of the village, working for food to eat and a place to sleep."

He stopped and studied her for a moment. "You remind me of Beatrice. She was also a bit hot-headed and reckless."

"I'm not reckless," Pearl insisted, whipping a glare at him.

"Really now?" The way you jump into my attacks when we're sparring, I think you want to get yourself hurt," Theseus laughed, and Pearl cracked a smile. "Beatrice always got the two of us in trouble. She worked hard most of the time, but there were some days when we would have gone hungry if not for Father Alexander's charity. She loved exploring and would bring me berries from deep in the forest while I toiled away doing both of our chores."

Theseus fell silent and looked up. Nightfall had brought out a sky full of stars. "Then one day…I was chopping wood and Beatrice dragged me away to go exploring in the forest. We went further than we had ever gone before, Beatrice running through the trees and me chasing after her, until we found the Black Hill. Of course we didn't know that at the time. All we saw was a large hill in the middle of a shallow lake. Ignorant of the danger we were in, we played along the water's edge, sword-fighting with sticks until they broke. As we jumped around, swinging at one another, we fell through a weak spot in the roof of a tunnel beneath us."

"A tunnel?" Pearl touched the ground, wary it would drop away any second.

"The Black Hill and the area around it sit on top of a network of tunnels. I can't say for what purpose, though I would guess they're meant for subterranean ambushes. I do know they don't reach far beyond the hill. In fact, Beatrice and I fell into the tunnel at its end. With the opening above us out of reach and nowhere else to go, we followed the tunnel down under the hill. It grew darker as we went deeper, so we had to run our hands along the walls to find our way. That we didn't lose each other was a miracle. Hours passed before we saw light again, though it wasn't sunlight or moonlight, but an indigo glow. In our wanderings, we had arrived in the deepest cavern, the chamber of the Black Heart."

"You've seen the Black Heart before? You know where it is?"

Theseus didn't hear her. "I remember...terror...stronger than anything I've ever felt before, as I stared at the Heart. As ignorant as I was of it, I knew to be afraid. Beatrice stabbed the Black Heart with the stick she had been playing with. Just walked up and stabbed it. No fear. Even now, I don't know why, but the Black Heart bled a black and blue liquid. We stood there, watching for some time, when we heard a low growl above us. The ceiling was covered in Khaous, hanging like bats. They crawled down the walls to gather around the Black Heart, not even noticing us. We reached the edge of the chamber when a roar rose from them, and they chased after us. We ran, not in any direction. Just away from them. Somehow we found our way back to the tunnel we fell in. We tried to reach the hole in the ceiling again, even though we knew it was too high. Beatrice stood me on her shoulders, and I reached for anything to grab, but I wasn't high enough. And then, I was lifted up and clung to a thick root. I reached back for my sister, but saw the Khaous swarming around her, lifting her off the ground and carrying her away. She reached for me, but…I couldn't. That was the last time I saw her, her face disappeared among the Khaous as they took her back into the tunnels."

"I don't even remember running back. The next thing I can remember is crashing into the church, trying to explain what happened through my sobbing. Somehow Father Alexander understood me and comforted me as best as he could. It was then that he told me about the Brotherhood." Theseus finished his story with a shudder. She opened her mouth to say something, but he continued. "He offered me justice for my sister, a path I committed myself to, so I could forget about the emptiness of my old life. And that's what I'm forcing onto your life, a decision I have no right making for you."

His eyes shimmered as tears threatened to well up, but with a quick wipe and a distracting cough removed any traces of them. "I hope you understand me better than before. Now, tell me a story, so I might know you better."

She told him every story she could about herself. She told him about the first time the other children had mocked her and how she eventually stood up for herself, making sure no one, save the arrogant and stupid, teased her to her face. The sounds of the Khaous filled the forest and the chill in the air turned cold, as she continued with stories about her vague memories of her mother, and how her father and her would pray for her mother and brother every night, a practice she felt guilty for failing to complete on a regular basis. "And almost every night, I have the same dream. I'm in a strange village. The sky is black and full of stars, like night, but the moon is blue and green. And there's music coming from one of the houses. It sounds like my mother's lullaby."

"You've mentioned your mother quite a bit."

"My father talked about her a lot. Every night, after we prayed for her and my brother, he would tell me how I had her hair or her laugh or something of that sort. I guess he saw more of her in me than he did himself."

"What was her name?"

"Judith." Theseus shook his head at the name and looked off into the distance. When Pearl didn't speak, he snapped, "Well, go on."

"Uh…well…before all of this, all I wanted to be was a Lamplighter, like my father. I wanted to fight the demons—sorry, Khaous—and to protect the town, just like he did…right until the end…"

"Do you miss him?"

"Every day," she managed to say before a sob escaped her lips. Tears rolled down her face, but she kept herself from crying any louder. "I miss him so much, Theseus."

Theseus let her cry, giving her the occasional pat on the shoulder. The worst passed, though tears still fell from her eyes. "You remind me of him. At least what parts of him I did know, which now doesn't seem like much. He never talked about his life before me,as though I was born and he just showed up to be my father. There were times, especially when he was fighting the serpent Khaous, when he became a completely different person. Not just how he acted, but how he looked. He would grow taller and more muscular. And I never would have suspected he could use magic. Can someone be attuned to ice?"

"Of course. Like lightning, ice is an impure element. Do you think that was his attunement?"

"I would assume so. Every spell he used was ice-based."

"Well that can't be right..." Theseus mumbled.

"Why not?" Her question gave Theseus a start and he looked at her with wide eyes, as though she had caught him doing something he didn't want her to see.

"No reason. Let's see, your father. George...Chaucer. I've only met him a few times, the last being when he arrived in the village. Before that, I had seen him work in Europe. I mentioned on the first night you came here that he relied on magic more than I think he should have, but that came with his duties to the Brotherhood. He was a specialist in demonology and containing demonic energy, usually called in for complicated exorcisms and creating powerful wards around people."

"Really? Did he ever rip a demon out of someone and have to fight it? Was he good?"

"The best. In London, when I first met him, he singlehandedly eradicated a hive of nightmare demons infesting the psyche of an orphanage. Not just the children inside, but the dreams of the building itself. Bottled one up and gave it to a Baroness of the Dreamscape."

"...Wow," Pearl could think of nothing else to say. "That's incredible."

"It may seem like a fairytale, full of adventures and heroes, but those rewarding moments are seldom and buried in a life of danger." He stopped with thoughtful hesitation. "Don't feel as though this is your only option. I know I told you that once you chose to be part of the Brotherhood, you couldn't leave, but give the word and I will take you back to London. I'll provide you with the means to start a new life, to follow any path you want."

"What I want is justice for my father. I want to destroy the Black Heart for taking him from me." She reached out to the forest, and clenched her fist.

"Ah, that's not justice. That's revenge, a short-sighted, unfulfilling, less wholesome motive. I would advise against it. Thinking higher than yourself will serve you better."

"Don't you want to avenge your sister?"

"I suppose I do. Doesn't make it just. Besides..." He rose to return inside, and gave her a pat on her shoulder. "I want you to be better than me."

Chapter 7

The violet seals on the Magic Room's floor gathered loose mana from the air to power themselves. Multiple, circular focal points marked where the Brothers had stood when they created the seals to prevent wanton summonings from damaging the rest of the house. Pearl thought about how much power they would gather after this day's session.

"Focus," Theseus commanded. "You can't afford to let your thoughts wander."

"Would…be…easier…without…your…yelling ." Sweat dripped down Pearl's forehead and into her eyes. It stung, but she ignored it. A series of rings made of pure mana floated in between her outstretched hands, interlocked but not touching one another. Outside of her body, Pearl's mana appeared as cloudy red glass and moved like molten ore. According to Theseus, mana's color varied from person to person, though it typically came in shades of blue. When Pearl questioned the color of her mana,

Theseus had no explanation, though the silence before admitting that suggested otherwise.

The first time she manipulated mana outside her body, Theseus had her create a ball of pure mana. The process varied from creating a ball of fire at one step, and proved much more challenging. Once she gathered the needed mana into her hand, she had to isolate it, so her body didn't attune it. It pained her cutting a fragment of mana off from the flow throughout her body, like severing a limb. She had lost count of the number of mana orbs that had unintentionally ignited.

But, as with everything Theseus taught her, she mastered it and graduated to different shapes and then complicated arrangements. One after another, she conquered them, albeit after many failures. However, maintaining the nine interlocking rings frustrated her. Nine times she had attempted to move the rings around without letting them touch while keeping them in the same space in the air, and nine times had the rings destabilized and fallen apart, the loose mana falling like mist to the floor.

"Con-cen-trate."

"Mm…trying…" Pearl grunted. She pushed the mana flow of her body and tried to take absolute control of it, but the harder she strained, the more her mana flow slipped out of her control. Something within her wavered and her heartbeat slammed against the inside of her chest. Her knees trembled, her vision blurred, and sounds muffled. Her body went numb and she didn't feel her body crash against the stone floor. Violet light filled her world. Theseus lifted her head up and pressed his hand onto her chest. Warmth spread from his hand into her body, then cooled. Her vision snapped back to focus and she snatched Theseus's collar to hold herself up as she gasped for breath. "What…what was…that?" What happened?"

"Magic withdraw." Theseus inspected her eyes and pressed two fingers against her neck to check her pulse. "It was bound to happen, though I'm surprised it took you this long."

"Withdraw? What does that mean?" Pearl's body temperature fluctuated with each brief, shallow breath, though another surge of mana remedied this.

"Expending too much mana or pulling too much mana into a part of your body will strain your mana flow. To prevent potentially fatal mana exhaustion, your mana flow retracts to your center. The sudden retraction leaves the rest of the body weakened, hence your collapse." Pearl stood up on her own accord, but Theseus caught her when she staggered. "I think that's all of the magic training we'll do for today. No need to push yourself any more tonight."

Pearl leaned on Theseus as she hobbled up the spiral staircase. She would take care not to push herself when they ventured to the Black Hill. Inspiration struck and an idea popped into her head. "What are the limits of magic?"

"Magic's chief restraint is its cost. The more powerful the spell, the more mana it requires."

"Could a group of individuals pool their mana together to cast an even more powerful spell?"

"Group spells do exist. A group of magi can channel mana between one another while chanting an incantation to invoke the spell they want. It requires those involved to chant in unison, and any mistake can be disastrous for all of them. There is another option, where one mage has others channeling mana into him—"

"Or her."

"—him or her...and then he—"

"Or she."

"—he or she casts the spell. Why?"

"I was thinking about the Black Hill. Couldn't you just craft a spell strong enough to destroy the entire hill and the Black Heart within it?"

Theseus chuckled, much to Pearl's irritation. "I'm sorry. I wasn't laughing at you. It's just...I too proposed such an idea during my training. The simplicity of the idea is refreshing. Often, the simplest solutions best the most complicated problems, but go overlooked, like Alexander the Great and the Gordian Knot. However, this is not one of those problems. Your lack of knowledge, on the other hand, is and can be corrected in the study. There's something to show you before I answer your question."

In the study, he helped Pearl into a chair by the large desk, then spread a map retrieved from one of the shelves flat across the table, wrestling to keep the corners down. Once the map laid flat, he slammed his hand upon it and closed his eyes. The map's image, a random assortment of lines rather than a map, glowed as Theseus infused them with mana. He lifted his hands and the image on the map rose with them. Pearl gaped as the image in front of her gained another dimension, transforming from a drawing into a sculpture, showing the depth of the Black Hill and its tunnels.

When Theseus spoke of the tunnels beneath the Hill, she imagined them near the surface and growing more complex the deeper they dove. But according to the map, numerous, complicated tunnels rested only a few feet underground. She traced all of the tunnels with her finger to see where they led, disappointed when she discovered that each of the deepest tunnels came to abrupt stops at the same depth.

"How did you get this map?" Pearl asked.

"I was abroad at the time, so I witnessed none of this. But when the Brotherhood deployed its finest battalion to Lightholme to destroy the Black Heart, the battalion's magi released magic probes to map out the tunnels upon entering. The battalion failed its mission with no survivors. At least, none left the Hill. Their probes, on the other hand, continued to survey the tunnels for several years until something destroyed all of them once they reached the same depth." He pointed to the sudden cut off in the tunnels. "I suspect these tunnels go even deeper, leading right to the Black Heart, and are probably guarded."

Pearl studied the map closer. "You can even see the tunnels becoming steeper where the probes were stopped."

"Precisely. You asked why we don't use magic to destroy the Black Hill. The answer is we have no idea where the Black Heart is within the tunnels and therefore don't know how much of the Hill we would need to demolish. If we try to blast it away, we may end up burying the Black Heart under a layer of rubble that would take years to clear. Not that we have the power between the two of us to destroy what we can see on the map."

"So that's out of the question," Pearl grumbled. Theseus pressed the image back into the map and rolled it back up, returning it to its spot on the shelf. "How can we succeed when a whole battalion of Brothers failed to destroy the Black Heart?"

"Because two people draw far less attention and make far less noise than a battalion. We're going to sneak into the Black Hill, quietly make our way to the Black Heart, and destroy it."

"Why not send just one person then? Wouldn't that be even better? Half the people, half the noise." Pearl imagined Theseus creeping his way through the darkness and driving his sword through a pulsing black heart."

"But also half the chance of success. Father Alexander developed this two person plan for Brother Gen and me. While one person could better avoid detection, a second person could provide additional protection and the mission can continue if one of the Brothers fall. The benefits outweigh the costs."

"What if we both fall? What happens if we don't destroy the Black Heart?"

"I don't know," Theseus admitted, a grim shadow falling over his face. "The Brotherhood would come looking for the Fire of God. It is the very heart of the Brotherhood and without it, the Brotherhood would likely collapse as the upper echelon breaks away. The Flame is stolen, all of us considered accomplices in its theft in the eyes of Yahweh, and they would be afraid of what the missing Flame would mean for them if He learned the Flame survived the Great Flood. Even if He reclaimed it, He would seek retribution, and the Brothers would scatter and hide themselves from His sight in order to survive."

"Are they all cowards?"

"Only a fool would not fear the anger of a god," Theseus warned her. "Their power is great, their reach far. We cannot fathom the scales of their might."

*   *   *

The chill of Fall replaced Summer's warmth, and the shorter days brought Nightfall earlier. Not wanting either of them to fall ill, Theseus moved their evening activities inside to the Magic Room.

"Meditation is the expansion of one's consciousness," Theseus reminded her as they slowed their breaths together. "You're spreading your mind out in all directions and opening it up. The wider and more open your mind is, the more mana you can absorb."

"Where does the mana in the air come from?" Pearl asked to Theseus's displeasure.

"Why must you ask questions when you should be silent?"" he grumbled. "The theory is that at the beginning of all things, there was a singular source of mana, which dispersed and is now shared by all things. At any time, throughout all existence, the amount of mana remains constant, for mana cannot be destroyed. When you cast a fireball, the mana used to create it doesn't disappear with the fireball. It disperses into the air around it. For a brief time, this mana is inactive and unusable, but over time it regains its potency."

"What caused the mana to disperse?"

"Later. I have entertained one question already. Now, hush and focus."

They sat on opposite sides of the room's seals. The metal door stood ajar, allowing fresh air and, more importantly, fresh mana to enter the room. Pearl slowed and deepened her breath as she crossed her legs and tilted her head up towards the ceiling. She thought of white snow to clear her mind and felt it stretch out beyond the confines of her body, stretching out of Lightholme into the forest in all directions. Her slow and powerful heartbeats shook the ground beneath her like the footsteps of a giant.

Then, something tugged at her mind, on the edge of her consciousness. Pearl's heart leapt in terror, but the thundering beat continued, another heart thumping in her mind. She pulled her mind back to her body, but something else pulled it away towards the other heartbeat, which grew louder and more grotesque the closer her consciousness drew. Pearl struggled to free her mind from this foreign presence and open her eyes. With the full force of her will, she lifted her eyelids.

Darkness. Nothing, but darkness. She raised her hand to her face to see if she had opened her eyes. The Magic Room, Theseus, everything else had fallen away. Everything save the heartbeat, echoing through the darkness. She found herself standing, but couldn't remember standing up.

"Hello?" Pearl called out, uncertain anyone would answer.

A hand grabbed her shoulder. She would have jumped, but its touch froze her in place. Warm breath slithered across her neck as someone behind her whispered into her ear. "Hello, Pearl. You have something of mine."

Venomous intent laced his calm voice, each word worming into her thoughts. She tried to answer, but her lips wouldn't move. Another hand, fire-hot, yet sending a chill down her spine, reached around

117

and covered her mouth. "Sh-sh-ssshush. Don't talk. Listen. You have something that belongs to me and I have something you want. Something you've wanted for oh so long."

He waited for her to respond and laughed when she didn't, his laughter swallowing her. He enjoyed his power over her. "What's the matter? Can't guess? What a shame...oh well, I thought you would be interested in seeing your family again."

The hand clenched her shoulder and twisted her around. A green and blue moon hung in the black, star-dotted night. Houses of different sizes and color, and made of different materials sat on the greenest grass Pearl had ever seen along a gray stone path wrapping around a lake-like patch of black stone. She looked around, bewildered by her sudden arrival in the place of her dreams, searching for the man who must have brought her here. But as she walked around, the impossibility of being here without sleeping dawned on her.

Music drifted through the air coming from the blue house to Pearl's left, just as it did in her dreams. She walked to the door and opened it, but found herself in her old room in New Bethlehem. It looked as it did when she left it to escort Mrs. Graham through the forest. She peeked out into the hallway and saw someone standing in the main room.

"Pearl." The voice came from every direction.

"Who..?" She studied the person in her house. "Father?"

The person turned their head as if they heard her. As she stepped closer, the person stretched, growing taller, thinner and, somehow, more familiar.

"Father?" The person looked at her, their face featureless and smooth.

"Pearl." The slender person grabbed their face and peeled it away like a mask, revealing the face of her father. Her smile faded when it reached up and grabbed its face again. She tried to speak, but nothing came out. The person lifted the mask of her father's face, and Theseus's face slept under it. Pearl raised her hand to his face and his eyes snapped open.

"Pearl!" Pearl jolted awake at the sound of her name and found herself looking up at Theseus.

Chapter 8

Theseus's fingers pressed firm against Pearl's head as he mumbled notes of what he felt to himself. His eyes, shut tight most of the time, relaxed at random times, like brief reprieves during a prolonged suffering. He released her head with a deep *huff*. "And yet another lesson added to your routine."

"What do you mean?" Pearl touched her head, trying to discern for herself whatever Theseus had discovered.

"Your mental defenses are feeble at best." They sat in one of the lower level rooms they had skipped during Pearl's tour of Lightholme. Though small, the room's white wooden floor, ceiling and walls distorted Pearl's perception and made its dimensions ambiguous. The wall right behind Theseus seemed miles away. She lost track of the door the moment it closed and disappeared into the wall. According to Theseus, the enchanted walls stopped mental attacks from entering or exiting the room. "Something in the Black Hill, no doubt the Black Heart, targeted you during your meditations when you're mentally most vulnerable. Bringing you to this room is the only reason you're even conscious right now. Here, we will train your mind to protect itself while you meditate or sleep, and exercise your conscious mental defenses."

"Meaning?"

"Your ability to protect your mind when you're awake." He ground his teeth together, and Pearl knew why. Every delay compounded against his patience, so every day he grew more irritable and anxious. At one point, he had suggested forcibly implanting knowledge into Pearl's mind to expedite her training, though he talked himself out of it moments after proposing the idea. "With enough training, you can turn these skills against others, attacking their minds with your own. Though, as weak as our mind is, that's not happening anytime soon."

"What's it like attacking someone's mind?"

Theseus took a deep breath and thought before he answered. "You expand your mind beyond your body, as if you were meditating, but then you give it a direction, a target, another mind. In order to do any damage, your mind must be strong enough to break through their mental defenses. Imagine a spear piercing a sheet of ice which grows thicker the stronger their mental defenses are. Once through, most assailants attempt to damage their target's mind enough to render them useless. However, a skilled psychic can shape the thoughts of others undetected and can even control weaker minds. It's a powerful skill to have, but few possess the mental capacity to accomplish even minor psychic feats. So stop squinting at me before you burst a damn blood vessel."

"Sorry. So…why did the Black Heart show me what it showed me? Why my dream and my old room? And why did it offer my family?"

"Uncertainty on your part makes its infiltration easier. If you can't distinguish an intrusion from your own thoughts, how can you protect yourself?" The man with no face still haunted Pearl's thoughts. She couldn't remember having ever seen him, yet something at the edge of remembrance gnawed at her attention. "As for its offer to reunite you with your family, it most likely wanted to invoke an emotional response and break any concentration you had on defending your mind. I'm sorry, Pearl. It was nothing, but an empty promise."

"Don't apologize. I didn't have my hopes up," she lied. "Teach me how to protect my mind."

The basics of mental defense proved easier said than done. Theseus would attempt to find a way into her mind, so to protect herself, she had to imagine an unbreakable, multi-sided solid object surrounding her. She imagined herself inside a hollow stone and waited for Theseus's assault. Despite proclaiming himself a weak psychic, having only a few basic techniques after a near-lifetime of practice, Theseus broke through Pearl's hollow stone within seconds. Pearl had expected a pointed thrust of thoughts at her mind, an overwhelming brute force like the Black Heart's attack. Instead, Theseus struck with a torrent, wrapping and circling around the stone, sawing it open. She tried again, this time wrapping her mind within a ball of metal, but Theseus hammered at the ball until it shattered open, despite Pearl's efforts to keep it whole. Blood dripped out of Pearl's nose as she thought of a place nothing could get into, some place safe.

An idea came to her, one she felt foolish for forgetting and she readied herself, giving Theseus the go ahead to attack her. He crashed against her defenses, first with a single, ordinary mental thrust, then with a chopping sensation, and then with a circular band wrapped around her that constricted and spun, trying to crush and cut at the same time. But her defenses stood and she pushed back to repel him. Theseus's face turned red with a shade of purple appearing on his cheeks as he strained to break through.

Then the attack stopped, its sudden absence surprising Pearl. Her concentration broken, Theseus's mental attack caught her off guard as it rushed at her, punching her in the forehead and throwing backwards onto her back. This attack differed from previous attacks, forcing images and voices into her mind instead of inflicting pain. The world around her broke away, and she found herself in New Bethlehem.

"Not again," Pearl grumbled in the vision. As Theseus had taught her to do in this situation, she focused on herself, and thought aloud, "I'm in the White Room. I'm in the White Room. I'm..."

"I missed you." A woman with dark brown hair stood in the doorway of the house in front of Pearl. She knew this woman and this house, but didn't know from where. Vague memories Theseus could utilize against her. Fog obscured the surroundings, those details unimportant to the memory. The woman stared at Pearl with sultry eyes and beckoned her closer with a single finger. A devilish air surrounded this woman, though more playful than sinister. "Let me show you how much."

"Oh," Pearl gasped, realizing she wasn't in one of her memories. Something had gone wrong, and she felt guilty for trespassing. Just as she wished to leave, the world melted away, revealing a new one underneath. Even the woman changed.

"I will not stand here while a group of old men and an outsider abandon a village to the Khaous without even trying to save it," yelled the woman, her hair now black and her skin paler, her narrow eyes glaring at Pearl. Pearl sat at a table of men, all with black hair and pale skin. They listened to the woman out of obligation, but their patience thinned. The woman pleaded to the elder man seated at the head of the table, next to Pearl. "Father, have you forgotten the words you taught me? The words of your father and his father? The words engraved on your blade? 'There is always light.'"

The scene shifted again. The man next to Pearl now sat on an elevated platform in front of her, looking down at her. Some time had passed since the last memory, as black streaked the man's gray hair. She could feel his gaze pressing down on her, and each of his words carried final, undebatable authority. "This boy will be raised by his people, by his true family, to carry on our traditions and heritage. He is your son no more."

Darkness flooded the world, the only light now a single, fallen candle next to her foot. Pearl stood over a beast with the body of a man and the head of a bull, her hands strangling the hilt of a sword driven into the beast's chest. It gasped for breath, but had stopped fighting some time ago. With a ragged cough, and deep, hoarse voice, it spoke. "I curse you, human. Enter my domain again, and it shall be your grave. Fire and blade will bear witness to your fall. This is my final vengeance. With my dying breath, I...curse...you..."

The memory ended with the jarring blink of an eye and Pearl crashed back into her body in the White Room. Blood coated her face from the nose down and her head pounded from the inside. It felt heavy and light at the same time. Her thoughts crawled at a sluggish pace. A loud thud drew her attention and she saw Theseus slumped against the wall, the blood dripping from his nose forming a small puddle on the ground. Pearl moved to help him, but her feet weighed her down like anchors and she dragged them as she crawled across the floor.

"Arrr yuuu wllll?" Pearl slurred.

"...Sorry..." Theseus gasped. He pushed off the wall, then fell back into it. He looked aged from the assault. "I'm afraid my own failings made this an ineffective lesson. As I said, my psychic abilities are not the best by any means and using them requires intense concentration. And mine faltered."

"What happened?" Pearl massaged her head with the palm of hand. "I saw images. Memories."

"During my final push, I lost focus and connected our minds by accident. Try to forget them. They're of little import and deserve no reflection." Theseus looked at the blood on his hand and on Pearl's face. He tried to wipe some off her face, but gave up soon after.

"What do we do now?"

"Let's wash up first. There's no point in continuing covered in blood. Clean up, put on some fresh clothes, then we'll return here to try again." As they climbed up the stairs, Theseus asked, "What was that tree you used to protect your mind?"

Pearl smiled to herself. "It's my secret place, my safe place, where nothing can get to me."

*   *   *

After another hour of tense faces and nose bleeds, they went for a silent walk through the forest to rest their minds. With Nightfall only an hour, they didn't venture far from Lightholme. Among the dense woods, they came across a clearing made just the night before, judging from the freshness of the fallen trees.

"This was some battle," Theseus broke the silence. "Something fought like hell here."

"But what?"

"When food is scarce during a hunt, the Khaous will fight amongst themselves to cull their numbers. The Khaous need to devour living flesh for some sort of sustenance, though the specifics are unclear, with dissection being impossible. A group probably came across a deer or some large prey and fought until their numbers could be sustained by their catch."

Deep cuts marked each of the standing trees ringing the clearing; so deep, Pearl didn't understand how they still stood. As she ran her fingers over one of the cuts, a buried memory stirred within her: Pearl running her hand over a similar cut in a similar clearing, while other people stood around her, looking at something among the trees. She remembered nothing more, but the memory left a dark impression of her, and she drew her sword.

"I don't like this. Something…there's a darkness here."

"Put that away. There's no need for it." Theseus rested his hand the hilt of his sword. "I'll admit, it's odd. Each of the trees fell to a single, clean blow. Not impossible, but I've never seen a Khaous take a tree down without any hacking and tearing. And look how the trees were cut from a central point…here…as though something stood its ground while the Khaous rushed in from all sides."

"But what else is out here?" Pearl felt the eyes of the forest upon her, though a scan of the forest's depths revealed nothing.

"Some time ago, Father Alexander created four beings to patrol the forest and hunt the Khaous. The Four Guardians, he called them. But they've been gone for years. The Ghost People could be out there still, though most native tribes moved west or north, and they avoid wandering too far from their homes. I've been all over the world and seen many things, but this new world is still strange to me. The furthest inland I've gone is to the Black Hill and that was by accident. We've yet to discover how far it stretches west. You ask what manner of beast and monster we shared these lands with? You'll know when you find them. Or when they find you."

This failed to comfort Pearl and she stayed close to Theseus, as she had done on her walks with her father, as they returned to Lightholme, the forest coming alive around them.

Chapter 9

"In the beginning, there was darkness," Pearl told the darkened room around her. "Darkness and a small orb of light."

"A 'pearl' of light, it is often said." She slashed out as she spun towards Theseus's voice behind her, but her sword cut nothing but air. She raised her blade into a defensive position and pivoted one slow step at a time, ready for an attack from anywhere.

"This pearl of light, the light of Order, contained all of existence. All that was, is, and will be. The darkness of Chaos surrounding the pearl desired to be the only thing in reality and attacked it, stabbing, pushing, crushing, doing all it could to destroy Order. But the pearl endured, every assault upon it a failure."

A blade's edge whistled closer from her right. Her Forewarn kicked in and Pearl raised her sword in time to block the attack. Sparks jumped from the clashing blades and illuminated Theseus's face for a brief moment, his eyes full of excitement and an almost wicked smile on his face. Then he and his blade disappeared back into the darkness.

"Chaos stabbed Order with all of its force and for the first time, it pierced into the orb. It did not expect what came next." Pearl raised her foot, focused her mana into it, and stomped down. A small wave of fire rolled out in every direction from her foot, and in the light, she saw Theseus and lunged at him. They fought, attacking, blocking, and parrying, but never giving an inch to each other, until the flames crashed and died against the wall. Pearl leapt away from Theseus and listened for his footsteps. "The orb shattered and everything within exploded out throwing Chaos back."

A week ago, Theseus had approached Pearl about undergoing the First Fight, the final test in becoming a Sister of the Flame, named so as it marked an initiate's first real fight in service of the Brotherhood and reminded them of the battles to come. The test combined a demonstration of her knowledge of the Brotherhood's lore and history, and a trial by combat against Theseus. Pearl had accepted the challenge on the spot and since that day, she had trained on her own, so Theseus couldn't learn what techniques she planned to use against him. Now, after what felt like hours of fighting and recitation, only one part of the Brotherhood's lore remained: the beginning of existence. Her Forewarn had kept her alive so far, though gaining an advantage vexed her as Theseus could disappear into the shadows. "Released from its orb form, Order expanded. And as it expanded, it created, guided by the singular mind and soul that held it together as an orb."

"The Presence." The cracking of lightning drowned out the echoes of Theseus's voice and the bolts dancing around him illuminated his position on the opposite side of the room. With a thrust of his hand, he shot the lightning at her. She dropped her sword and threw up her arms to create a shield of pure mana. As the lightning fizzled away against the shield, Theseus rushed towards her. Pearl kicked her sword off the ground up into her hand, snatching it in the dark. But Theseus never attacked.

"Yes, the Presence. The origin of all souls and minds. As existence and Order stretched out in every direction, so too did the Presence." Fighting in the dark had grown tiresome for Pearl. Though she didn't know the layout of this room, Theseus's reason for choosing this room, she remembered seeing torches on the wall before Theseus's lightning had died away.

Mana gathered in her hand and ignited. She threw the fireball and chased it to the wall, reaching the wall just after the fireball burst against it. She shuffled along the wall, her body pressed against it, feeling the space above her head until her hand brushed against the wooden shaft of the torch and the cold iron mount holding it on the wall. She removed it with caution, careful not to alert Theseus to her position. "Spread too thin, the Presence, Order, and all existence shattered, and their many different pieces scattered throughout the fledgling universe."

She covered her mouth. Her voice. Theseus followed the sound of her voice to attack her. But she couldn't stop her recitation. *Too hell with it,* she thought, and lit the torch. It flared to life, illuminating Theseus lunging at her. Pearl parried his attack away and swung the torch at Theseus. The fire licked his coat's edge before he jumped back into the shadows.

"As the pieces of existence continued to break apart in an expanding universe, multiple realms formed in the tears created by this expansion. And it was in the space between these realms that Chaos settled." Pearl kept her back against the wall as she made her way to the next torch, lit it, and moved on to the next one. Now and then, a torch would go out as Theseus tried to return the room to total darkness, his movements sporadic to keep them unpredictable. Pearl noticed something in the dark, but her torchlight blinded her. Moving the torch behind her, she could see specks of faint, red light glowing in the dark and moving around.

She threw her torch aside and rushed at the specks, slashing at them. They twisted away and Theseus parried her sword out of her hands. Her Forewarn made her jump backwards and she heard the swish of a sword passing right in front of her. She channeled mana into the red specks, the embers on Theseus's jacket, and ignited them, fire erupting up his side. He danced away from Pearl, his swears drowning out the roar of the fire as he tried to pat it out. Pearl chased him down and, with a "Hee-yah!", struck his forearm with her palm, making Theseus drop his sword. She kicked it away before continuing her assault, landing several powerful blows, though Theseus protected himself from the worst, despite being preoccupied with his burning jacket. A jump kick to the chest knocked Theseus off his feet, but he rolled out of the way when Pearl tried to stomp on him. He jumped to his feet, threw off his jacket, and ignited all torches in the room with a clap of his hands.

"Scared of the dark?" Pearl mocked him with a cruel smile.

"Just the things that go bump in it, you little monster," Theseus chuckled. He lowered his stance and raised his arms in front of his body. Don't forget your recitation."

"As far as we know, there are three realms. Our realm, the Mortal realm, and the realm of the gods, the Celestial Spheres, with the Chaos realm laying between and around them." While faster on her feet, Pearl's punches and kicks couldn't compare to Theseus's raw strength, and with him on guard now, she would have push harder to knock him off balance. *Focus on key spots*, she told herself when her blows didn't even faze Theseus. Between his swinging, crushing blows, Pearl darted in and struck at his joints. "The remnants of the Presence coalesced into lifeforms which would one day become gods. With only a fraction of the power the Presence possessed, these proto-gods couldn't travel the universe and settled in nearby growing planetary systems, claiming newborn planets as their own. As they shaped these planets, they grew more powerful, more unique, more individual, becoming the gods they are today. Once powerful enough, they were able to journey to the Celestial Spheres and claim spheres for themselves. This led to the creation of the different pantheons and, eventually, religion—agh!"

A solid blow to the head surprised Pearl and threw her off her feet. She hit the ground and recovered, rolling backwards into her stance, just in time to knock away Theseus's fist. She spun along the length of his arm and chopped at his neck, but he ducked under it. Pearl leaned back and kicked at his face. He caught her foot with his hand and wrapped his other arm around her leg. He pushed her off balance and threw her leg up to drop her on her back. Again, she rolled off her back onto her feet.

Theseus didn't pursue her and gathered lightning around his body. He flung a bolt at her before she could gather any mana for a shield. She cartwheeled to dodge the first bolt, and dove to evade the second. She fumbled into a kneeling position and shot a fireball, but a third bolt reduced it to a cloud of embers. The bolt was too fast to avoid, so Pearl caught it, a thin, glove-like layer of mana protecting her hand. Theseus's mana within the lightning attack and burned the mana over her hand, like warring armies of ants. With an agonized scream, Pearl forced the lightning into a ball and launched it back at Theseus. To her groaning dismay, the lightning ball sailed pass Theseus and crashed into the wall behind him, breaking off a large chunk of stone.

Exhaustion washed over Pearl's body, but only for a moment. Theseus rushed forward and her second wind kicked in. He tackled her, all of his weight thrown on top of her. She caught him, weight shifting from her front foot to her back, and threw him off of her. He twisted in midair and landed on his feet with a stumble.

Now, Pearl shouted in her thoughts. Mana gathered over her whole body sparked, covering her in fire. She threw her arms out at Theseus and the fire flew at him. He waved his hands in front of him, the air becoming misty as he created a mana shield. The blaze surrounded the shield and pushed against it, trying to break through. Pearl channeled her little remaining mana into the flames and directed it to the weak spots in Theseus's shield. She could feel Theseus pushing from within, reinforcing his shield and trying to break free. She concentrated as hard as she could, keeping Theseus stuck within his shield, but with a primal roar, Theseus expanded his shield, extinguishing the flames on top of him. The shield kept growing, smashing into Pearl and shoving her across the room into a wall. The shield and the wall crushed the air out of Pearl's body. Spots of light formed in her vision before the shield dispersed.

She fell to the ground, coughing and gasping for breath. Her neck strained to lift her heavy head. Theseus had retrieved his sword and stood over her. Pearl searched the room for hers and saw it laying against the wall to her right. Her body exhausted, she had a slim chance of beating Theseus to it. She struggled to her feet, her legs shaking the whole time.

A slim chance indeed. Theseus walked to his left, cutting off her path to her sword. She swore under her breath and weighed her options. Weaponless, her body sore and tired, with no mana, she would need to force him to make a mistake and then take advantage of it. The problem laid in Theseus. Despite the burns on his discarded jacket, he looked no worse than when the fight had started, the occasional deep breath the only sign he fought at all.

"Surrender, Pearl. I've won. You put up a good fight and there's no shame in losing." Pearl clenched her fist so hard, she drew blood from her palm. She wanted to beat him or, at the least, make him look like he had to try to beat her.

"No. I won't."

"What do you plan to do?" Theseus asked. Pearl didn't answer, her silence speaking her defiance. He sighed. "If your wish is to suffer a greater loss, I will grant you that."

He took cautious steps towards her, watching if she would make a move, and when she didn't, he rushed towards her, his sword ready to strike. Pearl's Bloodlust fed off her burning frustration, roared out of her and pushed her to charge straight at Theseus. Her faraway Forewarn tried to warn her of Theseus's sword, but she ignored it, her focus locked on Theseus's throat. In her Bloodlust-induced bestial frenzy, she hungered to rip it out. She no longer noticed his movements, seeing him only as a target.

She heard the clanging of metal, then a punch to her gut knocked the wind and the Bloodlust out of her. Theseus followed through with his punch by lifting Pearl off the ground, then grabbing her and throwing her down. Pearl gurgled in pain with no air to scream. The Bloodlust's sudden removal left her mind somewhat vacant, until her thoughts returned in fractions.

"takin...upid...sks." Theseus's words came in and out as Pearl's senses readjusted. "And...or what? A stupid test?"

"What?" She tried to sit up, but Theseus kept her on her back as he inspected her eyes.

"I'm saying cruel things about you, girl," he growled. "You have no idea when to give up or when to consider another method, and end up taking stupid risks. This is only a test. No need to get yourself killed over it."

"Didn't want to fail," Pearl admitted.

"You're reckless. You gave away your position when you lit that torch, and, worst of all, you lost control of your Bloodlust," Theseus lectured, counting her faults with his fingers. He retrieved Pearl's sword from the other side of the room, incinerating his scorched jacket with a barrage of lightning on the way back. "If I really wanted to kill you, I would have."

139

Pearl waited a moment. "But did I fail?" She pressed him for an answer as he lifted her to her feet in silence. "My recitation suffered from constant stops and a few missing details, but I got through most of it. I struck you a fair number of times, putting you on your heels more often than not."

"I don't care about the recitation." Theseus returned her sword and helped walk her out of the room. "More of a formality. I won't need a historian in the Black Hill. I'll need a fighter, a weapon. Despite some minor faults, you're well learned in combat and magic, and you mind is sharp, always searching for options, though you often take the dangerous path when cornered."

Pearl stopped and stared at him. "I passed?"

"Yes."

"I'm a Sister of the Brotherhood?" A smile spread across her face.

Theseus smiled. "Yes."

Joy lifted Pearl off her feet, but her body couldn't handle the jump and she almost collapsed upon landing. She thanked Theseus over and over again without breathing. She hugged him, surprising Theseus, but he returned the gesture, which comforted Pearl more than she thought it would. Breaking the embrace disappointed her, but she would never admit it.

"Are you ready, Pearl?"

With her basic training complete, they would spend every day from now until they reached the Black Hill preparing for the mission. She had a duty now, and she felt the responsibility settling on her shoulders. Though she knew nothing of the Brotherhood's quests of old, she knew the dangers of the Black Hill made their mission one of, if not the, most perilous. She held her head up, her smile not as steady as she would have liked. "Yes. I'm ready."

Chapter 10

Theseus slammed his hand onto the ground, the force of the blow shaking Pearl's feet. She sensed his mana channeling into the stone beneath them, shaping it into its desired form. As he lifted his hand off the ground, a human shaped statue with wider arms, legs, and body rose up, identical to the other three he had created already.

"What are they?"

"They're stone constructs." Theseus pulled for red gemstones from his pocket and clenched them tight in his fists, pooling his mana into them. Though Pearl could now detect concentrations of mana, she didn't need this ability to know filling the gems had drained Theseus. She saw it in the bags under his eyes and heard it in his haggard breath. "Similar to golems, but made of stone, as the name would suggest. The crystalline properties of gemstones allow them to store large amounts of mana. And, if enchanted, they can absorb mana from the air around them, just like our bodies. They'll serve as power sources for the constructs and the spells animating and sustaining them."

"And why are you making them?" Pearl took note of the morning sun's position over the tree tops. Despite the early hour, they had a long way to go and Theseus had yet to address their lack of weapons, much to Pearl's worry. They did carry lanterns containing half of the Fire of God each, and the warmth spreading from Pearl's through her body and soul brought some comfort to her worries.

Once Theseus pushed the last gem into the last construct, all four quaked to life, then resumed their motionless state, as if nothing had happened. But when Theseus moved around, the four constructs' heads turned to follow him. When he commanded them to patrol the perimeter of the house and awaited their return, they remained still, as though they hadn't heard him. Then, with the grinding of stone, they stomped to the tree line and began their guard, staggering their patrol until they were equally spaced around the circle clearing. They marched at a perfect, uniform pace, never gaining on one another.

"Without the Flame to power the Eye, they'll be Lightholme's only defense during our absence. Besides, there's no flame other than Yahweh's own that I would carry through the tunnels of the Black Hill." With the security of Lightholme in as fine

143

hands as any they would find, Theseus and Pearl set out into the forest. She glanced back at the house which had become her home for maybe the last time. Theseus had warned her their chances of success were not favorable, barring some divine act, and she wondered if she would ever see her new home again.

By midday, the lingering heat of summer emerged weak from its struggle with the morning's autumn chill. Orange leaves carpeted the forest floor and hung for dear life from the branches above. Piles of leaves rolled apart with every breeze. The seldom present wildlife scurried about preparing for the coming winter months.

Theseus admitted the night before he would rather deal with colder temperatures if it meant additional time to prepare Pearl, but he wanted to embark before the harvest's end to avoid the strange magics that occur naturally during that time. So, instead of waiting and risking a surge in activity from the Black Hill, they settled on early Fall. Pearl took time to admire the beauty around her, but after an hour, she noticed the sun still rising to her left.

"Why are we heading South?"

"We need to stop in New Bethlehem."

"What's there that you could want? The demons...the Khaous tore the town apart and anything still standing probably burned down. It will be a miracle if anything survived that night." In the quiet of the woods, she heard the howls of the Khaous, the roar of the flames, and the cries of the villagers. She recognized the lack of choices she had that night, but the memory of running away haunted her nonetheless.

"Weapons. Or, I should say, better weapons, stored in the tunnels beneath the church." Theseus walked with comfortable familiarity, the path clear to him despite his confessed fifteen year absence from the town. Pearl had no recollection of this part of the forest from her ride to Lightholme, and she stayed close to Theseus, the vast strangeness of the forest overwhelming her. The trees stared at her, every leaf an eye.

"It feels like something is watching us." She sought the solace of his logical perspective.

"Something is watching us. Something always is, and will be, watching you from just out of sight. Nothing is without its cost. Not even a walk through the woods."

Pearl kept her thoughts to herself for the rest of the walk.

*   *   *

Nothing remained of New Bethlehem. The four rows of houses and shops arching around the town square had been reduced to rubble. Weeds climbed their way up through the rotting lumber towards the sun, which slipped behind a thin scattering of clouds. Wild flowers grew among the crops in the farmlands to the east and west. The trees encircling the town, tall, thick elms, stood like watchtowers and formed a natural wall to protect the town. But they had failed, and had instead successfully concealed the dangers beyond.

In the silence, Pearl heard her breath's hissing escape through her teeth. The paths and town square, previously worn down to mud and dirt by foot traffic, had grown green after months of disuse. A cool breeze stirred a small cloud of dust and dry dirt, then the grave stillness returned. Pearl's jacket, given to her at the beginning of her Lamplighter training, hung heavy on her. She, the last Lamplighter, had failed in her sole duty of protecting the town. She pushed the thought to the back of her mind, but her jacket grew no lighter.

"Damn it." Theseus inspected the largest pile of debris, where the church once stood. "The bloody door's buried."

"There's always the door in the woods," Pearl reminded him.

"Not anymore." Theseus lifted a wood beam off the pile and tossed it to the side. "As a contingency, the stairs of the second entrance were lined with runed parchment on the bottom, which would explode unless recharged with mana every three days. In the event of the experiment being compromised, the detonation would destroy the stairs and cause the tunnel to cave in. This entrance's mechanical lock meant it required no contingencies. Despite appearances, this is the best path."

"What experiment?"

"One of Father Alexander's projects, nothing to worry about." He heaved a larger beam out of the way, and it landed with a cacophony of cracking and snaps. When Pearl moved to help, he raised a hand to stop her. "Stay there. I appreciate the offer but I don't want you getting hurt. Tell me about the town. I haven't been here in a while. Not since you were born, perhaps."

"Well, there were shops over there," Pearl pointed to the closest row of destroyed buildings. "The baker, the blacksmith, the carpenter. We didn't have any proper money, so we just traded what we had and what we could do."

"Gods, you're dull," Theseus groaned. "What was <u>living</u> in the town like, girl?"

"Well, be specific next time," Pearl jabbed back. "It wasn't fun, for me. Most people hated me. Some of the children my age were nice enough, but these two boys, Duncan and Pat, would scare them away. Duncan the Glutton and Pat the Rat, I called them. They tried to make my life hell, but I wouldn't let them. The adults didn't give a damn about me, except Michael Crowley, the man who trained the young Lamplighters. The only peaceful times were when my father and I took our morning walks. No one to whisper behind my back. No ugly stares and no one turning away from me. Just the quiet mornings. Then at night, the Lamplighters would go throughout the town and light the candles in the lanterns. Some nights, the trainees would follow them as part of their training. Everything we did was part of our training."

"Let me guess," Theseus huffed, tossing aside a pile of lumber. "Basic chores meant to build your strength?"

"Exactly," Pearl nodded. Theseus looked at the woods littered around him and under his feet.

"Damn, this is going to take longer than I thought. Why don't you scout the area? Search around, and report anything of note. I'll call for you when I have this clear." Pearl watched him move rubble around for several minutes before walking south to the river, the town's water source. She couldn't tell whether he wanted to be left alone or just wanted to keep her occupied, but she knew he didn't care about what she would find, if she found anything at all. Over a small hill and down a sharp decline, she reached the river. The mud and sand of the riverbank laid unmarked, though the lack of animal tracks surprised her. She checked all of the tree hollows and dens where the other children would play and hide, and found them all empty, as she expected.

No survivors…save Pearl. The memories of that night crept back into her mind like a guilty secret. The people of New Bethlehem suffering and dying, their screams filling the night and drawing more Khaous upon them. The Khaous descending upon the town like ravenous beast, snarling, growling, salivating…She…she could hear them. Her haunted thoughts mixed with reality, and she felt the Khaous around her, waiting in the branches for her return.

She needed to escape. She fell to her knees and clamored across the bank to the water's edge. She plunged her hand into the river, the sun-warmed surface belying the cold beneath, and clawed for a stone resting on the bottom. She wrapped her fingers around a stone so smooth it felt slimy, and clenched it tight as she ran to her tree, the hollow beneath vacant. No one else, neither man nor animal, ever came to this tree. Children would tell ghost stories about the tree and how the hollow was the unholy gate Pearl (or Pearl's mother, depending on the storyteller) had

149

exited Hell through. Despite knowing the story's origins, adults shared it in terrified whispers as truth.

To Pearl, it was her safe hideaway, where nothing could hurt her. Not even her own memories. She pulled her knees into her chest, pressed the stone against her heart, and listened to the river with her eyes shut. The imaginary screams and Khaous sounds faded away as the river babbled over rocks it had worn smooth. She chuckled. Even with no one around to bully her, she had come here. Some things never change. But others do. Just as New Bethlehem was no more, one day this tree would no longer stand, and she would lose her hollow. She looked at the stone in her hand and decided to leave it behind with a message to whoever found it. She focused mana into the tip of her finger and wrote upon the stone with the ease of quill on paper. She finished the last word just as Theseus called for her, and placed the stone down in the hollow's center.

A ring of debris encompassed Theseus as he waited for her at the top of the stairs to the tunnels. Large chunks of the wooden altar still sat upon the secret door it had hid from those who had prayed before it. Pearl followed Theseus down and found the tunnels lit, the torches still burning since the day she left. Though, like Pearl's father, Theseus could have led her in complete darkness as he moved with certainty through the turns of the hallways. With no markings on the doors, how Theseus found the door he wanted baffled Pearl

"This would be the armory." Weapons of varying shapes and sizes covered the walls and filled several chests below. A wooden table to her left had several weapons sprawled across it, abandoned before anyone had a chance to return them to their proper places. A fireplace in the corner lit the entire room, brown logs resting on top of the fire, as if someone had just thrown them on. When she asked about this, Theseus couldn't answer her. She turned her attention back to the wall to distract herself from the eerie possibilities.

"Why are there so many?" Several short swords hung right next to each other, identical in almost every way. "Do you really need so many of the same sword?"

"Shape is their only similarity." He picked a longsword off the wall, held it, then took a few practice swings before placing it back. "Father Alexander, Brother Gen, and, for a time, I enchanted these weapons to mimic various God Artifacts."

"God Artifacts? Like the Flame?" She copied Theseus as she examined one of the shortswords. She hovered her hand over the blade and focused mana into her palm to make it sensitive to the spells and enchantments around and within the sword. She couldn't discern the specifics of the enchantments, but could tell fresh mana, only a few years old, had recreated ancient magics, an old tale in a dead language rewritten with fresh ink. After some practice swings, she replaced the sword. "So there are more than one Artifact?"

"Hundreds, probably thousands, possibly millions. Anything created, blessed, favored, or even touched by a divine being could be considered an Artifact. A transfer of energy occurs when a god interacts with an item made by mortal hands, since each originate from a different realm, whether the god meant to empower it or not. If a god drank from a mortal cup, the owner of said cup may find it never empties or it turns water into wine. While some Artifacts are named and remembered throughout history, most go unnoticed and forgotten. The Brotherhood, in addition to guarding the Fire of God and combating the forces of Chaos, sends it agents around the world to find Artifacts, named and unnamed, before they can fall into the wrong hands. More often than not, the Artifacts found are weapons with incredible and destructive powers. Brothers and Sisters educated in ancient magic work to replicate these powers and enchant other weapons with them, though the copied enchantments are never as powerful as the original. But they're still useful for the Brotherhood's endeavors. The powers of every weapon in here originated from the might of gods."

"Wow," Pearl gasped, stunned by the potential power within each weapon on the wall. "How do you know what kind of magic every weapon has?"

"Father Alexander kept records of that in a book, which should be somewhere in this room. And there are also these." A scrap of paper hung by a string from the hilt of the sword in his hand. "These will tell you everything you need to know about each weapon.

Pearl found the book on the only table in the room, but when she told him, Theseus ignored her, opening a chest and removing its contents. As she flipped through the book, she looked at the weapons also on the table: a few knives, a bow with a single arrow, two pistols, and a bastard sword with a golden blade and a black hilt. Her eyes kept wandering back to the sword, and when she did break her gaze away from it, she looked for it in the book. Each page featured a different weapon including a detailed illustration and an extensive list of specifics, like the weapon's dimensions, weight, ornaments, materials, colors, and so on.

She flipped through the entire book, but couldn't find the sword's entry nor did the sword have a tag. As with the short sword, she waved her hand over the blade and sensed the magic within, not knowing what it did. But she did know the original, ancient mana fueled enchantments just as old. She held the blade up to her face to study the unrecognizable runes carved into it. A fire seemed to flicker within the steel, becoming more alive the longer she stared at her reflection. Heat distorted the air around the sword, but it cooled her hand. It felt comfortable, the hilt long enough to grip with both hands if she wanted.

I don't want this sword. She didn't want to wield a weapon if she didn't know what it would do in the middle of a fight. But her training taught her the best weapon would feel like an extension of her body, and the sword already felt like a part of her. The sword whispered to her in a bygone tongue, asking her to wield it. It should have unnerved her, but the blade felt natural in her hand. She wrapped the sword's simple black sheath around her waist, and slid the sword away with a click.

"Ragenoz Rako." The words escaped her lips.

"What did you say?" Theseus shouted as he rummaged through another chest, pulling out a pair of golden, jeweled gloves.

"Nothing." She didn't know what she had just said or how she knew them. She tried to remember the words, but couldn't. "What are those?"

"They're called 'Titan Gloves.'" He slipped them on, grabbed two longswords off the wall closest to him, and swung them with no strain, as if he held thin branches fallen from a dead tree. He slung one of them onto his back and returned the other. "Once activated, the gloves allow the wielder to hold heavy weapons in each hand, making them as light as knives. Plus, they make the wearer as strong as a Titan when they're wielding lighter weapons." He gestured at Pearl's sword as he removed the gloves. "What have you got there?"

"A bastard sword." All she knew of the blade.

"Ah, one and a half handed sword. A very middle ground weapon. Versatile. That might come in handy. Make sure that's not your only weapon. Consider something with some range to it. Throwing knives, a lance, a bow, anything that can hit that which your sword can't."

In the end, Pearl decided to take a bow made of white wood and a matching quiver of arrows. According to Father Alexander's book, the bow guided its archer, making it near impossible to miss, and the arrows, with a bit of mana to ignite them, turned into bolts of burning light. Theseus took the

155

two pistols from the table where Pearl found her golden sword. "I made these before I started working on the rifle model. Couldn't figure out how to make the rifle sturdy enough, so I lent them to Gen to see if he could crack it."

"It fires mana blasts, just like the rifle?"

"Correct. Mana flows from me into the chamber, where it's shaped into a sphere, and then fired. It shoots as fast as I can pull the trigger, which can be dangerous. If I'm not mindful, I could shoot myself to exhaustion." He pulled the longsword, wide bladed with a simple handguard giving it the appearance of a cross, off his back and ran it across his throat. Pearl screamed, reaching out to stop him, but he laughed as he revealed his uncut neck. "This is Caliburnus Minor. The blade can never harm me, and while it is in my possession, all but my severe wounds will heal faster."

"I have something for you, Pearl." He sheathed his sword and searched through one of the piles of weapons he made. From among the swords, axes, and other weapons, Theseus pulled out a necklace, a ruby veiled with gold set in a dark metal base on a chain made of the same metal. When Pearl placed it around her neck, the ruby pulled some mana from her body, before reversing the flow back into her. Theseus placed an identical necklace, save for its sapphire

156

gem, around his neck. "It's called a 'Hungering Stone.' Just as your body naturally absorbs the mana in the air around you, the Stone does so at an accelerated rate, increasing the flow of mana into your body and refilling your mana stores faster. You should already feel it feeding you mana."

Before Pearl could thank him, Theseus turned away and picked up two identical swords he had set aside. He threw the one in his left hand to Pearl, and drew his sword to show it to Pearl. The slender blade, sharp on only one side, had a slight curve to it. Pearl drew her sword and noticed hers had a circular, silver guard and a dark blue hilt, while Theseus's had a square, gold guard and a red hilt. Though light in her hand, Pearl could tell the blade could cut through most materials and block even the strongest blows without breaking. "They're called 'katanas,' used in the country of Japan in the Far East. I spent a long time there during my travels for the Brotherhood. Lived there actually, but…circumstances demanded otherwise. My…friend gave me this katana as a gift. She named it 'Akuma no Satsugai-Sha' or 'the Slayer of Demons.' With every blow this blade deals to a Khaous, I become stronger and faster."

Theseus stared at the light dancing on the blade before pointing to the katana in Pearl's hands. "Years after I received my blade, I created one of my

157

own and copied my blade's magic into the new one. It...I...The..." Theseus seemed stuck in his thoughts, his tongue incapable of producing words. "I wanted to see if I could replicate the magic as Father Alexander had done with all of the weapons in this room. It...I was not wholly successful, as your blade's magic is partially bound to my blood. So, in your hands, it will not have as great an effect, but it will still augment your strength and speed. Not to mention, it's a damn fine blade, if I may say so."

"What's its name?"

"...Hānta no Musuko. Son of the Hunter."

"It's amazing. Thank you." A sword hung from each of Pearl's hips and she strapped her new bow and quiver onto her back. When Theseus suggested she arm herself with a few more weapons, she refused. "I have my speed, not your strength. I don't need any extra weapons or armor weighing me down."

Theseus couldn't deny this. Not that much fit Pearl anyway, all of the equipment and armor created for men. Gloves fell off her hands and her feet shuffled within every pair of boots she tried without moving the boots an inch. Her simple cloth shoes with their flexible, yet stable leather soles, black cloth pants, and white cloth shirt satisfied her needs. She abandoned the wide-brimmed hat of the

Lamplighters, which obscured her vision looking up, and tied her hair back into a tail to keep it under control. At Theseus's suggestion, she wore a pair of fingerless leather gloves that reached to her elbow.

Theseus, on the other hand, covered himself with weapons and equipment. His longsword strapped to his back, his katana hanging on his left hip, his two pistols tucked into his belt, the Titan Gloves slipped over his hands, a chainmail shirt beneath a leather vest on his chest, and several throwing knives concealed inside his jacket. He walked over to a golden shield hanging on the wall and stared at his reflection until another face, a woman's, appeared on the shield surface.

"Greetings, Argonaut. It draws closer," the woman's face on the shield sang, before she disappeared. With a sigh, Theseus lifted the shield off the wall and placed it on his back.

"Ready?" he asked. Pearl nodded and followed him out of the room, staring at her reflection in the shield. After a few seconds, the woman's face appeared on the shield.

"Greetings, jewel. It will come with the end of the next cycle."

Once outside, Theseus estimated they had a few hours of sunlight before they had to prepare a camp for Nightfall. "Let's try to put as much distance between us and these ruins before then. Let's follow the sun."

Pearl refused to look back as they entered the forest once again, but the screams of the dead called out for her, filling the woods with echoes only she could hear. She shifted her jacket and pulled it shut to fight the chill crawling over her.

Chapter 11

The sensation of being watched returned the moment they left New Bethlehem. Theseus laughed when Pearl alerted him to this, but as the hours passed and they journeyed deeper into the forests, Pearl noticed his head turning from side to side more and more often. His right hand rested on the hilt of his katana and Pearl sensed the mana gathering in his left palm. Pearl watched their rear, her hands resting on both of her swords. She saw nothing among the trees, but every time she looked, she swore something moved beyond her field of vision before she could see it.

"Stop!" Theseus's hand caught Pearl's shoulder like a vice and pulled her backwards onto her rear.

"Why the hell—?!" Pearl shouted as she stood, rubbing her buttocks.

"Watch where you're going, instead of worrying about our stalker." They stood at the edge of a deep pit trap, filled with sharpened logs standing erect on the bottom. The scattered bones of those animals unfortunate enough to have fallen in and the pit's decomposing grass cover littered the floor between the log spikes. "If it hasn't attacked us yet, I doubt it ever will."

"Who dug this hole?" They walked along the pit's edge to circumvent it.

"The villagers of New Bethlehem. They knew the Khaous came from the forest, but didn't know how to deter their attacks, so they created these primitive defenses."

She remembered the childhood warning of not going far into the woods. "They didn't want us going deep into the woods because they didn't want us falling into the traps."

"I'm sure they just didn't want you getting lost after Nightfall. These traps were quickly forgotten after Father Alexander created the Lamplighters." Once on the other side, they continued west. An hour before Nightfall, they stopped in a small clearing to camp for the night. On one side of the clearing, a large fallen tree provided some measure of protection as a small wall. On the opposite side, a thinning among the trees allowed them to see anything approaching them, though they didn't need to worry about an attack. Theseus took both of the lanterns and adjusted the blinders to cast a shell of light around them, shielding them from any Khaous once Nightfall fell, much like the lamps of New Bethlehem. A layer of fallen leaves, most of them from the fallen tree, acted as a thin, unforgiving bed over the grass kept short by the animals of the forest.

They ate the night's rations of their provisions: dried meats and berries, roasted nuts, cheese, and a thin, dry bread of Theseus's own invention. He claimed it never staled or went bad, though Pearl wished it would do either or both, just to add some flavor. They washed all of this down with careful sips from their waterskins. *This might be our last supper,* Pearl thought. Though she knew many, there was no dish she would rather have. A breeze shook loose a shower of leaves over their little camp, the chill biting at Pearl's coat. Then the forest returned to its silence, as it waited for Nightfall.

"I have an idea." Theseus stared at the lanterns, his eyes shining with their brilliant light. "Gather some firewood. Fallen sticks if you can find them. If not, cut some from the trees. I'm going to hunt for some fresh meat, so we can have a proper meal tonight."

The idea of a hot dinner warmed Pearl and she jumped to her feet. By the time Theseus rose to his feet, Pearl already had a handful of broken sticks. Her enthusiasm waned as she moved out of the lantern light and the sensation of being watched returned stronger than before, raising the hairs on the back of her neck. A malicious aura radiated from something nearby. Rustling in the trees above drew her attention and she dropped the sticks in her hand to draw her sword.

"Theseus," she called out, but only the rustling replied. Through a hole in the foliage, Pearl saw the figure of a creature more than half her size leap from one branch to another. Something on its forelimb shone in the dying light of day. It circled her from above, watching her sword.

"Theseus." The creature ignored her cry and instead looked out into the forest away from their camp. It raised its human-like head, as though it heard something else. Then it pounced at Pearl.

"Theseus," she screamed as the creature landed on top of her and the two of them fell to the ground. The creature's hands, one of them hard and cold like metal, struggled to take hold of Pearl's arms to stop the wild swings of her sword. Pearl managed to raise a knee between her and the creature, and kicked it off of her. She leapt to her feet and raised her sword at the creature. A boy, about half Pearl's age, stood before her. He kept thrusting his arms out at Pearl, begging her to stop, though he never spoke a word. Slim muscles, more than a boy his age should have, toned his tan body. Black fuzz layered the top of his head. He wore a shirt and a pair of trousers, both made of deer skin and lined with fur, as well as an armlet made of a white metal, but no shoes. An upside down white handprint covered his face like a mask, making his dark brown eyes stand out.

"Who...who are you?" The boy didn't answer, and looked away at something Pearl couldn't see. He ran to her side and tried to pull her back towards the camp. "What are you doing?"

Theseus ran into the clearing, his Titan Gloves on and a sword in each hand. He placed himself in front of Pearl and the boy, without noticing the latter, defending them from the forest. "I heard you scream. Are you okay? Were you attacked? Where is it?"

"Theseus, there's nothing out there." She pointed to the boy. "Nothing except him."

"Theseus turned and noticed the boy for the first time. "Oh, him."

"Who is he?"

"A native of this area. One of the Ghost People."

"Ghost People? I didn't know there were other people in these lands." In New Bethlehem, during what served as schooling, the children learned they lived in unclaimed, unsettled land, belonging to no one.

"Since long before we knew this land existed, the Ghost People called these woods their home, though I don't know how far their land stretches." Theseus grabbed the boy's right hand and studied his armlet. It seemed unremarkable to Pearl, but Theseus took great interest in it. "Where did you get this?"

"What's wrong? It's just an armlet."

"But I don't recognize the metal or the craftsmanship. IT appears to have seams in it, as though it can come apart." To the boy, he asked again, "Where did you get this?"

The boy remained silent. His eyes moved from Theseus to Pearl, then to something behind them. His eyes widened and he grabbed Theseus and Pearl by the arm, trying to pull them back to their camp. Pearl broke free, turned around, and saw nothing.

"Gather up the wood." Theseus walked back to the lanterns. "It's too late to go hunting or fishing, but at least we can be warm tonight."

Pearl kept an eye on the boy as she picked up the sticks she had dropped, but he paid her no mind and scanned the trees, expecting to see something.

"What's your name?" Pearl wanted to break the silence handing in the air, but the boy didn't answer. "Do you even understand me?"

The boy nodded.

"Then will you say something?" The boy shook his head.

"And why not?" The boy didn't answer her and resumed his watch. His head started to turn to the right, when it snapped back to look past Pearl. He leapt forward and pulled on Pearl hard enough to shake the sticks out of her arms.

"Why did you do that?" She stomped her foot and looked down on the boy, her hands resting on her hips. The boy took a step away from her, then pointed over her shoulder. "Would you stop? You keep looking and pointing, but there's never anything there. You better pray to God there really is something behind me or I'll—"

A slender man twice Pearl's height, with pale skin and arms reaching down to his knees and dressed in his best black clothing, stood behind her. Pearl felt his gaze, even though his head lacked any features or indents meant for his ears, mouth, nose, or eyes. Whispers filled her head, drowning out the rest of the world. A long buried memory clawed its way to the light and a name came to her.

"The Grey King," Theseus's voice cut through the whispers. Pearl shook them out of her head, the forgotten memory remaining lost. Theseus, with the boy hiding behind him, approached the Grey King. "Grey King, we met once, long ago. Do you remember? It was shortly after your creation and on the eve of my departure."

The words 'Grey King' echoed from the depths of her mind, but she didn't understand their significance. The figure, the Grey King, stared at her, even as it answered Theseus's question with a nod. Magic surrounded him, rippling the air like water.

"Who…what is it?"

"I mentioned the Four Guardians of the Black Hill some time ago. In an effort to combat the Khaous around New Bethlehem, Father Alexander performed a powerful and arcane ritual to create four homunculi, artificial beings, with powers beyond any homunculi before them. Once created and released, the Guardians wandered the forest, killing any Khaous they encountered. Unbound to their creators by design, they were rarely seen after their creation. It was assumed they had disappeared into the western lands. Yet, here one stands." Theseus gestured at the Grey King. "I'll sleep easier tonight, knowing a Guardian still hunts the Khaous in these woods."

As Theseus returned to his leaf bed, the boy tugged Pearl's arm, urging her to follow. She flicked free of his grasp and picked up the twice dropped sticks. With the boy and the Grey King, the two things in the forest watching them present, Pearl felt safe, though something about the Grey King killing

Khaous disturbed Pearl. A wave of cool washed over her, the way a light breeze feels on a hot summer day, comfortable and peaceful. A faint humming filled the air, and Pearl assumed it came from her. The boy still pulling on her arm, didn't annoy her so much anymore. His touch grew lighter and lighter, and soon he let go of her completely. The humming and the soft voices speaking comforting words to her in a language she couldn't understand silenced all else. The forest faded away and she opened her arms to the serenity promised to her. She felt nothing, not even the ground under her feet.

The Grey King moved closer to her, its long arms branching into long, shadowy tendrils wrapping around her. She danced within them, jumping and twirling with joy. The Black Hill held nothing but death for her. All she needed she had here with the Grey King. She wished Theseus and the boy would join her, but they busied themselves in the lantern light, Theseus speaking to the boy and the boy gesturing towards Pearl with aggressive urgency. Theseus looked at Pearl, his eyes widening, his mouth moving in wide motions as he yelled. Why yell? With everything at peace, what warranted yelling? Everything… peaceful… good… sleepy… Her eyes and body heavy with sleep, Pearl fell backwards, certain the Grey King would catch her. His many arms collapsed upon her like a cold, but welcomed blanket.

Chapter 12

Pearl floated in a sea of darkness. With no horizon, sky and sea fused together as one. A lone star shone on Pearl. She couldn't see him, but she knew the Grey King watched over her, bringing peace and safety. She said his name aloud over and over again, hearing the word leave her mouth and hearing nothing at the same time. The star's light stirred a memory within her as she spoke his name. A forest grew around her and she stood next to a woman. She too knew of the Grey King's power and grace, and took Pearl to him.

No, a voice within her said. *Berries. We were looking for berries.* Berries…That's why Pearl had gone with Mrs. Graham and the others into the forest. But they had gone too far…

"Pearl!"

Pearl opened her eyes after what felt like a prolonged blink, and scanned her surroundings. The forest, existing as vast singular entity like an ocean, threatened to consume all intruders. In New Bethlehem, it always seemed ready to wash over their homes and erase all trace of the colony. This far from the town, it felt like Pearl and her small group had drawn the forest's full attention. The trees, armored in gray bark, towered over them and reached out with limbs coated with thick layers of dark green leaves. Each was an exact replica of some primordial monolithic tree, though distinct by the scars the demons had left behind.

The foliage's hungering shade marked the hunting grounds of the demons, which had preyed on the creatures of the woods long enough to drive them to near oblivion. The overlooked smaller animals survived as timid beasts, hiding whenever they heard or saw something larger than a deer moving through the trees. The natural predators, wolves, wildcats, and bears, had long since left the area around the town, so one could walk through the forest during the day without fear of running into one.

Not that anyone ever felt safe in the forest, regardless of the time of day, and these thoughts didn't ease Pearl's mind as she realized how far the village they had gone. Something didn't feel right, an odd sort of memory permeating her thoughts. Had she been here before? Her hand squeezed the hilt of her sword, but once conscious of this, she let go, though her hand continued to hover over it. *Stay calm,* she thought to herself. *Don't show that you're nervous. Stay calm for them.*

"Is everything alright, dear?" Mrs. Graham asked. A soft woman, every part of her body cushioned by flesh, Abigail Graham retained some of the beauty the loss of her husband had drained from her. She never spoke ill of Pearl and would greet her with a smile when they crossed paths in town. Her own misery had taught her to see the misery in others, and she had no reason to add to their pain. It only made sense that Pearl enjoyed the woman's company.

"Yes, Mrs. Graham. Just thinking about how deep in the forest we are," Pearl reassured, her voice steady while her hands shook. But the others could sense her anxieties.

"Coward. I should be the leader," Duncan mumbled loud enough for everyone to hear. He swung his sword, a long, wide blade he had chosen based on the impractical notion that bigger equaled better and without insight of his own physical limits, at a low branch without regard for those around him. Pat the Rat had distanced himself from Duncan a while ago after one of Duncan's backswings missed him by an inch, but stood close enough to provide verbal support.

173

"You should." Pat glared at Pearl with his beady eyes. The other boy and girl remained silent at the edge of the group, trying hard to make the others forget them.

"Crowley put me in charge because you two are idiots," Pearl reminded them without looking back. She turned towards Mrs. Graham. "Why do we have to go this deep into the forest for berries?"

Mrs. Graham chuckled. "When you were younger, you children ate all of the good berries near town. All that grows on those bushes now are tiny, bitter berries, so I have to travel far from town to find any good ones."

Mrs. Graham hadn't picked a single berry so far and they continued going deeper into the forest. Pearl kept an eye on the sunlight coming through the leaves. Close to midday, it should have brought her comfort, but didn't. Only her sword comforted her, but the others would notice if she kept fidgeting with it. Duncan and Pat needed little to undermine their assignment, so she refused to give them a reason. Still, she couldn't move her hand far from her blade. Something out of sight watched them, moving beyond her field of vision every time she turned her head.

For the past few months, people in the town had been walking off into the woods, never to be seen again. Prior to disappearing, each of the missing individuals had mentioned hearing whispers in a strange language, and complained of sudden head pains and occasional memory loss. Despite the concern this had stirred in the townsfolk, nothing was done about it, until the number of disappearances jumped to twelve people gone in as many days.

In order to keep control of the situation, the Lamplighters had announced a town-wide lockdown and curfew. No one could leave the town without permission from the Lamplighter council. Even then, a Lamplighter escort had to accompany them. This morning, when the Lamplighters gathered in the town square for their assignment, Michael Crowley had assigned Pearl to Mrs. Graham. "Despite what my brother and the rest of them might think, you have the potential to be a great Lamplighter. But first you need to learn how to lead." He had stolen a glance at Duncan and Pat, and added, "And no lesson should be without its challenges."

"Stupid chore," Duncan complained as he waddled to keep pace behind Pearl. No doubt"Of course they'd make you the leader, witch-bitch."

"Heh 'witch-bitch,'" Pat chuckled, ever looking to remain on Duncan's good side. On the cusp of manhood, his voice squeaked and body oil gave his face a dirty sheen. Both them smelled, neither having bathed in weeks.

"Shut up, Duncan." Pearl rolled her eyes at his new name for her. Not only did it insult her, it rhymed too, meaning Duncan and Pat would use it for at least the next week or so. Unless they came up with a new, even wittier one, which Pearl doubted since it had taken them years to discover that 'witch' and 'bitch' rhymed. Years spent torturing Pearl with other cruel names and bullying away any child Pearl tried to befriend. It had hurt Pearl when she was younger, but it had lost its sting with time. That hadn't dissuaded Duncan the Glutton and Pat the Rat, nor had Pearl ceased using the insulting titles she had given them.

She knew Crowley had assigned her this specific task for a reason. Frederick had united those who distrusted Pearl into a cult of hate and threatened to take retribution into their own hands. Crowley, and no doubt her father, probably wanted to get Pearl as far from the town as possible until they could pacify Frederick and his followers. Though knowing Frederick, his hate would persist beyond all others.

Mrs. Graham ignored several bushes dotted with berries and they journeyed deeper into the woods than any before them, at least in Pearl's mind.

While she relished the excitement of an adventure, a palpable dread darkened the world. The leaves above suffocated the sunlight and an ominous dim settled around them. The scars on the tree grew more abundant, some low to the ground, some marking the highest branches, all left by fang and claw. Fallen trees, their roots still clutching dirt, marked the paths of the largest demons. For those who had only heard the demons and never seen them, here laid the proof of their existence. Holding her sword failed to comfort her now, so Pearl drew it, ready to fight.

"Ooo," Duncan jeered with a wave of his chubby fingers. "Look at the scaredy-cat. What's the matter, witch-bitch? Afraid something might get you while the sun is out? Like a rabbit?" This gave Pat a good laugh, a squeaking hiccup-like sound.

"That's it," Pearl growled to herself. She turned around and pointed her sword at Duncan. He stumbled backwards, his size and weight making his retreat awkward. "All you do is moan and complain. The forest is filled with all...kinds of dangerous...things..." She trailed off as she counted heads. Duncan, Pat, Mrs. Graham. "Where are the other two?"

Duncan and Pat looked around, just noticing the absence of their comrades. Wordless since leaving town, they could have disappeared at any time.

Movement out of the corner of her eye made Pearl jump, as Mrs. Graham scratched her head. Pearl shook with a rush of energy and took breathes to calm herself. "Mrs. Graham, did you see where our friends went?"

Mrs. Graham didn't respond, preoccupied with her own thoughts and whispering to herself. Pearl opened her mouth to ask again when Mrs. Graham responded, "Not much further. We'll be home soon. Very soon."

Pearl saw her fears reflected on Duncan and Pat's faces. She glanced down at her sword and, with a nod, instructed the other two to draw their swords. Duncan dripped with anxious sweat and Pat's trembling hands made his sword waver like a bough in the wind. They looked to Pearl for guidance. For now, Pearl kept an eye on Mrs. Graham, who walked away. They followed her, a few paces behind, until she stopped in the middle of a clearing.

A storm-like force had thrown trees around and snapped them in two like twigs. Among the usual tears and scratches left by demons, Pearl noticed unusual cleaner, blade-like cuts in the trees, some so clean, they had left the exposed wood as smooth as polished wood. A fight had taken place here, but who would fight the demons this far into the woods?

"Ah, these berries will do nicely," Mrs. Graham announced, pushing aside a large stick to kneel next to a bush. Pearl studied her for a few seconds, then gestured for Duncan and Pat to keep an eye on her while Pearl scouted around the clearing. The trees felled by clean cuts had done so with a single blow each, lacking any sign of hacking. While woodchips and dust littered the soil around the trees cut down by demons, she found none by the other fallen trees. Sap still seeped from every cut. Whatever happened here had happened last night, when the demons hunted the forest, or maybe even an hour ago. Pearl shuttered at the thought and scanned the trees around her for any threats.

"Everyone, we're heading back to town." Pearl felt something staring at her to her right, and turned to find her missing comrades standing before. "There you are. We're going back to—"

"The Grey King rises," the two droned in unison. Their vacant gaze reached deep into Pearl's being. She raised her sword at them, or whoever stood there. They took no notice of the blade. "The Grey King rises."

This time, Pearl heard two more voices join in. Duncan and Pat stared at Pearl, the same emptiness in their eyes. She swung her sword towards them and stepped back to keep an eye on all four of them. They remained still, except for their soulless eyes, which followed her. She needed to get Mrs. Graham away from them and back to town. One of the other Lamplighters would know what to do, and if not, Father Alexander would. She saw movement to her left, but before she could react, something heavy hit her in the back of the head. The blow sounded like a knock on a thick, wooden door. The world spun as Pearl fell to the ground and, before the world went dark, Pearl saw Mrs. Graham holding a large, club-like branch.

*   *   *

Nearby voices woke Pearl up, and she willed her shut eyelids apart. Her blurred vision failed to discern her location, but the rustling of leaves above and the soft grass beneath her meant welcomed her back to the forest. Night had fallen. Instincts guided her hand towards her sword, but fear chilled her when she discovered it missing. She reached out to search for it, but as soon as she moved, her head spun in two different directions inside and out. The welt on the back of her head throbbed with every heartbeat and weighed like a second head. Jumbled thoughts coalesced as her vision cleared, and she discovered her blade was nowhere nearby.

"I awaited your arrival for hours, sire." Pearl froze, her hands still groping the ground for her misplaced sword. Mrs. Graham's voice came from behind her, but she spoke to someone else, hidden behind a tree or the tree itself. Pearl's fellow Lamplighters knelt in reverence behind Mrs. Graham. "I would have waited days. And look, I've brought acolytes, converts to your will."

"Mrs...Mrs.Graham?" The words tumbled out of her mouth as her head exploded with pain. Worms grew inside her skull and chewed their way out. Her ears ached, as if suffering some deafening roar, but Pearl heard nothing, not even her own screaming. She roll around on the ground, smacking her head against the earth to gain even a temporary reprieve from the agony.

Then, in the silence, she heard it. A voice whispering in her ears-no, in her head-in a language she had never heard before, words not of this world. Quiet at first, the whispering grew into a roar, like the winds of a faraway storm lumbering closer. It tried to tell her something, but she couldn't understand. Not as though she could at the moment, her body spasming in pain. She flailed around helpless, like a fish on land. Someone spoke nearby, but Pearl's screams, now audible, drowned it out. The tears in Pearl's eyes smeared Mrs. Graham and the four Lamplighters, but the figure they knelt before appeared pristine in Pearl's vision.

"Hhhaaalllppp mmmeeeeee," Pearl grunted through gritted teeth. Only the figure looked at her, as if noticing her for the first time. He, or she, dressed in fine, black clothing and had a bald, pale head somewhat hidden among the leaves of the trees around it, standing twice as tall as Pearl. As the figure stared at Pearl, the air around it rippled like water and the ripples grew wider as they drew closer. They swallowed Pearl whole, and it felt like the ground beneath her had punched her whole body, throwing her into a tree.

She fell to the ground and laid as still as she could while trying to catch the breath knocked out of her lungs. The whispering had stopped, but the pain had not. She commanded her body to get up and fight, but it wouldn't move. She could only watch as the tall figure's arms stretched out and wrapped around Mrs. Graham. She accepted its embrace with a calm and quiet stillness. The others didn't reacting, four kneeling statues awaiting the experience Mrs. Graham underwent.

A growling filled the air. The figure stopped, retracted its arms, and looked at the trees to Pearl's right, where the growl rumbled in the back of a beast's throat. Mrs. Graham dropped to the ground and laid like a discarded doll. Branches and sticks snapped as the growling grew closer, each snap causing Pearl's heart to skip a beat. Even if she could move her body, she wouldn't have. Better to play dead than to draw the attention of whatever new threat had entered the clearing on light feet, which she felt with her head pressed against the ground.

She couldn't see it, but heard it sniff the air above her head. It thought little of her, and approached the tall figure, its paw landing inches away from her face as it walked over her. The wolf shaped demon, three times larger than any wolf, stood on its hind legs. Its black flesh and fur allowed it to blend in with the darkness of the forest. Its bulky forelegs, now serving as arms, ended in finger-like toes with knife-like claws. Mrs. Graham and the others snuck away into the trees as the demon confronted the tall figure.

Pearl's attention pulled towards the figure, as though a small voice told her to look at it, but she kept her eyes on the tree Mrs. Graham had ducked behind. If Pearl could get to her, they could run back to the town. Dangerous without a sword, but she had run out of options. An eerie silence fell upon the clearing as the wind died, and the demon and the figure in black studied each other, waiting for the other to make a move.

A gust of wind howled into the clearing and the wolf-demon arched its head back, joining its voice with the wind. It pounced at the figure and the two tumbled out of sight. Pearl, body and mind still aching, brought herself to her knees and then, with a growl, to her feet. She swayed, her legs weak and her balance lost, but steadied herself enough to walk towards Mrs. Graham. A dim glimmer of moonlight on the ground caught her eye, and she allowed herself a quiet cheer when she found her sword. A rush of strength and confidence filled her body as she wrapped her fingers around the hilt. She could do this. She could save Mrs. Graham and the others.

"Mrs. Graham," Pearl called out as she approached the tree the woman hid behind. But when she looked around the trunk, she found no one. She checked around the other trees, but again, no one there. "Mrs. Graham? Duncan? Pat? Anyone?"

A feral, yet still human battle cry answered her. Pearl spun around and raised her sword to face a charging Mrs. Graham. Rage twisted the older woman's face as she swung a tree branch too large for her to hold. Pearl ducked and spun behind Mrs. Graham, not wanting to hurt the woman. The other four formed a semicircle around her, their swords drawn. Pearl positioned herself against a tree, so nothing could attack her from behind. Her fellow Lamplighters, slow to follow her, could take their time, since she had nowhere to go.

"What the hell is wrong with you?" Pearl barked. No one answered. They waiting for Mrs. Graham to take her place at the head of the group.

"You won't stop us from being with him," Mrs. Graham snarled, her glare pushing against the center of Pearl's chest. "He has risen to save us. We are destined to become him. Only the Grey King can save us! And you won't stop us!"

Weapons raised and ready to strike, the five of them rushed Pearl together. She readied herself as best as she could, ignoring the fact she had never fought this many opponents at once. Duncan and Pat's eyes lacked their usual glint of hubris and the other two Lamplighters showed none of the fear typical of those forced to spar the 'witch-spawn.' Pearl parried a blow from her right and twirled around the tree behind her, putting it between them and her.

Duncan chased after her first, leading the way with a slash at her head. Of all times to have it, he had gotten the strength to wield his heavy sword and Pearl just managed to duck under it. The blade buried itself deep into the tree and Duncan struggled to free it, paying no attention to Pearl and leaving himself vulnerable. Despite her disdain, Pearl didn't want to kill him, but took some pleasure in kicking him as hard as she could in his stomach. The blow knocked

185

him off his feet and his girth brought him down hard on his back.

Pat and the girl came from either side of the tree. Pearl stepped back to avoid an overhead slash from Pat and raised her sword to block another one from the girl behind her. Pearl spun around and whipped her fist into the side of the girl's face, stunning her. Pat pulled his sword back for a thrust, so Peal stepped forward and rammed her hilt into Pat's ribs. Pearl couldn't help but smile when Pat's body gave a soft crack. She pulled him closer and headbutted him away. The other girl recovered from the blow to the face and circled around Pearl, as the last boy approached Pearl from the side.

Parrying away a slash from the boy, Pearl blocked another attack from the girl. They exchanged blows for several moments that lasted hours, before Pearl kicked the boy's legs out from under him and punched the girl square in the nose. With another punch, the girl joined Duncan, Pat, and the third boy on the ground, all out cold. Pearl surveyed the damage she had dealt and took a deep breath. One more left.

Mrs. Graham waiting for Pearl in the clearing. Though no different than before, the woman appeared more feral. Her body shook with every breath. The branch she wielded touched the ground, its weight taxing on Mrs. Graham's thin arms, but she raised it when she saw Pearl. A growl rolled out from Mrs. Graham's clenched teeth as Pearl raised her sword. "Mrs. Graham. I'm taking all of you back to the town, willing or not."

The ultimatum fell on deaf ears. Mrs. Graham let out another roar and lifted the branch over her head as she rushed at Pearl. However, she only took a few steps before coming to a stop. The emotion drained from her face until she looked like a frightened child lost in the woods. She stared at something deep in the forest Pearl couldn't see, then ran off into the forest without warning. Pearl raised an arm to stop the woman, then heard a growl coming from the direction Mrs. Graham had stared in.

The wolf-demon limped into the clearing, panting and wounded from its fight with the slender figure. Dark mist floated out of its wounds and dissipated into the air around it. It caught Pearl's scent and eyed her like a chunk of meat, as if recognizing her from before. A growl rolled out from its throat as it circled her. Pearl kept her sword between the two of them as she recalled the lessons about what to do if you ever fought a demon. Three things came to mind: 'Stay on your feet,' 'Hold onto your sword,' and 'Don't die.' The rest had remained in town, a world away.

"Come on then," she coaxed. She didn't want to prolong the inevitable any more. She swore the demon smiled before lunging at her with teeth bared and gnashing. It leapt out of the way of her first slash, and lunged again as she turned to face it. Once it realized how much faster it could move than Pearl, the demon changed its tactics. It leapt from side to side to throw Pearl off balance as she tried to protect herself. She lost track of it for a moment and then it disappeared.

A burst of warm air on the back of her neck told her where the demon had gone and she jumped away. The demon's claws raked across her back, and she fell to the ground, shaking in pain when she tumbled onto her back. What remained of the clothes on her back drank up the blood from her cuts and stuck to her skin. She raised her sword at the demon as she struggled to her feet. The wolf-demon took its time pursuing her, each step a chance for her to stand and fight again. The threat of her sword didn't faze the demon, which didn't hesitate to get within the weapon's reach when it knew it could just jump away. Pearl stood up anyway, ready to die in battle like a true Lamplighter.

Over the demon's shoulder, Pearl saw a shadow, as silent and foreboding as a dark spectre, reach out with arms that splintered into numerous, shapeless limbs. The demon howled, a sound full of anguish and sorrow, as the shadow's limbs pierced its body and it exploded into a cloud of black mist. The tall, slender man, the Grey King, stepped forward as the black mist parted for him and stared at Pearl with his eyeless face.

She walked backwards as fast as she could to get away from him, tripping over her feet and falling into a tree. The pain from her back hitting the rough bark, which would have brought her to her knees otherwise, couldn't compare to her body's desire to escape the Grey King. He crept closer to Pearl, each step it took lasting seconds that stretched across hours, and her heart slammed against the wall of her chest. He paused, then swooped down to the ground like a hawk before arching back up to Pearl's face.

Ithasnofacewhereisitsface. The jumbled thought bolted through Pearl's head. Its head lacked any feature, just pale skin wrapped around a skull. Their faces only inches apart, Pearl couldn't feel its breath, if it breathed at all. She wanted to look away, but couldn't. A voice whispered in her head, telling her all would be well. Though she didn't believe the voice, Pearl felt a smile stretch across her face.

"Yes," she answered a question in her head, unsure if she had said it aloud. "I'll come with you." Pearl never saw her join them, yet Mrs. Graham knelt next to her. The woman offered Pearl a hand up, a false serenity on her face.

"Pearl!" A familiar voice filled the world, and a flash of light blinded Pearl. Screams of pain replaced the whispers in her head, ripping her mind open from within. Mrs. Graham screeched in a language full of gurgling, hissing, and hacking sounds. Pearl tried to make sense of it all, but the burst of light had darkened the rest of the world, leaving her unable to see anything but simple shapes once more. The Grey King coiled, swayed, and twisted like a serpent to avoid the arrows of light coming from a small figure on the far side of the clearing.

Pearl ignored the pain in her body and mind, and struggled to her feet. She readied her sword as she staggered towards the Grey King, unconcerned about the child-size figure shooting at him. Just another problem she would deal with if the need arose. She drew close and stabbed out with a shout, half battle cry, half pained scream. Movement came from her right and her arm shook as the blade struck its mark. As her eyes readjusted to the dark, she heard her blade slide forward with a squish and felt warm blood on her hand.

"Not you..." Pearl whimpered. Mrs. Graham stood in front of her, her mouth and eyes open, Pearl's blade pierced through her stomach. The red

stain on her dress grew the longer Pearl stared at it.
Mrs. Graham reached out and pulled Pearl towards
her, driving the sword deeper into her gut. She
gasped, but smiled as she looked into Pearl's eyes.

"Thank—" Mrs. Graham collapsed onto Pearl
with her last word. Pearl let out a short scream before
pushing the dead woman off her blade. The effort
threw her off balance, her body too weak to catch
herself, the fall hurting her entire body. She wanted to
sleep, despite the present danger. Everything felt
heavy and kept her pinned to the ground. She closed
her eyes for a second, or a minute, or an hour. She
couldn't tell. When she opened them, the Grey King
stood over her.

"Pearl!" She didn't know who could be yelling.
The arrows of light had stopped flying and darkness
had reclaimed the night. She closed her eyes again
and when she opened them, the Grey King's no-face
waited a hair's width away from her own. Her eyes
started to close again, coaxed by the returning
whispers, when she heard the crack of thunder and
witnessed a bolt of lightning strike the slender figure
in the arm.

"Pearl!" The slender figure twisted towards the
source of the bolt, then swooped away from the
lightning. Pearl turned her head and watched a man
with fierce eyes and a white beard that sparked with

lightning coming towards them. He threw lightning bolts like stones, each thrown with roaring fury. In the space behind the man, a tear formed in midair. Not on anything, just hovering above the ground. It opened like a maw, and white light poured into the night. No one but Pearl noticed it. More tears formed, peeling apart the world around her.

"Pearl! Fight it!" Pearl's eyes couldn't stay open any longer. The image of a tall, powerful bearded man with sparks dancing on his arms burned into her memory as she fell unconscious.

Then she remembered. "This…already happened. This isn't real. Something's…"

The Grey King. Pieces fell into place in her fractured memory. He had invaded her mind, just as he had done to Mrs. Graham and the others, and when that failed, he removed himself from her recollection. Who knows how many times he had done that already?

She steeled her mind, picturing the hollow tree, and sensed the roots the Grey King's mad whispers had planted in her thoughts. His hold on her faltered, some distraction pulling his efforts elsewhere. As her grasp on her mind returned to her, reality ripped apart and light devoured everything.

Chapter 13

"Pearl!" The light collapsed and narrowed into a bolt shooting past her. The darkness around her retreated, as the Grey King twisted away, and a pained screaming struck Pearl's mind. Theseus hurried to Pearl's side, but the boy lunged past them towards the Grey King, who's splintered arms aimed at the boy like a legion of spears. A white metal glove replaced the boy's armlet, and the boy used it to shoot bolts of light at the Grey King. But the fallen Guardian's body bent around them, like smoke curling around piercing arrows.

"He made me forget…he made them…she…" Pearl's mind still reeled from the whispers and screams. "Why is the Grey King attacking us?"

"I don't know. I…just don't know." She heard a whip crack, and the boy crashed to the ground. Theseus drew his swords, as the gems on his Titan Gloves flashed to life, and charged the Grey King with a roar. Pearl's arms, weak and shaking like a newborn calf's legs, couldn't lift her to her feet, forcing her to watch.

The Grey King's boneless body twisted to avoid Theseus's swords and his branching arms forced Theseus onto the defensive as he struggled to protect himself. The boy leapt into the trees, bolts of light from his glove raining down upon the faceless Grey King, who glared at the boy. A scream of pain, the first sound Pearl heard him make, erupted from the small limp figure falling from the tree. Theseus dropped his sword and dove to catch the boy.

"Theseus," Pearl's voice had no strength and her cry came out as a whisper. The Grey King stalked towards Theseus and the boy, his arms pulled back and pointed at them, lances ready to launch. *They're all I have.* "You bastard. No more."

In one motion, Pearl sprung to her feet and drew golden Ragenoz Rako. The Grey King turned to her as she charged, and her Forewarn remained silent as one of his arms shot out at her. She relied on her training to deflect the first spear-like thrust and dance around the rest. She stabbed her sword into an arm stretching past her, cutting it into two curling strands, and the Grey King let out a psychic scream which sent Pearl reeling. He retracted his injured arm and took a moment to study the wound.

The runes on her sword glowed, dim at first, but growing brighter as the blade absorbed bits of the mana cut loose from the Grey King's wound. Pearl didn't understand why it happened, but she knew it didn't matter. She grasped her sword with both hands and resumed her assault. With the Grey King weaving out of the way of each slash and Pearl doing the same for each thrust of his tendrils, neither landed a blow, until Pearl ducked under an arm and severed it.

As it fell to the ground, the arm broke apart into fragments of mana her sword absorbed, the runes glowing brighter. Pearl leapt away, as did the Grey King, though it was more of a glide than an actual leap. The injured limb still attached to the Grey King grew and came to a point as nothing had happened. They both stood still, waiting for the other to make a move.

"Pearl, look out." Theseus pointed to Pearl's left. A cluster of the Grey King's arms arched around the trees to hit her from the side. A quick glance to the right revealed another cluster coming from that side as well. She flipped backwards out of the way, when a scream inside her head dropped her to her knees. Theseus and the boy also cried out and grabbed at their heads. The clusters crashed together where Pearl had stood, then shot out at her as one large cluster.

She struggled to stand and raise her sword above her head, but she couldn't direct her swing and just let it drop down.

The moment it cut into the arms, a wave of fire erupted from Ragenoz Rako, filling the night with blinding light and soothing warmth. The flames rolled out in all directions, passing over Pearl, Theseus, the boy, and the surrounding trees, but their fury fell solely upon the Grey King. The psychic screams tearing through her mind faded into painless, agonized wailing, as the firestorm consumed the Grey King. It burned out of existence a few seconds later, leaving the scorched Grey King behind, his body retracted to its most human-like state.

He shook with rage when his burns didn't heal like his limbs had and he unleashed a psychic shriek strong enough to throw Pearl onto her back several yards away from where she had stood. Her burst of strength from before now gone, she struggled to prop herself up on her elbows, and could go no higher. Prepared to face a killing blow, Pearl discovered with some surprise that the Grey King had retreated. The screaming in her head faded as he moved further away from them, until it fell silent.

"Are you two hurt?" Both Theseus and the boy shook their heads. "I thought the Grey King was our ally."

"He was." Theseus retrieved his swords and lifted the boy to his feet. The boy, though dazed and a little bruised, appeared uninjured. He wore his armlet again, but Pearl couldn't see where he kept his glove. "I don't know why he attacked us. Several rules were woven into his being during his creation. One of which being that he could bring no harm to humans. For obvious reasons. Could you imagine what he would do to people if unrestrained?"

"No need. I lived it." Pearl tapped the side of her head.

"Right. Well, thank the gods for that fire spell of yours."

"The flames weren't a spell," Pearl corrected. "They came from the sword." She handed him the sword and explained how the sword had absorbed the energy from the Grey King's wounds, causing the runes to glow brighter until they erupted with fire. He moved his hand over the blade to examine it.

"Then the blade absorbs and convert chaos energy into mana to fuel its magics. But that's impossible." He looked away in disgust and returned the sword to Pearl. "Damn it all."

Pearl held the golden sword away from her body. "What? Is there something wrong with this sword?"

"No. The fact the chaos energy came from the Grey King means his body has been corrupted by it. No doubt from years of fighting the Khaous. But that alone shouldn't have been enough. Something else..." He punched a fist into his other hand. "Damn. If he's corrupted, no doubt the others are as well. That's why they haven't been seen in years. Who knows where they are now and what they're doing." A branch snapping somewhere deep in the forest made all three of their heads twist in that direction. Theseus beckoned for them to follow. "Come. If the Guardians have been tainted by Chaos, the lanterns will protect us."

Sleep did not come easy as all three of them sat with their backs propped against the fallen tree, Pearl watching their left, Theseus their right, and the boy straight ahead. Fear chilled their blood, too cold for their meager fire to thaw. Nightfall came and went. They watched as Khaous stalked just beyond the lantern light, growling their frustrations at prey just out of reach, until the Khaous left them alone all together. Not that they cared. The idea of a wrathful Grey King watching them from the unperceivable black depths of the forest scared them more than anything. Their bodies tensed with every sound, and Pearl's hands hovered over her bastard sword's hilt.

Theseus fell asleep first, or at least he appeared to sleep. He laid silent with his eyes closed, but his hand rested near his swords. Their fire had died by that point, but the lanterns proved more than sufficient in lighting the night. Pearl yawned and her eyes felt heavy, but the boy sat alert and looked far from tired. He remained silent, even when spoken to, only nodding or shaking his head, or shrugging.

Pearl woke up, realizing she had fallen asleep, and looked around for whatever had awakened her. Theseus and the boy slept fast, their bodies collapsed next to each other against the log, their soft breaths lifting and dropping their shoulders. She scanned the trees around them, then dared to look over the fallen tree, but saw nothing. Then came the sound of something huge moving through the trees, stirring the forest to life. Startled birds took flight, silhouetted against the moonlight, as a ripping sound filled the air. Then the forest fell silent, and Pearl drew her katana out an inch.

"Theseus, boy, wake up." They didn't stir. Motion above the trees drew her eye. Something large and far away flew into the air, and grew larger each second. It looked like a tree, its roots still clinging to earth. "Good lord, it is. Incoming!"

The two of them turned in their sleep and awoke. His voice sluggish and drowsy, Theseus asked, "What is it?"

Pearl pointed to the sky. "Stay down!" Like thunder, the tree crashed down beyond their fallen tree, shaking the ground and tearing through smaller trees.

"What the hell was that?" A large stone falling to the ground just short of their camp answered his question. Theseus threw one of the lanterns to Pearl. "Run. Their aim is improving."

"Who?"

"The Khaous. Bastards realized they can't get to us themselves." A tree next to them exploded into splinters as a stone shot through it. "Move. Now."

"The Khaous can do that?" Pearl asked as they ran.

"They're not simple. They can learn. In older parts of the world, where they're been fighting men for much longer, some Khaous have learned to use crude weapons like wooden clubs. A damn thorn in the side."

"God, could things get worse?" She checked for the boy, but he no longer followed them. She looked up, but didn't see him in the trees, though the dimming light made it harder to see. With each step, the lantern's shutters closed a little and their shield of light grew weaker. Stopping to readjust the lanterns would take too long and leave the two of them exposed to the Khaous, who tightened their movements around Theseus and Pearl to cut off any escape routes.

Theseus shot a glance at Pearl, and nodded. She returned the gesture and they came to a stop, back to back, weapons drawn. Her katana, lighter than her bastard sword, shone with the dim, orange light of the shuttered lanterns. The Khaous didn't wait, falling upon them the moment they stopped. Pearl ducked under a claw and her sword bit off a chunk of a Khaous's body. With another slash and stab, the Khaous burst into a cloud of black mist, blowing away as she slashed through it at another one. As the next one fell, Pearl's blade felt lighter and it cut through Khaous like air.

"Theseus, the sword is working." She leapt over one Khaous and stabbed her blade into the chest of another. "I feel...so strong and fast."

"It...what?" Theseus froze for a moment. The roar of a charging Khaous moved him back into action. Bolts of light shot through the trees, killing Khaous and creating an opening. The boy leapt into the opening, and waved Theseus and Pearl through, holding off the Khaous with the beams from his glove.

"Go, go, go," Theseus barked, pushing Pearl past the boy, who no longer stood behind when she looked back. Instead, she saw the surviving monsters chasing them.

"They're gaining on us. Where are we going?"

"I don't know, but the boy keeps pointing this way, so that's where we go."

Pearl looked up. The boy jumped and strode from branch to branch above and ahead of them. He stopped every once and awhile to point forward.

"What's that?" Far ahead of them, two white boxes with black seams, similar to the boy's glove, waited like sentinels. A blur dropped from the trees and landed between Pearl and Theseus. Something caught Pearl's foot and she fell to the ground with an "oof." A grunt from Theseus told Pearl he had fallen as well. She looked back at her feet to see the boy holding onto hers and Theseus's ankles so tight, they couldn't shake free. Beyond the boy, the Khaous bore down on them. She kicked at him. "Let go of me."

When she started to pick herself up, the boy threw his body on top of hers, slamming her back to the ground. Before she could threaten him, the world lit up as white light streaked above them towards the Khaous. She followed the light back to its source, the two white boxes, opened to reveal a cluster of barrels firing bolts of light like the ones from the boy's glove.

The Khaous screamed as the bolts cut through them and they exploded into the mist of Chaos energy from which they spawned. The lights died away, but the boy stayed on top of Pearl, waiting. After a few seconds of silence, he pulled himself off and released Theseus's arm. The boy offered Pearl a hand up and she thanked him. Theseus examined the white boxes as they closed and sealed themselves.

"Some kind of cannon, with multiple, rapid firing barrels that activate when Khaous are nearby. Made from the same material as that glove of yours, boy. But why put it here?" He looked over the boxes and laughed. "Oh that's why. This is where you've brought us."

"Where?"

"Where every boy runs to when he finds himself in trouble." Theseus smiled. "Home."

Chapter 14

Despite the lateness of the hour, the village of the Ghost People bustled with frantic activity as men, women, and children, dressed in tan deer skins similar to the boy's, broke down their bark and hide covered buildings. Long structures designed for housing twenty or thirty people, though some could have housed up to fifty, came down with great urgency. They threw the pieces onto their backs and marched off into the forest like ants into an anthill.

"Why are they leaving?" Pearl asked. Bone white upside-down handprints painted upon tan faces studied them as they passed, unsure if friend or foe had entered what remained of their village. Either way, the villagers stayed out of their way.

"They're not leaving," Theseus corrected. "They're fleeing."

"From what?" Theseus didn't answer. Pearl noticed more white boxes positioned along the village's parameter. Poles, made of the white metal, staked throughout the village glowed with white light from their tips. Positioned so their lights overlapped, they reminded Pearl of New Bethlehem's lamps. The boy led them to the only untouched building, a small hut with enough space for a handful of people. A warm fire inside the hut made the early morning that much colder.

Their arrival unannounced, they waited outside, until a woman emerged from behind the deer hide door. She bore no white handprint on her face. Her skin, darkened and hardened by the sun, aged her appearance, though her hair retained a youthful, ebony color. Her dress made of dark pelts melded with the night, making it hard to discern her form. She took a sullen look at them, then smiled, her entire visage softening. She transformed from a stony crone to caring grandmother.

"Well, Ghost Boy, you've brought some interesting guests home with you." She spoke English better than Pearl.

Recognition flashed in Theseus's eyes. "You."

The woman lifted a hand to silence Theseus. "Last time we met, we were much younger."

"Pearl, this is—"

"Names are powerful things," the woman cut Theseus off. "All words carry magic, but names in particular can be dangerous. If you must, call me the Ghost Mother. Come inside."

The hut lacked nay furnishing beyond a rolled up sleeping mat in the corner. They sat around the fire in the middle of the room, Theseus and Pearl on one side, their backs to the doorway, and the Ghost Mother opposite them, the Ghost Boy standing at her side. The older woman moved with the caution of a woman twice her and Theseus's age, yet Pearl recognized the controlled movements of someone trying to appear frail and careful. She must have felt Pearl's eyes on her because she stared straight at Pearl, her piercing gaze reading the chapters of Pearl's life. Pearl didn't sense any incursions within her mind, but steeled her mental defenses anyway. She distrusted the Ghost Mother, but thoughts of her own mother stirred in her presence.

"I would welcome you to our village." The Ghost Mother spoke to Theseus, but continued to stare at Pearl. "But, as you saw, we are moving south. The winters here can be so cold."

"Ah, winter," Theseus pondered aloud, a smug smile crawling onto his face. The Ghost Mother smirked, but her eyes narrowed as they cut to Theseus. "Even though it's months away."

"When a man walks, he carries only his burdens. When a people walk, all burdens fall upon their shoulders. Travel takes time, especially with this

206

many people. But we both know you have other implications."

"What are you really running from?" Pearl blurted out. Theseus cringed at her, as if she had tripped over her own feet and landed flat on her face. The Ghost Mother looked at Pearl with withdrawn and distant eyes.

"Words born of ignorance are the spawn of fools, Pearl." Hearing the Ghost Mother say her name incited more unexplainable contempt in Pearl. "I pray you're strong enough to do more than flee should you ever confront the evils that cast shadows upon the Khaous."

"'Cast shadows upon'..? What do you mean?" Pearl looked at Theseus, but he kept his eyes forward. "There's something more powerful than the Khaous?"

The Ghost Mother straightened her back and took a deep breath. "'The Bright Ones.' That is our name for them. They arrived in a thundering metal craft that fell from the stars, but landed as softly as the feather of a dove. They looked human, and wore metal clothing that glowed. When they spoke, it was in a tongue none had ever heard, yet all could understand. We welcomed them as gods, and they accepted us as kin. We gifted them with food and clothing, all that we could provide. In exchange, they gave us weapons."

The Ghost Boy stepped forward and presented his armlet. In a series of *clicks*, the armlet unfolded around the Ghost Boy's hand and lower arm. "These gifts were to be used to slay the Khaous, a task the Bright Ones charged onto us and a task for which we were already equipped. For years, we had been fighting the Khaous with ancient magics known only to our people. Or, at least, to the people we used to be. It had insured our survival for many years, but the cost was growing. When word came of a northern tribe surrendering their minds and bodies to their beast gods in order to fight off the Khaous, we accepted the Bright Ones as our masters and their weapons as our own. We were fools to think these new gods and their tools did not come with a price of their own, a price made clear in the Hill of the Shadow Heart."

"The Black Hill," Theseus translated.

"I figured that out by myself." Pearl's face reddened. She couldn't stand the idea of this woman thinking less of her, a confusing thought given her distrust of the Ghost Mother.

The Ghost Mother smiled, as if she had read Pearl's inner confusion, but continued her tale. "The Bright Ones returned to the stars in their craft, three remaining behind to aid our people. They sought to destroy the Shadow Heart and called for the warriors to follow them. All who entered the tunnels, the Ghost Boy's parents among them, never returned. My father, the chief, had walked besides the Bright Ones into the hill, refusing to send his men anywhere he would not go. My mother, after months of waiting for his return, died of a broken heart, and it fell to me to lead my people. Fearing the retribution of the Bright Ones, we forsook our names, the name of our people, the power the gods had given us, our history, everything that shaped us. When they return, they will find nothing but ghosts."

"Why would these people come for you?" Theseus asked.

"Because they are gods," she corrected him. Wind rolled through the door cover, causing the fire to flicker. The Ghost Mother stared over Pearl and Theseus as though a frightful visitor had entered with the wind. She tried to whisper, but her fear only made her words louder. "Beings whose very words had power in them. You've seen what their weapons can do and they freely gave them to us. No being does that unless they're certain their gifts can do them no harm."

"You didn't kill the Bright Ones," Pearl pointed out. "Why should you be punished?"

"Why wouldn't we be punished? How many times in the tales have displeased gods acted irrationally? How many times are the innocent punished by their hands for minor slights against them? We had accepted them as blood, so who else will they think guilty for the loss of their brethren?"

"Pearl, no more," Theseus commanded. "It is not our place to judge anyone from hiding from divine vengeance. We, more than any others, know better." Certain Pearl wouldn't speak out, he asked the Ghost Mother, "Could you afford to leave behind one of your huts? We need shelter for the night."

"You may have this one." The Ghost Mother stood with grace and speed rivaling Pearl's, her need for deception gone. "My ghosts journey to our new home, yet I am still here. As my father before me, I do not allow them to venture where I would not. Heh. It is the one thing no one can ever escape: being our parents' children." She began to leave, but stopped at the door. "Pearl, join me outside."

Pearl looked to Theseus for guidance, but his face told her he had none to give. With a sigh, she followed the Ghost Mother outside, the Ghost Boy tailing both of them. A sentry just outside the hut's opening followed Pearl with his eyes, making it clear he wasn't here for her protection. Besides him, the hut was protected by four white boxes positioned in a square around it, as well as three of the glowing poles planted in a triangle formation. They watched in silence as a dozen men, oblivious of their audience, took apart the few remaining buildings.

"Why is he called the 'Ghost Boy'? Are all boys named 'Ghost Boy'?" Pearl asked first.

"The children are named at birth, but bear the title 'The Ghost of…' Had you been born among us, you would have been as 'The Ghost of Pearl.' The Ghost Boy was no different, until the day he abandoned all names and took a vow of silence. No one knows why he did it, but I suspect the suffering was too great when he truly came to understand the depth of his loss. He taught himself to move unnoticed and silently, much to the irritation of some of the other villagers, and the name 'Ghost Boy' has been with him ever since."

"Come here." The Ghost Mother drew Pearl closer, held her head still, and stared into her eyes. Her gaze locked Pearl's eyes forward until she released Pearl several seconds later. "Thank you."

"What just happened? I didn't feel anything happen."

"You shouldn't have. Reading souls reveals as much as reading minds, without such invasive tactics. Yours revealed all it wanted to and nothing more,

keeping your secrets safe. Go now. Rest. And tell
Theseus I have questions for him."

Theseus was spreading their sleeping mats out
when Pearl reentered the hut, and left without a word
when she told him of the Ghost Mother's request.
Pearl tried to settle in, but the mat did little to soften
the ground. While sleep eluded her, she waited for
Theseus to return. Despite conversing just outside,
Theseus and the Ghost Mother's hushed tones hid
their words. After an hour of whispers, Theseus
returned and laid on his mat.

"What did you talk about?"

"Things I'm well aware of." He extinguished
the fire with a wave of his hand and turned away.

*   *   *

A man wearing a white suit stood before Pearl.
Wings of burnt white feathers sprouted from his back.
Behind him, half hidden by his wings knelt two
people. He gestured to them and asked, "Want to
make a trade?"

Pearl awoke soaked in sweat and wrestling
with the blankets constricting and choking her. She
tore them aside and stumbled out of the hut gasping
for air. Cool morning mist, illuminated by the dim
light of a sunrise trying to break through it, hung
heavy on the trees and grass. As she took several
deep breathes, Pearl discovered their hut stood alone.

Where a village once stood, a large, green clearing remained. The sentry from the night before still stood by the door, one of the white metal poles in his hand. The Ghost People had taken the other poles and the white boxes in the night, so his was the last one. He locked eyes with Pearl one last time, then walked away without a word, disappearing into the mist. She returned to the hut and shook Theseus awake. "Theseus, it's morning."

He growled several curses at her and swung a slow, lazy fist at her, which she leaned out of the way to avoid. He continued to growl as he rolled off his mat and the two of them prepared their packs.

"Last night, the Ghost Mother offered to adopt you as a Ghost Person," Theseus told her with a sleepy grumble. "You would have gone south with them instead of going to the Black Hill."

"Did you tell her that I want to go to the Black Hill?" She secured her swords onto her belt and her bow and quiver onto her back. "That you already offered to take me away?"

"You're still here, aren't you?" Theseus chuckled. "She would have taken you away as you slept if I had told her to, but I knew you would hunt me down for such an insult."

When they pulled back the deer hide door, they found the Ghost Boy waiting for them outside.

He pointed to his chest, then to the two of them, and then raised three fingers to them.

"Does he…does he want to come with us, Theseus?"

"I think he does."

"Do you want to come with us?" Pearl asked the Ghost Boy, who nodded. "Are you certain? Wouldn't you rather be with your people? Your family?"

He doesn't have a family, Pearl recalled. His story was much like hers and Theseus's. The Ghost Boy shook his head, pointed at Theseus, then Pearl, and then himself. She mirrored the Boy's actions, then held out her hand.

"We're his family now," Pearl informed Theseus. The Ghost Boy grinned and took Pearl's hand.

Chapter 15

The Black Hill looked like any other grassy knoll, albeit taller and steeper. The clear moat-like lake around it was knee-deep and devoid of any life. But without other hills beside it, the singular Black Hill stood like a silent, invasive monolith. The air here pulled at Pearl's breath, as if it was choking her. Two large doors, made of the darkest wood Pearl had ever seen, were embedded on the Hill's eastern face, perpetual shadows hanging over the hillside and reminding Pearl of the darkness within. But as foreboding as they appeared, Pearl doubted their purpose.

"Aren't doors useless here?" Pearl, Theseus, and the Ghost Boy observed the Hill from the tree line, a timber wall circumventing the Hill about a hundred yards away from its base. The similarities to the wall of trees that surrounded New Bethlehem haunted Pearl. The screams of that night threatened to return, but she took a deep breath and pushed them away. "I thought the Khaous could materialize anywhere during Nightfall."

"The Hill itself is largely hollow and structurally unstable, so the Brotherhood had to build up a wooden framework to prevent it from collapsing. That opening is the only secure entry to the tunnels from the surface. The doors themselves are the focus of a binding spell trapping the Khaous spawning within the Black Hill. The number of Khaous the Black Heart can create is proportionate to distance. The further away…"

"The fewer Khaous it's able to create," Pearl finished. "So the Black Heart has limits."

"Exactly. This is the hope we must cling to." Theseus patted her on the shoulder. "When the doors were built, the wood was brown. Over time, the Chaos energy within corrupted it."

The Ghost Boy remained close to Pearl's side as they crossed the wooden bridge over the lake to the doors, which grew more ominous as they drew closer. The morning sun glimmered on the lake as a light breeze shook ripples loose across the surface. Theseus stopped just before the door and held out his hand. The air between him and the door shimmer with heat, and the two doors opened with the sound of wood splitting, followed by a long, low moaning.

Stagnant air rushed out as fresh air blew past them to replace it. The sunlight shone straight through the doors into the Hill's interior, but couldn't illuminate the devouring black beyond the doors. But when Theseus and Pearl raised their lanterns, the darkness fled from the Fire of God. Joining them, the Ghost Boy created an orb of light in the palm of his glove. Their combined radiance reached to the ceiling high above them and stretched out in all directions, revealing a honeycomb-like structure of tunnels digging into the earth below them. With another wooden groan, the doors closed shut behind them, making them the sole beacon of light.

"Let's see where we need to go." Theseus unrolled his map of the tunnels, and Pearl took note of the differences in their actual surroundings. Something had dug countless new tunnels, more than those mapped by the Brotherhood. Nonetheless, Theseus found the tunnel entrance they had to go through and followed the route traced on the map. Pearl and the Ghost Boy kept an eye out for any Khaous lurking in the shadows, but Pearl's Forewarn remained silent and they saw nothing but rocks fallen from the ceiling. The absence of the Khaous became more haunting than their presence.

The path winded almost at random, down into the earth, and then arched out to the right, far out from under the actual hill above ground. When it cut back under the hill, the path split into three tunnels and they took the rightmost one. The next break in the path had six other tunnels, stacking like honeycombs. As they continued downward, they found themselves entering larger caverns with an increasing selection of tunnels to explore. However, since the original tunnel stayed in the same physical location, they could follow the map. When at last they reached the edge of their map, where the Brotherhood's probes had stopped tracing, Pearl couldn't find a reason why. Beyond the line on the map stood more tunnel, the only noticeable change being the tunnel's steeper decline.

"We've been walking these tunnels for hours and this is the first piece of fungi I've seen." Theseus raised his lantern to reveal a patch of black moss with dark purple tumors on the wall. "Conditions are no different here than they are anywhere else, so why or how is it growing here?"

Pearl and the Ghost Boy ate from their provisions as Theseus investigated the area where the probes failed, mumbling to himself the whole time. Then, with a cheer, he announced, "Ha! There's a barrier here. Invisible, but here nonetheless, stopping any magic from crossing through it."

"Why did it stop the probes then?" Pearl asked as Theseus sat down and dug into his food provisions. "And what about our weapons? Can they get through?"

"I've been through the barrier several times, and my Titan Gloves still respond to my will, so our weapons will be able to pass through," he explained between bites. "And the probes were conjured, constructs created from mana, lacking any mechanical components."

"So it's mana that can't get through." She stood up, faced the direction of the invisible barrier, and threw a fireball at it. The spell exploded against the unseen wall, the boom echoing throughout the tunnel. The flames skirted along the barrier and onto the tunnel's walls, extinguishing against the stone. Several fungus patches ignited and burned away, leaving a bitter smoke in the air.

"What the hell did you do that for, girl?" Theseus roared, uncovering his ears he had shielded before the explosion. The Ghost Boy glared at Pearl as well.

"I wanted to see whether barrier negates a spell's mana to stop it or simply stops it like a shield," Pearl confessed. "It's the latter. I'm sorry."

"You couldn't have taken my word for it?" He stared at her in befuddlement. "You've just alerted whatever is here to our presence."

"But we haven't seen anything," Pearl countered.

"And that's what we want. Otherwise, we would be fighting every step forward." Pearl heard the explosion's echo returning from the tunnel's end ahead of them. By the time it reached her, it sounded like the rolling of distant thunder.

"I'm sorry, Theseus. I am."

"Maybe we got lucky," he sighed as he lifted his pack onto his back. "Let's get moving."

The tunnel spiraled downward, growing steeper until they had to walk on their heels to slow themselves, and a growing weight fell upon them. A weight pressed harder on them the deeper they journeyed, the air growing thicker with moisture and spores from the dark fungi. The darkness itself had grown heavier, crushing against their circle of light until it could only illuminate the three of them. Their march slowed to a crawl as breathing became more demanding, the airborne spores and shadows choking them.

When she thought she could bear no more, Pearl felt a breath of cool, fresh air brush past her. The spores grew sparse and a dim light ahead of them alleviate the pressing darkness. As they drew closer to it, the light ahead brightened and the tunnel floor leveled out until it laid flat around the last turn. The tunnel ended in a wide, squat opening which Pearl and the Ghost Boy could walk through, but Theseus needed to bend over to pass. All three came to a stop on the other side as they looked out at the cavern beyond.

"How?" escaped Pearl's lips with her breath. Before them waited a mountainous dome carved into the earth, an entire underground world of which Pearl couldn't see the opposite side. Small clouds gathered at the faraway ceiling around a ball of blue light shining over the landscape below. The landing they stood on led to a long, slope ending at an empty field. Beyond the field, covering almost the entire floor of the cavern, awaited a labyrinth of black stone.

From here, she could see the twists and turns leading to the center of the maze, the only part covered by a stone roof. Even at a distance, the walls towered high. The entrance opened wide, a hungering maw ready to devour all who entered. A vague memory drifted into her mind: a dying monster and his curse. Pearl looked at Theseus, his face as grim and still as the stone of the labyrinth. She touched his arm and he leapt out of whatever thoughts trapped his mind.

"I'm fine," he answered.

"Does any of this look familiar?" Pearl changed the subject.

"None of this," Theseus admitted. "I didn't see much of it the last time I was here, but this…none of this was here."

The Ghost Boy stood in wide eye silence when his glove pinged, a song like pebbles dropping into a metal pot. He pointed at the blackened and rugged plain at the bottom of the slope.

"You heard the boy. Let's get a move on," Theseus forced a chuckle to Pearl. Before Theseus could take a step, the Ghost Boy grabbed Theseus and pointed to Theseus's katana and Pearl's bastard sword. Weapons drawn, they descended the slope to the plain below. The ground crackled underfoot, and when Pearl looked down, the ground looked back. Hundreds of skulls watched them tiptoe across the thick layer of bones covering the earth as they tried their best to not disturb the dead.

The Ghost Boy's glove went silent and he dug through the bones, pulling out several bands like his armlet of varied sizes. He snapped one on his other wrist, another around his head, a wide one around his waist, and two on his ankles. He concentrated on his new armlet and, after a few seconds, it expanded into a matching glove. He smiled and walked without cracking single bone.

In the center of the field of bones, Pearl's Forewarn sent a shiver up her spine and she came to a halt, scanning the area for danger. Theseus froze as well and the gems on his Titan Gloves lit up, their colors dancing upon the bones around him. A clattering arose around the bones, low and quiet at first, growing more excited by the second. The bones bounced and bumped around into small piles with skulls on top, then rose to form erect, animated skeletons. Only a few skeletons were complete, most of them missing arms, legs, ribs, and skulls. A handful wore the clothes and armor they had worn in life, but all armed themselves with swords, daggers, and even the jagged bones of themselves and their comrades.

"What...who are they?" Pearl asked with trembling voice. The skeletons stalked closer, trying to separate her from Theseus. She leapt through the closing gap between the skeletons to Theseus's side.

"Those that came before us. The members of both the Brotherhood's and the Ghost People's assaults." She felt something brush up against her. The Ghost Boy had somehow made his way to them and the three of them stood back to back to back. "There's necromancy at play. The bones must have been enchanted to reanimate when someone crosses through them."

Pearl's Forewarn yelped a warning as a skeleton lunged towards her with a bone fragment. She sidestepped the stab, severed the skeleton's arm, she brought her sword down onto its head. Ragenoz Rako crunched through its skull and shattered through the skeleton's ribs. Whatever magic held the skeleton together dissipated and it scattered apart on the ground. Theseus roared behind her, and more bones snapped under the force of his attacks. The Ghost Boy's gloves fired bolts of light with the sound of soft gunshots, piercing through the skeletons and cutting them in half.

"Fight to the labyrinth's opening," Theseus commanded as he cut down several skeletons with a wide sweep of his katana. Together, he and Pearl broke the line of skeletons in front of them, while the Ghost Boy covered their rear.

"What now? Run and have them chase us?" Pearl asked as they drew closer to the labyrinth.

"That's all we can do." He glanced over his shoulder, then turned back to cleave three skeletons apart. "Just beyond the entrance, the labyrinth's path splits in two. We'll make a choke point down the right path and hold our ground there. I'll be damned if I die here."

Pearl swung her sword at a skeleton rushing her, but her sword almost flew out of her hand as it cut through empty air. All of the skeletons broke apart on their own and their bones fell motionless onto the ground. Theseus and the Ghost Boy held themselves from leaping into the now non-existent battle. Before they could say anything, the bones started clattering and shaking again. They bounced across the field and gathered into a single, titanic pile. Chaos energy condensed and blew past them, sucked in by a whirlwind surrounding the bones.

As the energy soaked into the bones, the eyes of every skull turned towards them and two giant arms made of hundred bones each took hold of the ground. A pair of squatting legs formed on the sides of the pile. A gaping maw on the front opened and closed like a fish gasping on dry land. Several skulls clustered together, their eyes and mouths glowing red, creating two eyes that shifted around until the weight of their gaze fell upon Pearl, Theseus, and the Ghost Boy.

"What is that?" The monster heard Pearl and roared, the bones in its mouth vibrating to produce the sound. It lifted itself up, bones rolling over its form to complete its body.

"A bone construct, and a damn big one." His wide eyes shot towards the labyrinth. The bone construct opened its mouth and a bright, purple ball of energy gather inside, electrifying the air. The Ghost Boy's metal glove beeped with frantic urgency. "Run now. Now!"

The construct thrusted its head forward and unleashed an earthshaking stream of chaotic energy that carved through the ground as it chased after them. Pearl pushed herself to run faster, the sounds of screams filling her head. *No,* she thought. *Forget that. Focus on the now.* Something caught her foot and she flipped over onto her rear. An *oomf* from Theseus told her he too had fallen, but he quickly pushed himself to his feet. The Ghost Boy, still on his feet, slid to a stop, his gloved hands digging into the dirt to slow himself down. A black stone wall had risen from the ground, tripping them as they ran past, and closed off the entrance to the maze. The construct's blast crashed against the wall with the sound of heavy rain, loose energy sparking over the top.

"Safe, but trapped," Pearl sighed.

"The Black Heart is watching us," Theseus replied. "It doesn't want us to leave."

The ground shook once more as another black wall shot up, separating Pearl from Theseus and the Ghost Boy. She stared at the wall, unable to comprehend its existence. She touched it, ran her hand over it, yet still couldn't believe it was in front of her.

"Pearl!" Theseus's worried voice carried over the wall. "Are you hurt?"

"No, I'm not hurt. Just…stuck over here. I'm going to try and get over."

"Won't work. The boy just tried to jump over and some kind of a barrier stopped him. I don't think anything is supposed to move over the walls." Theseus, and the world, fell silent. "Pearl, you're on your own for now. These paths must connect somewhere deeper in the maze. Keep moving forward until we find one another."

"Wha—?" Pearl slammed her fist against the wall. "No. No. I can't."

"Don't panic," Theseus tried to calm her. "This is exactly what you trained for, and you're stronger than you believe. I'll find yo—we'll find you. Just keep moving and keep fighting."

The path forward disappeared around the corner not too far ahead. Pearl took a deep breath and drew her swords. "Hurry, Theseus."

She charged into the labyrinth, the walls stirring with life as the Khaous crawled down towards her.

Chapter 16

Hantā no Musuko ate well, turning the Chaos energy of the scores of Khaous Pearl had slain into additional speed and strength. But no matter how many she killed, she couldn't outrun the waves of Khaous pouring over the walls. The black soil packed underfoot allowed her to speed around corners without fear of losing her footing, but she ran without knowing her direction, her course, or her current location. She fled when she could, but when she fought, she spun, twirled, and pivoted as she swung her blades, often losing track of her heading. The scratches on the walls looked familiar as she passed them, but the Khaous gave her no time to regain her bearings.

The runes on Ragenoz Rako shone with a warm, bright orange light, but the blade had yet to release its torrent of flames. She wondered how much Chaos energy the Grey King contained, but the thought vanished as she ducked under a swiping claw. She severed the claw and lunged at the Khaous, leaping through its body as she slashed it into a black mist cloud. The cloud obscured her vision, but she could have sworn a rectangular stone had risen to close off a path further down the left wall. The right path remained open, so she followed it. She turned the corner in time to see walls rising out of the ground, sealing off all but an opening at the left end of the path. Someone wanted her to go somewhere specific, manipulating the labyrinth to direct her path.

"Not like you're giving me a choice," Pearl grumbled as the Khaous closed in behind her. Turns slowed them, and sometimes a few of them would crash into a wall, blocking the path until the fallen Khaous moved or another Khaous destroyed them. Certain she would lose the Khaous, she took every turn she could. Her legs and lungs screamed for a moment's rest. She turned into the opened path and found it brimming with Khaous skulking towards her. The Khaous chasing her caught up and blocked off her only escape.

"Damn it," she roared and raised a sword to each of the approaching hordes. They took their time, letting her suffer in anticipation. They ignored her yells to just get it over with, if they could understand her at all. Pearl didn't know what happened to those the Khaous consumed, but she didn't want to find out. Lizard-like Khaous the size of wolves darted out from among their taller brethren and beelined towards Pearl.

Her katana's enhancement had faded without being fed, but not enough to render her an easy target. She cut down the first wave with a flurry of slashes, their energy fueling her and her weapons. She begged the runes to unleash their fire, but they responded with a warm glow and cool silence. The remaining Khaous, monstrous amalgamations of man and beast, lumbered towards her. One Khaous had the face and horns of a bull, the body and arms of a man, and the lower half a snake. Another looked and squatted like a frog, but with the face of an eyeless old woman.

"I need the flames now," she pleaded with her bastard sword. She concentrated on the blade and tried to feed it with her own energy. The blade refused her mana, but another energy within her flowed into it. The world slowed and her arms dropped from their sudden weight, but the runes on the sword glowed brighter as Ragenoz Rako drained the Chaos energy her katana had consumed. Slower and weaker, she dropped Hantā no Musuko and grasped the bastard sword with both hands. "Fire. Now."

Nothing happened.

A shadow fell over her and she looked up to see a large fist falling down on her. With nowhere to run, she stabbed up. The tip of the blade grazed the Khaous's flesh and the whole sword erupted, fire washing out in every direction, swallowing every Khaous it passed over. For Pearl, they felt like a cool summer breeze. Some of the ache in her body subsided, but her lungs still screamed for air. She took several deep breathes and watched with a gleeful smile as the flames move down each of the paths and around the corner. Shrieks from incinerated Khaous echoed up from other parts of the maze. The labyrinth fell quiet for the first time since she saw it and Pearl sat down to rest, allowing herself a short, "Ha."

"Pearl." A whisper came through the wall behind her. She leapt to her feet, kicked her katana up into her hand, and stood ready. The wall slid into the earth and beyond it was a long, straight path leading to cavern wall. The lack of anything suspicious made the path that much more suspicious. She considered ignoring the new path, but, as the thought crossed her mind, stones rose up to seal off the other two paths.

"Bugger," Pearl cursed under her breath and walked down the path to an obvious trap. Reflected light coming from a small round pool of water danced on the cavern's wall.

"Pearl," whispered the pool. Pearl couldn't see the bottom, but saw hundreds of what looked like white blankets gliding below the surface. She looked closer and one looked back at her. It drifted towards her through the water as if moving through molasses. The features and the details of its body formed until George Chaucer floated on the other side of the surface.

"Father..?" Pearl couldn't believe her eyes.

"Pearl." Her father spoke without moving his mouth. He reached up to her, the pool's surface a barrier he couldn't pass. His face shook as Pearl's tears rippled the water. So much had happened since he died and she had forgotten just how much she missed him. But now, the feeling poured into her and burned inside, and she reached out to him.

"I wouldn't do that." A man snatched her wrist before she touched the water. She recognized the voice, but from where she couldn't say. She twisted to her feet and raised her sword.

"Who—" The sight of the man shook her and stopped her words. A tall, slim, clean shaven man with a head of short, messy blonde hair stood behind her, wearing a blood red shirt under a spotless white jacket, a pair of white pants, and a pair of polished black shoes. He bore no weapons, save for his reassuring and venomous smile. She knew him, but she had never seen him in real life. "You? You're the man from my dreams."

"Which proved oddly challenging. Though nothing I couldn't handle." He shot a wink at her, then gazed down into the water. "The connection you have with that other individual kept interfering. I managed to take it over one time, but you woke before we could speak. Then, another entity trying to get into your mind tried to block me out. In the end, as always, I was too quick and too clever for them. Yet all that effort proved pointless since you awake anytime something strange occurs in your dreams. You don't sleep much, do you, Pearl?"

"Who are you and what do you want?" Her grip on Ragenoz Rako tightened.

"For a start, I want to help you get him back." The man pointed to George Chaucer floating just below the water's surface.

"You can do that?" Pearl lowered her sword, but not completely.

"There is little I can't do, my dear," the man gloated. He enjoyed looking down at Pearl. "However, all that I do comes with a price."

"And what's that?" She had to know what it would take to get her father back.

The man chuckled, as if he expected the question. "An eye for an eye, a soul for a soul."

"My...soul?" She raised her sword.

"Pearl, my dear." Seeing her hesitation, he wrapped his arm around her. Pearl wanted to shrug it off, but his words dazed her. "This water, it is not the simple liquid you drink. The Khaous bring the souls they have devoured to these cursed pools and leave them trapped like fireflies in glass jars. But this jar has no holes to let air in and the bugs, suffocating and suffering, do not die once, but over and over again as they are broken down. After a year of soaking in these pools, the souls forget much of their lives. Within a decade, they forget their own names. After a score, they lose all sense of identity. These timeframes are considerably short for the younger victims, and I do see several souls down there about your age. I wonder, what do they still remember?"

"I..." She wanted to save her father. Everything she had done to this point she did to avenge his death.

"Are you listening, Pearl?" the man coaxed her. "Your father's soul, his identity, is being digested."

"No." She dipped under his arm and backed away from him. His smile disappeared for a moment, but he forced it back, though rage filled his eyes.

"No?" he repeated, his cheerful voice laced with malice. "No? Do you realize what you are refusing? I could bring this man back to you."

"My father would not want me to sell my soul for him."

"Your soul would stay with you," the man clarified. "It would just belong to me."

"It doesn't matter." The man's calm façade melted when he heard this. He rushed towards her and lifted her into the air by her arms.

"Listen to me," he growled. The labyrinth trembled somewhere on another side of the maze. The man's black ring glowed with impossible black light, an illuminating void. "No one refuses me. Tell me what your soul is worth and it is yours, but I will not be refused."

"You can't have my soul." Pearl tried to hide her fear, but she could see it in her reflection in the man's eyes. He noticed her looking at his eyes, and the fire in them cooled as he set her down. He backed away from her and adjusted his jacket. His ring dimmed and the trembling throughout the labyrinth settled.

"What about the truth?" he offered, his voice cool and steady.

"The truth?" She hadn't expected another offer.

"The truth." He smiled again, but it had loss its charm, leaving only its venom. "You live in a world of mysteries and forgotten histories. Hasn't your perception of the world been shaken by the knowledge you've gained under Theseus's tutelage? So what about the mysteries of <u>your</u> life? Wouldn't you like those truths?"

"Anything that I can learn on my own, I will." She backed up to the water's edge. "Besides, I'm used to being in the dark about things."

"What are you doing?" the man demanded as Pearl knelt down and rolled up her sleeve.

"Getting my father back." Pearl's hand shot down towards the water, but stopped an inch above the surface. Somehow, the man had run to her and grabbed her wrist before she could touch the water.

"Stupid girl." He threw her several feet away from the pool with an effortless shove. "After all I've told you about the water, you would touch it? At the slightest touch, the water would pull your soul right out of your body and what good would it be to me in there?"

"Why do you want my soul so bad?" Pearl's eyes glanced down at Ragenoz Rako sitting next to the pool's edge, shaken from her grip by the throw.

"I value anything that was promised to me." The man dusted off the knees of his white pants.

"Many years ago, most likely on the day of your birth, your mother wrote your name in my book. A fine gesture, to be sure, but of little substance. A name must be written with its bearer's own blood. I am owed a debt, but cannot collect until you die or we strike a deal."

"My...mother..?" The word caught in Pearl's throat and a sadness filled her, though not the longing she expected. She looked at the man, as if for the first time. "Who are you?"

He took pride in announcing himself. "I am the Man in Black. I am the Fallen One. I am the Serpent of the Garden. I am the Devil. I am the Satan. I am Lucifer of the Morningstar."

Pearl's katana flashed through the air, a metallic blur. Lucifer raised his arm and the blade stopped against his sleeve without even cutting it. He pushed the sword away, a small motion, but strong enough to disarm Pearl.

"But I insist you call me 'Lucifer.'" The attack didn't even faze him. Pearl stared wide-eyed at the ineffectiveness of her strike. She could do him no harm. "And who are you?"

"I—wha..? You know who I am," she stammered, still shocked and now confused. "Pearl Chaucer."

"Chaucer…" Lucifer considered this. "No doubt your father's name. Or was it your mother's? She's had so many. They're impossible to remember."

Before Pearl could say anything, he continued," No, that's right. No one is really a 'Chaucer.' Not your mother nor your father." He pointed to her father's ghost. "Nor this man."

It took several long moments for his words to set in. "'This man'? This man is father, George—"

"Mallory," Lucifer cut in, reveling in her confusion. "George Mallory. A demonologist of the Brotherhood of the Stolen Flame, assigned to protect you from your mother when you were a year old."

"No," Pearl denied. "No, he was my father. He is my father. He wouldn't have lied…to me…why would he need to protect me from my mother?"

Lucifer retrieved and returned Pearl's swords. Close to Pearl, he stroked her hair, his sweet, calming scent clashed with the sinister air surrounding him. "This is the woman who wrote your name in my Black Book. Judith Sexton is a dangerous woman, one of many traits you seem to have inherited from her."

Pearl recognized her mother's first name, but not 'Sexton.' Questions filled her head, and she knew only one way to get rid of them. "Who are the Sextons?"

"Oh, you want answers? I told you they would cost your soul, but I am enjoying how baffling this is for you, so I'll give you some for free. The Sextons, your mother's family, is an ancient lineage. Your forbearers settled in England while the country was under Roman rule, and not long after, pledged eternal fealty to me. And they have served me well ever since."

"But…" Pearl looked at soul floating below the pool's surface. "What about my father?"

"George Mallory is not your father," Lucifer delighted in reminding her. "Your mother used the name 'Chaucer' to hide her heritage. George Mallory assumed the name as his own to quell the suspicions surrounding you and your mother, and to protect you from any harsh retribution."

The ghost of George Mallory stared back at Pearl, his eyes full of hollow recognition. Trying to remember her pained him, and yet he bore the suffering. "What about my brother?"

"Half-brother, since you only share a mother," Lucifer teased. "Seems your mother can be very…persuasive, even with the most steadfast men. Mr. Mallory included." His wicked laugh cracked like a whip. "'Who are you?' indeed. A bastard child, abandoned by her mother, oblivious of her true father, and lied to her entire life by a man posing as her father. Can you feel it? The veil lifting from your eyes. The foundation of your life falling away as you discover what you truly are."

"And what is that?" His words assaulted Pearl's mind, making it hard to think.

"Nothing." His voice lost its faux cheer, replaced by somber monotone. "You are nothing. Vengeance brought you here, but you have nothing to avenge. You suffered the 'witchspawn' title your whole life because you thought it the unjustified hatred of a fearful people. But you are a witchspawn and they had every right to fear and hate you. So will you fight for them? Or will you fight for a Brotherhood you know nothing about? Do you truly believe in this mysterious group you joined?"

"Shut up." She covered her ears and dropped to her knees. "Just shut up…please…shut up and tell me what you want…"

"You know what I want, but let me tell you what I can give you," Lucifer knelt down next to her. "I have a need for you. I can give you a purpose. Give me your soul and I will rebuild your life. Sign with your blood in the Black Book and I will bring you to your mother and your brother."

The offer enticed her, despite its poison. "My mother and my brother?"

"Yes, your family." Pearl thought on this. She longed to ask her mother why she never came back for her, and to meet a brother she had never met.

"Pearl." She whipped her head towards the pool of water. George Mallory's ghost still waded just under the surface, almost out of sight, but Pearl could feel his eyes on her. A sense of security came over her, the same feeling she would get whenever her father stood between her and Crowley. She smiled as she remembered how big he seemed to grow whenever someone threatened her, but would look so meek and little afterwards. Her thoughts moved to Theseus, and how he had stood between her and the Khaous chasing her out of the forest. Theseus searching for her with the Ghost Boy at his side. Theseus offering to abandon his duties and take her to England to start a new life, not once, but twice. The Ghost Mother had made a similar offer. Yet here she stood, speaking to the Devil in a maze in a cavern underground.

"Here I stand." She didn't remember standing up. While not her true father, George Mallory had raised and protected her like one for as long as Pearl could remember. She loved him like a father, and he had loved her like a daughter. His assignment to protect Pearl had ended once her mother disappeared, but he had remained for Pearl. She touched her katana Theseus had given—no, entrusted to—to her. He had trained her in the ways of the sword, but how she used it fell on her. Subjected to the opinions and instructions of others for so long, she had forgotten her choices shaped her actions, as Theseus had told her so many times before. So she made another choice.

"No."

"No?" Lucifer echoed as if he had never heard the word before. "No what?"

"You can't have my soul." With a swift pull, she drew Ragenoz Rako and raised it at Lucifer, who remained where he was, unfazed by her sudden moves. Pearl circled and kept an eye on him.

"So you've chosen a life devoid of purpose." The labyrinth shook as his ring glowed with dark light.

"I've chosen to give purpose to my life, to follow my own path." She smiled at George Mallory's ghost. "That's what he would want. That's what Theseus would want. And that's what I want."

"And your mother and brother?" This gave Pearl pause, but it passed.

"If they are alive, I will find them on my own." The rumbling grew louder and closer, accompanied by the sound of crumbling stone and shattering walls.

"You fail to understand me. I will have what I am owed. A soul is still a soul, whether given

242

willingly or stripped from a corpse, and yours belongs to me." His voice lost any trace of goodwill, the cold poison of every word bit and stung like insects. "I would say 'good bye,' but I'm sure I will see you again shortly."

Her Forewarn gave a short scream for her to move backwards as far and as fast as possible. As she backflipped away, the wall to her left exploded inward as something charged through it. When the dust cleared, Pearl gasped in the face of the giant bone construct towering over her, its tail of spines lashing about. It glared at her, slammed its hands into the ground, and roared, energy gathering in its mouth.

Not this time. Pearled thrusted her sword into the ground, swung her bow off her back, and nocked an arrow. As she held the arrow, she could feel the mana within becoming excited and the arrow glowed. She loosed it and in midflight the arrow turned into pure light and shot forward with a burst of acceleration. Struck dead in the chest, the bone construct staggered backwards, the energy in its mouth dissipating. Every shot she fired pushed the construct back another few feet. She drew one more arrow, held it longer than any of the arrows she had shot already, waiting until the arrow's mana grew so excited the wood cracked, then fired it at the construct's head.

The force of the shot tipped the construct over and it fell into the pool behind it, sending a spray of water into the air. An eerie moan echoed out as the souls in the water fell like rain. Pearl readied her bow, prepared for the monster's reemergence. Two claws, each the size of a bear, breached the pool's surface and dug into the ground as the construct pulled itself out of the half-empty pool with a clattering roar. The waters had combined with the construct's bones, running beneath the outer shell of bones and pooling within its ribcage.

Pearl loosed a charged arrow, but before the arrow struck, a tendril of water surged out, blocking the arrow, then snaking back into the construct. Before Pearl could draw another arrow, a narrow bone fragment longer than her arm shot through the bow, breaking it in half, and pierced into the ground behind her. A quick shout from her Forewarn and a slight lean out of the way had spared Pearl the bow's fate.

Discarding the two bow fragments, she pulled Ragenoz Rako out of the dirt. The bone construct thrusted its arms forward and they stretched out towards Pearl, two jets of bone and water. Pearl smiled, remembering the fight against the Grey King.

She spun out of the way and cut into one of the arms as it rushed past her. The force of the water almost knocked her sword out of her hands, but she held tight. Though the bones lacked any Chaos energy in or around them, the energy saturated the water and her sword devoured it. The blade's dark runes ignited with life. The construct's arms closed in around her, wrapping into a ring to constrict her. She slashed in a circle to free herself, the water falling inert to the ground. The bones, controlled by a different magic, crawled through the dirt to return to the monster, no matter how much she smashed them.

It roared at her and once again gathered energy into its mouth, but Pearl charged forward, not giving it the time it needed. The construct reared back as Pearl leapt up at its head, and unleashed a stream of purple energy. Pearl swung down on the blast, splitting it around her and absorbing a portion of the energy into the runes. She hung in the air, her descent halted by the force of the attack, the back of her jacket flapping behind her like a pair of wings. Then, she felt the glowing warmth of Ragenoz Rako.

Fire like the wings of a great bird fanned out from the blade and wrapped around the construct. Water boiled and evaporated, bones burned and crumbled into char. The monster flailed around, trying to extinguish the flames enveloping its body, its agonized cries drawing Pearl's sympathy. She rushed under its arms and stabbed into the skulls composing its head. The red light in the skull's eye sockets snapped to darkness, and what remained of the construct's body crumbled into an unmoving pyre. Pearl crawled out from among the bones and found herself face to face with her father. Freed from their watery prison, the other souls ascended to the cavern ceiling, taking no notice of their savior. George Mallory watched them, then turned back to Pearl.

"Pearl." He stroke her cheek, his touch like a drop of cold rain, but Pearl felt its warm love.

"Father." She wiped a tear from her eye as he joined the others on their final journey. When he faded from sight, she climbed over the rubble of the fallen wall and walked along the path on the other side, unafraid of being attacked.

Chapter 17

An eerie calm had filled Pearl. The labyrinth, grave and silent like a crypt, remained empty since her fight with the bone construct. The Khaous no longer attacked her, though she suspected the Black Heart held them back. She found no trace of Theseus or the Ghost Boy either, and continued wandering the maze, using the position of the cavern's sun as a reference point. Despite the ominous silence, Pearl knew the peace wouldn't last forever and her arms hung ready by her swords.

The soft pitter-patter of small feet drawing closer stirred Pearl's Forewarn and it rung a warning. Pearl pressed herself against the wall and drew Ragenoz Rako, careful not to make a sound. She reached the corner and peeked around. A young girl, about eleven or twelve years old, wearing a white dress that made her midnight black hair even darker, skipped down the path away from Pearl, then disappeared down a path to the left. A faint giggling floated through the air, though it sounded like an echo from much further away. The giggling faded like a specter, replaced by the sound of heavy footsteps running towards her position from her right. She made herself as small as possible against the wall, ready to lunge out. Theseus's sudden appearance stunned Pearl silent, her mouth and tongue tumbling over sounds as she tried to call out. He searched the area with a frantic back and forth of his eyes, overlooking Pearl not an arm's length away.

"Damn," he swore as the ever quiet Ghost Boy joined him. "Lost her. Boy, can you find her?"

The Ghost Boy's face tensed as he focused on his gloves. He released a burst of held breath and shook his head in failure. Theseus stood still, listening for something to give him direction.

"Theseus," Pearl blurted, finding her voice and stepping out from the wall. Theseus spun towards Pearl and a smile spread across his face when he saw her. He ran to her, lifted her up into his arms, and embraced her tight, cracking her back. She laughed and coughed at the same time, overjoyed to see him, despite his arms crushing her. He set her down and, with wet eyes, inspected her body for injuries. A few red scratches covered her body and her clothes had suffered some minor tears.

"What happened to you?" She told him about running from the Khaous, the moving walls, the pool of souls, the bone construct, and her conversation with Lucifer. Theseus stiffened when she mentioned the Devil telling the truth about George Mallory.

"But you already knew that, didn't you?" Pearl questioned.

Theseus took a moment. "Yes. I knew George Mallory wasn't your father. I just…didn't want to distract you while we were training. Pearl, you have to believe me, I wanted to tell you the truth—"

"It's okay, Theseus," Pearl reassured him with a hug. "It's hard to understand, but I'm making my peace with it. More so than ever. We need to focus on our mission."

"And you spoke with the Devil himself?" Theseus didn't let her go. "Consider yourself lucky. If he wanted to, he could kill you with a look. Gods willing you never see him again. But should such a day come, speak as little as possible. His serpent's tongue will twist your words against you."

"Theseus, all is well."

"And thank the gods for that." He squeezed her tighter. The Ghost Boy walked up next to Pearl and wrapped his arms around her waist. She ran her hand across his short, rough hair and hugged him back. "Who were you chasing?"

"The girl," Theseus remembered as he broke away from Pearl and scanned the ground for footprints.

"She went this way." Pearl led the way, and as they turned down the path, they saw the girl waiting for them at the other end. She ran off out of sight to the left and when they followed, the three found her waiting for them again. The moment she saw them, she took off down another path, and every time they turned the corner after her, no matter how long the path, she waited for them at the opposite end.

"After we got separated from you, the boy and I wandered around," Theseus told Pearl as they chased the girl. "We didn't encounter any Khaous, but got lost nonetheless. Then she showed up and we followed after her."

"Why?"

"Why what?"

"Why did you follow her in the first place? Why are you still following her?"

Theseus didn't answer. They reached the halfway point when the girl ran right, and Pearl grew certain they had caught up with her. But her heart sunk when they turned the next corner and saw the girl for them at the end of a long straight away.

"Because it's Beatrice," Theseus answered Pearl's question at last. His stone cold voice sent a chill down Pearl's back. He scowled, his eyes pointed straight forward. "I know how it sounds, but it's her. She's wearing the dress she wore that day we fell into the tunnels. She has Beatrice's hair. Hell, she's even the same age."

"But you told me Beatrice died forty years ago," Pearl reminded him.

"I don't know how, but I know it's her," he repeated, not hearing Pearl. He didn't hesitate to enter the covered part of labyrinth, running head long into the shadows. A dim purple light coming from somewhere deeper in the maze illuminated the paths just enough for them to see the girl disappear around corners and to stop them from running into the walls crawling with life.

Theseus drew his katana and signaled for the others to arm themselves. The Ghost Boy's armlets snapped and clicked into their glove forms. Pearl still held Ragenoz Rako in her hand, the runes getting brighter as the blade ate the Chaos energy thickening the air. They turned the final corner and found the girl waiting for them, but she didn't run away as they stepped closer. Her back to them, she stared into the expansive room laying before her. A large, pulsing construct dominated the center of the room, its black, fleshy material giving it the appearance of a large muscle or organ.

"It's a heart," Pearl gasped. "It's the Black Heart." Veins, glowing with bright purple energy rooted into the ceiling and floor, shook every time the Heart pumped its contents. Every beat sounded like a deep drum and reverberated off the walls until the chamber growled. The Black Heart exhaled excess Chaos energy in a thick, sparking cloud, and shimmers of heat twisted around it. The Artifact glowed with strange dark violet light and the small girl cast a large shadow over the three of them. Theseus approached the girl one step at a time, holding up a hand to stay Pearl and the Ghost Boy.

"Beatrice?" he whispered. The girl remained motionless.

"Theseus," Pearl whispered and took a step towards him.

"Shhh," he hushed her, his glare silencing her. Pearl stepped back and kept her mouth shut. Theseus turned back to the small girl and reached out to her. "Beatrice? Is that you?"

The girl nodded, but didn't face Theseus. His voice wavered as tears rolled down his face. "Beatrice…I thought I had lost you forever. Gods, Beatrice, I've missed you so much. I'm so sorry I left you."

He dropped to his knees, the weight of his joy and sorrow too much for his legs to bear. He wrapped

his arms around her and pulled her close. The girl fell
through his arms and collapsed apart onto the floor.
The silence falling over Theseus haunted the
immediate area around him. Pearl tried to shrug it off,
but it pressed down on her. The Ghost Boy fidgeted.
Theseus stared at the small lump of a person in front
of him and reached down to pick her up. He froze
when his shaking fingers grazed her white dress, then
he grasped and jerked it aside, revealing a pile of
bones, decades old.

"No…" Theseus gasped as he touched the
bones, denying their existence. The girl's hair still laid
on top of her skull, but when Theseus touched it, the
hairs turned into black snakes, which slithered away
before burrowing into the ground. "No. What
happened?"

A loud, sharp hiss from the Black Heart
answered him. A seam appeared in the surface of the
Heart facing them, a brighter purple light shining
through it. The Black Heart's pulse slowed and it
peeled open to reveal a girl, curled up in the fetal
position, hovering in the Heart's core. She uncurled
and floated to the ground like a feather. She wore
nothing, though the bright light within the Heart
shadowed her body features. When her toes touched
the ground, a black dress flowed down from over her
shoulders and covered her. She looked identical to the

young girl they had followed through the maze, though a couple years older. A black ribbon choker with a deep purple amethyst jewel embedded in silver wrapped around her neck. She opened her eyes, the same color as her choker's jewel, and looked at the three of them. Her eyes stopped on Theseus and she covered her mouth as she gasped his name. "Theseus…"

Theseus took a step towards her. "Beatrice..? Is it truly you?"

"Yes, brother. Yes, it's me," she sobbed with a smile on her face. They ran to each other and Beatrice leapt up into his arms to embrace him. Theseus spun her around and threatened to never let her go. Pearl couldn't help, but smile. She wanted to join them, but the Ghost Boy grabbed her arm. She tugged to break free, but he held fast. His blank face gave no clues to his reasons or intentions, but the last time he had held her back, the danger had been real.

"Look at you, Theseus," Beatrice laughed as she tugged at the gray hairs conquering his brown hair. Her fingers traced some of the wrinkles on his face. Theseus always looked youthful for his age, but next to the young Beatrice, he seemed as old as Father Alexander. "You're so…old. What happened? How long has it been?"

"Forty years," he confessed. "And look at me? Look at you. You've barely aged at all since…" He hesitated, his face growing grim. "You're not going to break into a pile of bones too, are you?"

"No, silly," she giggled.

"How are you alive?" he inquired as he inspected her hair with his fingers. "It's been forty years. How are you so young? How did you survive down here for so long?"

"The Black Heart," Beatrice pointed to the still and silent Artifact. "I don't know why, but the monsters brought me here and put me inside the Heart. I entered a quasi-sleep state, awake and asleep at the same time. I could see things happening around me, but I didn't know how long they happened. And the energies within kept me from aging." Worry flashed across her face. "Does this mean I'm going to become one of them? Am I going to become a monster?"

"I don't know, but I'll be damned if I let that happen to you. I just got you back and I won't lose you again. I'll take you back to my house, and Pearl and I will remove the Chaos energy from your body." He glared at the Black Heart. "After we destroy this abomination."

"What?" Beatrice snapped. Her hair lifted off her head, like the fur on the back of a cornered beast.

"No, you can't do that. You can't destroy the Black Heart."

Surprised, Theseus observed Beatrice like a sick child. "Why not?"

"Because if you destroy the Black Heart, you'll kill me," Beatrice informed him. Theseus studied her, then the Black Heart, searching for some way to save his sister and complete his mission. Pearl and the Ghost Boy looked at the Black Heart as well, which had remained motionless since Beatrice emerged.

"We'll take you back to Lightholme now," Theseus suggested, drawing closer to the Black Heart. "We'll remove the Chaos energy from your body, sever your connection to the Black Heart, and then destroy it."

"It won't work," Beatrice assured him. The pile of bones and white dress at Pearl's feet disturbed her. Something didn't make sense. "I'm forever tied to the Black Heart."

The Khaous had taken Beatrice and, according to Beatrice, placed her within the Black Heart, but according to Theseus, Beatrice had stabbed it with a stick. The Black Heart had deflated and fallen to pieces. So the Khaous couldn't have taken her to it, and if they had, how come her bones laid here?

"Theseus," Pearl cried out as the truth came to her. But before she could warn him, a loud series of clicking and snapping came from behind her. The bands around the Ghost Boy's ankles, waist, and forehead unfolded and covered his entire body in white armor until he looked like a miniature knight. He raised both of his hands at Beatrice and, before Theseus or Pearl could call him off, he fired a powerful combined blast of white light from his gloves. The beam pushed Beatrice through the Black Heart and into the wall on the opposite side of the chamber, a good thirty yards away.

"Boy, what the hell do you thinking you're doing?" Theseus roared as he drew his longsword and pointed at the Ghost Boy's throat. The Ghost Boy didn't move, standing statuesque. "Why the hell did you attack my sister?"

The Ghost Boy didn't reply, though Pearl heard a soft voice coming from inside his helm. Theseus ran towards the pile of rubble burying his sister. "Beatrice. Beatrice, say something."

"Theseus, it's not Beatrice," Pearl shouted, and pointed to the pile of bones and the ragged white dress. "This is Beatrice."

"What are you talking about?" He didn't wait for an answer and called for his sister again. "Beatrice."

"Beatrice died and these are her bones. Whoever that is, she is not your sister."

"No, she's alive, if that damned boy hasn't killed her," Theseus cursed. The Ghost Boy remained still, though his armor shook a little every few seconds. Pearl leaned in to listen to the soft voice inside his helm. She hoped for the boy's voice, but instead heard a woman's, her speech stilted, with syllables coming in spurts and jerks.

"Lan-guage lo-cal-iz-a-tion…com-plee-t…lan-guage des-ig-na-tion: Sec-ond Earth: Early Common/English…" the woman's voice announced. "Genome mapping…initiating…synapses calibration…initiating…"

Beatrice let out a battle shriek as she blew away the pile of rocks on top of her with a burst of purple energy. She looked as if nothing had happened, her silk dress without a dirt smudge or tear in it. She shot Pearl a smug smile.

"Beatrice," Theseus sighed in relief. "You're alright."

"More than alright," Beatrice scolded him, and waved a hand at Pearl. "Not that you would care. You always were a lousy playmate."

"What?" Theseus asked, confused and taken aback. Beatrice ignored him as she walked towards Pearl.

"Theseus, that's not Beatri—ah!" Dark Chaos energy snaked up Pearl's legs to her head and

258

wrapped around her like chains, forcing her arms against her side and lifting her off the ground. Beatrice waved her hand at the Ghost Boy, but stopped when she saw he couldn't move.

"Oh dear, it seems his armor is stuck," Beatrice laughed as she flicked the Ghost Boy's head, producing a solid ringing. "I don't expect him to be too much trouble."

"Beatrice, what are you doing?" Theseus barked, the gems on his Titan Gloves glowing. Though armed with both of his swords, he kept them pointed away from Beatrice.

"You abandoned me down here," Beatrice barked back. She raised her hand above her head. Chaos energy crackled up her arm and into her palm, they stretched out into a crooked, purple thunderbolt. She swung the thunderbolt with flourish and the energy solidified into a long, crooked, black sword. "Left me to die alone in the dark. And then you come here, and try to have your little minion kill me?"

She swung her sword over her head, down at Theseus. He raised his longsword to block, but the power of Beatrice's sword forced him to his knees. He grunted as he pushed her blade to the side and it clawed into the ground. He spun away and raised his swords at her. "Beatrice, please. I'm not trying to hurt you. I want to help you."

"Liar," Beatrice shrieked. She swung across at his chest and he leapt back to avoid it. Pearl strained against the Chaos energy, struggling to reach her bastard sword. With the slightest cut, Ragenoz Rako could devour the strands of energy and free her. Theseus leapt back several more yards. Black bones emerged out of Beatrice's back, and shorter, thinner bones branched out from them. Chaos energy spread out between the bones, forming the violet membrane of her bat wings.

With a single powerful flap, she launched forward, her feet only a hand's width off the ground. She closed the distance between her and Theseus in seconds. Theseus did all he could to protect himself from her unholy speed and power, but she knocked his swords aside and kicked him in the chest, throwing him backwards. He slid to a stop just short of Pearl. Slow to get to his feet, he used his swords to prop himself up.

"Theseus, are you okay?" Pearl asked. He didn't hear her, his eyes out of focus as he searched for meaning.

"Why?" he asked no one. "Why is she doing this?"

If Pearl could have moved her legs, she would have kicked him. "Would you just shut it and listen to me? That's not Beatrice. Your sister died. Maybe not when the Khaous got her or when she was placed in the Black Heart, if any of that is true, but at some point in time she died. She, this thing you're fighting, is the Black Heart."

"What?!?" Theseus didn't believe her at first, but the idea dawned on him as he studied Beatrice with clear eyes.

"I don't know how, but I think the Black Heart took the form of your sister and is using her memories to torment you," Pearl suggested. "She was telling the truth when she said that she would die if you destroyed the Black Heart, because she is the Black Heart. She doesn't care who we are. She's going to kill us. You don't have to hold back. You can't hold back. You saw what the Ghost Boy was able to do to her. Nothing."

Strength returned to Theseus's body as he straightened his back and lifted his swords at Beatrice, who laughed at him. "What is this? A second wind?"

"Theseus," Pearl smiled.

"Pearl?"

"Kill this bitch." He nodded with a smirk, then let out a roar as he lunged at Beatrice. She raised her sword just in time to catch both his blades, her eyes wide with shock. Theseus didn't wait long to attack again, spinning around and striking out at Beatrice, forcing her to take a step back. Not giving her time to mount a counterattack, he attacked her with speed and power the likes of which he had never shown before. Beatrice blocked every attack at the beginning, but as she tired, cuts appeared on her dress. Black blood poured from her wounds and the blood-soaked silk stuck to her body. Pearl's body ached as her Bloodlust wanted her to take advantage of the injured Beatrice. Theseus's Bloodlust must have burned within him as his attacks became more aggressive.

Beatrice jumped back to put some ground between them, but quick Theseus pursued her, a wolf closing in on wounded prey. She swung her sword at his head, he slid under her blade and rammed his shoulder into her neck. She stumbled backwards, coughing, hacking, and grabbing at her throat. Her blade fell out of her hands and crashed to the ground, cracking the floor. Theseus charged forward, ready to deliver the killing blow. Beatrice raised her arm in an effort to block the slash, then let out a breathless gasp as the blade passed through the flesh and bone of her arm, and sliced her throat open. She tried to cover the wound and hold back the torrent of black blood pouring forth. Her panicked eyes looked to Theseus for help, but he just watched before he walked behind her and kicked her legs out from under her.

"How dare you?" he growled, his entire body shaking with rage, as he grabbed both sides of her head. "How dare you take her form!? I want you to die. Die a thousand deaths, and know it will never be enough for taking my sister from me."

The room grew dark as Theseus's hands glowed with dancing sparks of blinding lightning, casting sinister shadows onto his face.

"Please," Beatrice wheezed. "Theseus…no…"

"You don't get to call me that," he growled. Beatrice's skull glowed as Theseus channeled lightning into it. Light shone out of her eyes and mouth, and from her came an inhuman scream, a sound from an ancient nightmare, discordant bellows and shrieks reverberating together in an unnatural chorus. Even when she fell silent, the lasting echo warped into a haunting overtone. When Theseus released Beatrice, she fell to the ground, lifeless, her head charred black. He stood over her, still shaking, his breath haggard and primal. Then he broke and fell to his knees, sobbing.

"Forgive me," he wept. "Forgive me, Beatrice."

Chapter 18

The Chaos magic bindings around Pearl faded, dropping her to the ground. The Ghost Boy's armor, still frozen like a statue, trapped the Boy within it. He couldn't go anywhere, so Pearl went to Theseus first. He knelt beside the body of fake Beatrice and wept. His head hung low, and he clawed at the dirt to get a hold of it before it completely fell out from beneath him. The ground had drunken its fill of Beatrice's black blood and a small pool formed, rippling as Theseus's tears fell into it.

"I've killed her again." Pearl placed a hand on his shoulder and let him cry. He punched the ground and Pearl heard the snapping of bones. "It wasn't her. I know that. But it's like I've killed her again. The damn thing soiled everything. Can't even celebrate the fact that it's gone."

Seeing Theseus cry pained Pearl, so she dropped to his side and embraced him. If nothing else, she hoped it helped. He wrapped his arms around her and hugged her tight, sobbing into her shoulder.

"Theseus, we need to help get the Ghost Boy out of his armor. He's stuck in it," Pearl said after a minute or two. The simple task would distract him from his grief.

Theseus wiped his eyes clean, stood up, and took a deep breath. Besides his red eyes, he had returned to his old self. He looked over at the Ghost Boy and rolled up his sleeves. "Damn boy. More trouble than he's worth."

They laughed, but stopped as another voice laughed with them. Before Pearl's Forewarn could alert her, a purple light flashed behind her and Theseus fell forward, howling in pain. Something grabbed Pearl by her neck and threw her towards the Ghost Boy. She tumbled in midair, and found herself upside down when the Chaos energy chains wrapped around her again. Theseus squirmed in agony on the ground. The blast had blown off most of his left knee, the two halves of the leg connected by ragged strands of burnt flesh.

"What's the matter, brother?" Beatrice cackled. Though her silk dress remained torn, her body showing no trace of the previous fight. Her wings had faded, replaced by eight serpents sprouting from her back, each one with black scales and deep purple eyes. The serpents shot out at Theseus, four of them wrapping around his arms, waist, and neck, while the other four bit at him, driving their fangs deep into his body, but not tearing away any flesh. Theseus shouted curses, and fought to free himself, but to no avail. "I bet you relished the idea of killing me again, but I'm afraid that game has gotten boring for me."

"Shut up," he growled through gritted teeth.

"Oh, but we have so much to talk about," she giggled as she drew him close and whispered into his ear.

Pearl tried to free her arms, but the chains didn't give an inch, no matter how hard she pushed against them. With her weapons out of reach, she would have to rely on her own strength. She dug deep within herself for the power to break free, but found none.

"Damn it," she swore, her blood boiling. All of that training and preparation rendered worthless by some bloody chains. After facing the Khaous, the Grey King, the skeletons, the bone construct, and the literal Devil, she refused to die like this. Her anger and frustration ignited something in her, a fresh, white-hot brand burning Pearl's very soul, but the pain it inflicted only made Pearl stronger. As her efforts to free herself continued in vain, her frustration grew, and so too did her suffering and strength increase. "God damn it!"

The burning within her exploded throughout her body, giving her new strength laced with wickedness and fueled by sin. But she didn't have time to worry about that. With a roar, she tore apart the chains holding her. She flipped over as she fell, and she had both of her swords drawn before she touched the ground.

"Put him down, you monster," Pearl barked, wasting no time as she charged at Beatrice.

"Gladly," Beatrice smiled as she threw Theseus at Pearl, who dropped to her knees and slid under him. Beatrice raised her left hand and Chaos energy gathered in her palm once more. This time when she waved it, the energy transformed into a large axe with a single, black, rectangular blade with a crook edge and a long, crooked shaft of the axe that appeared too thin to hold its blade. Pearl lunged at Beatrice, who swung her axe as though it were a twig. Pearl expected as much and leapt out of the way as the axe crunched deep into the stone floor. Beatrice lifted it free with a brief tug, but not brief enough.

Pearl closed in on her left and swung to kill with her katana. The serpents on Beatrice's back straightened out into the rigid bones again, reforming her bat wings. With a single flap, Beatrice jumped away and pushed Pearl with a gust of wind. Pearl anchored herself by stabbing her swords into the ground and once the wind stopped, she gathered mana into her hands. There was no time to pull her swords free, as Beatrice swooped down towards her, body twisted back like a spring, ready to attack. With crazed eyes, Beatrice swung her axe with the snap of a snare. Pearl threw her arms forward and fire roared forth from her hands to swallow Beatrice whole like a dragon's maw. The firestorm burned on its own and Beatrice disappeared within it, though Pearl still heard agonized shrieks over the blaze. She had time, probably seconds, to retrieve her swords. Her spell, no matter how powerful, was not enough to end Beatrice.

"Pearl, wait..." Theseus moaned, still in pain. She didn't have time to listen. Beatrice blew the flames around her away with the beating of her wings. Tall, thin cyclones of fire swirled themselves out of life. She took flight, moving without any display of pain, the singes on her body more for show.

"Impressive, but for your sake, I hope that wasn't your trump card," Beatrice mocked, hovering in the air even as her wings turned back into serpents. "'Impressive' won't kill me."

The serpents shot down at Pearl like falling arrows, their heads turning into spear points. Pearl stood her ground and slashed at the serpents as they fell, deflecting half of them into the ground around her and severing three more, each cut paining Beatrice. The last serpent pierced through Pearl just under her ribs and out her lower back. She cried out, the pain threatening to send her to her knees, but she couldn't afford to fall. As bad as it hurt, it hadn't struck hit anything vital, or at least she hoped.

She cut the serpent-lance going through her with Ragenoz Rako, the blade drinking the Chaos energy as if dying of thirst. The glow of the blade's runes reassured Pearl and the augmented strength from Hantā no Musuko kept her on her feet. Beatrice retracted the remaining four serpents back to her side and, with a burst of violet energy regrew the serpents she had lost. She screamed at Pearl, "Why do you want to help him? He's done nothing but lie to you, and yet you fight to protect him?"

"Because I care about him." Ignoring her wound, Pearl readied herself for another attack. "And because it's the just thing to do. As is killing you."

"Why must you do that? Do you even think you can? I've played a round of existence before, and when it was over, I hadn't lost." Beatrice challenged her. "I am a survivor, all of what you call 'Chaos' survived the end of what came before. Haven't you ever considered that Chaos has as much claim to this plane as Order does?"

"None of that matters." It was an unwavering answer, strong and sure, without a trace of compromise. Her swords ate at the Chaos energy in the air, and she could feel herself becoming stronger and nimbler. She channeled energy from her bastard sword into her katana, making herself stronger until both blades felt absent in her hands. "Your existence threatens all there is, was, or will be. You took away everyone I've ever known. You took away my home. And you killed my father."

"Ah, I love that game. Vengeance," Beatrice chided, a wicked smile creeping onto her face.

"No, justice," Pearl corrected.

"Oh." The smile on Beatrice's face soured into a scowl. "Now you have to die." With a harpy's cry and fury, Beatrice rushed at battle-ready Pearl. The crooked axe fell upon the golden bastard sword, and Pearl's katana darted out for a bite of flesh. The serpents shot out, but instead of spear, they struck Pearl like stones, pushing her away from Beatrice. A memory of the people of New Bethlehem throwing stones at her younger self stirred Pearl's anger, causing the brand within her to burn brighter, making her stronger.

"Isn't that interesting?" Beatrice remarked. "Someone else has placed their mark upon you. Won't they be disappointed when I take their toy from them." The battle raged further into its stalemate, neither side giving an inch. Pearl never tired, as new strength flowed from her blades as they fed on the Chaos energy in the air. That she could block Beatrice's large axe with a single blade hardened Beatrice's scowl and filled her eyes with unholy frenzy. The two clashed their weapons together, their faces only a breath apart.

Pearl grimaced as she tried to push Beatrice back. Beatrice's wicked smile slithered onto her face, and Pearl let out a sharp cry as something stabbed into her right arm, the shock of the pain making her drop Ragenoz Rako. Beatrice kicked the sword away, and it clanged into the shadows to Pearl's right. One of Beatrice's serpents had sunken its fangs deep into Pearl's wrist. With a quick swipe of her remaining blade, Pearl freed herself of the serpent and sent Beatrice reeling with a kick fueled by her anger at having fallen for such a simple ploy.

Without Ragenoz Rako in her hand, the energy she had channeled from it into her katana would fade, taking her augmented strength with it. Folly lied in any attempt to find the blade while leaving herself vulnerable. She gripped Hantā no Musuko with both hands and rushed Beatrice. Though able to swing the single blade stronger with two hands, Pearl couldn't breach Beatrice's defense.

Too straightforward, Pearl noticed in her approach. She disengaged, and prepared for Beatrice to come to her. Furious Beatrice lunged forward, axe raised above her head, and brought it down at Pearl. The axe sunk deep into the ground as Pearl hopped out of the way at the last moment. Before Beatrice could retrieve her weapon, Pearl leapt onto the axe handle, ran up its length, and kicked Beatrice's chin. Teeth cracked under the force and Beatrice's head snapped backwards. Pearl's momentum carried her past Beatrice and as she rolled out of her landing, she gathered mana into her hand. A short thrust of Pearl's arm shot a fireball that struck Beatrice square in the face.

"Aaaaaah! You bastard," Beatrice swore blinded by the fire. Pearl rushed forward to deliver the killing blow, Beatrice laughed and waved her hand at Pearl. The serpents on her back arched out and, despite a nimble display of avoidance, bound Pearl by her limbs. "Do you think I need eyes to play this game? Do you think I suffer your pathetic mortal rules and limitations?"

Pearl opened her mouth to curse Beatrice, but a bile tasting serpent wrapped around her face and gagged her. With a wave of her hand, Beatrice undid the damage done to her face. She lifted her axe above her head and the Chaos energy composing it crackled back into its original ball state. Her smile mocked Pearl and she waved farewell, as the serpents lifted Pearl into the air and flung her across the room. Pearl flipped about through the air with no way to straighten herself. She crashed onto the ground and tumbled into Theseus, who had propped himself up on his arms.

"Good. Now we can all play together," Beatrice bellowed. She pointed the pulsing Chaos energy in her hand at them. The serpents focused on them as well and opened their mouths, light purple sparks forming inside. Beatrice glared into Pearl's eyes. "Where is your justice?"

The ball of energy in Beatrice's hand grew, sending out a wave of heat that brushed against Pearl. Her Forewarn screamed for her to protect herself, but she threw herself onto Theseus to shield him. A *boom* echoed throughout the cavern, accompanied by the sound of multiple high pitch *pops*, as Beatrice and her serpents unleashed torrents of energy, and Pearl braced for impact. Metal armor clanked, stone cracked, and the air filled with a soft humming and the sound of rain pounding on a roof. But the blast never came. Pearl picked her head up, looked to

Beatrice, and found the Ghost Boy, mobile in his armor, standing before her. A barrier of orange light projected from his raised hand shielded all of them and remained steady under the pressure of Beatrice's large beam of Chaos energy and her serpents' dart-like shots. When the attack ceased, he pulled his arms back as though about to punch something, and the barrier disappeared.

"Projected Hard Light Shields: Stability Level: 72 percent. Shield Regeneration: 100 percent: 30 cycles: Five minutes," announced the warbling female voice coming from inside the Ghost Boy's armor. The eyes of his helm and the seams of his armor glowed orange. He glanced back to check on Pearl and Theseus, and reassured them with a silent nod. His attention turned to Beatrice and the female voice identified her. "Target acquired. Omega-class anomaly detected."

"And what is this?" Beatrice asked Pearl as she laughed at the Ghost Boy, having no idea what to make of him. "A little boy pretending to be your knight in shining armor?"

"Hunter-Champion Subcategory: Orion: Protocols: HCO-0000: Annihilation: Engage." His armor's arms, legs, and body panels hissed as they loosened and opened, revealing an array of gun-like barrels. The Ghost Boy aimed his arms at Beatrice and unleashed a thunderous storm of bolts of white light. Clusters of bolts arched at Beatrice, covering her possible escape routes, while most shot straight at her. Regardless of their path, every bolt struck Beatrice before she could defend herself, and burst on impact with blinding light. Pearl covered her eyes from the light, and heard, then felt, something slam into one of the stone walls, which cracked and crumbled, the debris bouncing over the cavern floor.

Once the Ghost Boy stopped firing and the light faded, Pearl uncovered her eyes. The Ghost Boy's assault had thrown Beatrice backwards and as she pulled herself out of the demolished wall, her injured and disheveled appearance lacked any of the façade she had displayed earlier. The rips and tears in her dress didn't repair themselves, and the singed strands of her hair and the burns on her body still smoldered. She glared at the Ghost Boy, trying to kill him with the look alone for hurting her.

"Stupid, little bastard," she growled. "What the hell are you?"

"I am a hunter." These were the first words Pearl had ever heard the Ghost Boy speak, and it took her a moment to realize that. His voice had some lower tones, but the general higher pitch of his voice betrayed his youth, which Pearl would have chuckled in any other situation. But in the here and now, having just put Beatrice through a wall, he stood a wolf among sheep. He stabbed a finger at Beatrice. His helm made his words metallic and harsh. "And you are my prey."

Beatrice let out a harpy screech as she summoned her axe again and charged at the Ghost Boy. He made no move other than to raise his arm to block the axe and remained where he stood despite the blow's force. He pulled back his fist and punched Beatrice in her stomach, cracking something within her. She coughed up some blood onto his helmet and he punched her chin, lifting her off the ground. He leapt up and knocked her back to the ground with a hammer swing of his fists. Before she could get up, he landed on her, stomping her into the ground. A groan rolled out of Beatrice's mouth as the Ghost Boy pounded her face, coating his fists with black blood.

He stood up and watched her laying on the ground. She didn't move, blood gurgling out of her mouth and her nose whistling as she tried to breath, and didn't struggle as the Ghost Boy grabbed her and lifted her above his head. With a metallic roar, he threw her up to the ceiling and then fired a blast of white light that caught her midflight. She crashed through the ceiling and disappeared into the darkness beyond.

"Target tracking: engaged," the voice inside the Ghost Boy's helm announced. The voice hiccupped for a second, as though it interrupted. "Hunter-Champion AI: Vocalized Updates: Silent." Fire erupted from the bottom of the Ghost Boy's feet and roared as he flew after Beatrice. Pearl watched the hole in the ceiling, waiting to see if Beatrice or the Ghost Boy would return, as she retrieved her swords.

"Theseus, are you okay?" She returned to his side and examined his wounds. The fraction of knee remaining, a few burnt strips of flesh, kept his lower left leg attached to his body. The blast had cauterized the wounds crisp and black.

"Just fine, actually. I never liked that leg anyway. How the hell do you think I'm doing?" he barked. Before she could respond, he waved his hand to silence her. "Nevermind that. Listen, Pearl, listen to me. You can't kill Beatrice."

"What? What do you mean? That's what we came here to do."

"I know," he coughed. His hand hovered above his missing knee and strands of golden energy flowed down to the wound. He sighed in relief as his pain faded. His eyes focused on Pearl, though his pupils shook back and forth. "We still have to kill it. But you can't be the one to do it. None of us can, but you especially."

"Why?"

"Because it wants you to kill it." He propped himself up on his elbows. "Beatrice—it told me. Steel and magic can't destroy the Black Heart, not truly at least. It channels through and possesses whatever kills it. That's why it took Beatrice's form. When she stabbed it with that stick long ago, she killed it. The monsters weren't chasing the two of us through the tunnels all those years ago. They needed to bring Beatrice to the remains, so the Black Heart could take over her body. It must have rejected her original human body and created a new one, which is why the one you and I chased through the maze was just bones."

"But why does it want me to kill it?" She looked at the hole in the ceiling. The Ghost Boy still hadn't return. "And why not just let me kill it?"

"I don't know," he confessed. He looked around for something. "It's been watching you your whole life. All of you, the people of New Bethlehem, looking for a new host. Why it chose you, she—it didn't say. As to why it hasn't let you kill it…perhaps…when it possessed Beatrice, her mind shaped its will. That is, we are seeing the Black Heart's will translated through a child's thoughts. It's matured some in these past years, but not enough to break free of Beatrice's love of games. Their bond was facilitated by the stick Beatrice had been playing with. We're fighting a god-like entity blinded by its power so much so, it can't stop toying with us long enough to realize how easy it could achieve its goals."

"So how do we kill it?" Theseus reached over to her belt and ripped off the lantern containing her half of the Fire of God. Despite the dented iron and cracked glass, the lantern remained intact, the Flame waving undisturbed inside.

"With this," he growled, a wolfish grin spreading across his face. "The Fire of God is pure enough and powerful enough to consume the Black Heart without being corrupted, and since it is neither a human made weapon nor a casted spell, the Black Heart will have no way to channel into your body and possess. We'll probably need to unite both halves, just to be sure. But I lost my lantern earlier."

After a quick search, Pearl found Theseus's lantern covered in rocky debris against a wall, its light signaling its location. With Theseus's help and instruction, she reunited the two halves by pouring the oddly water-like Flame from his lantern into hers.

"Now all we need is for the Ghost Boy to bring Beatrice here. How do we contact him?"

"Why not just talk to him?" Beatrice's voice suggested through haggard breath. Her return silent and unnoticed, she stood behind Pearl, the damage from the battle still fresh. The Ghost Boy's bolts had burned her hair into short and ragged mess. Her ruined silk dress revealed grievous wounds bleeding over her entire body. Her left eye sat at the bottom of a large crater crushed into her face, and her left arm hung limp at her side. In her right hand, she held the Ghost Boy by the collar of his armor, his arms and legs dangling down into the dirt, and his head hanging down, making him look like a child's doll. She threw the Ghost Boy towards Pearl and he crashed into a pile of lifeless armor at Pearl's feet.

"Ghost Boy," Pearl cried as she knelt down beside him. She lowered her head down to his helm and heard his troubled breath. She sighed and smiled. Strands of metal strings wrapped in different colored coatings protrude from the large tears in his armor. But as Pearl stared at the damage, the metal strings pulled themselves back into place and the armor itself started to grow back.

"Is he alive? I only wanted to break him so no one else could play with him. He's going to pay for being such an insufferable pain in my ass." She growled and, with a shout, unleashed a wave of energy over her body. Her hair flicked back to its full length, a new silk dress cascaded over her body, and her wounds washed away like dirt. Though her eyes filled with undying anger, Beatrice looked exhausted, and she panted for breath. Realizing the extent of her exhaustion only stirred Beatrice's wrath more and she directed it all at Pearl. "I've wasted enough time with all of you. You know what I want and I know you won't do it. As always, Theseus has spoiled all of the fun. One last game then, Pearl, with only one rule: kill me, or you all die."

Chaos energy sparked up Beatrice's raised arms and rolled off her fingertips, dispersing into the air. The entire labyrinth shook, loosening debris from the broken ceiling, as the thundering of a stampede surrounded them, growing louder as it drew closer. Stone cracked as the Khaous broke away large sections of the ceiling and walls to pour into the chamber. Pearl drew Ragenoz Rako as she dropped back to protect Theseus and the Ghost Boy from the swarm rushing towards them. She slew the Khaous with ease, pulling energy from the bastard sword as she slayed the Khaous, replenishing her strength and making it easier to kill other Khaous. But no matter how many she took down, more crawled into the chamber. Theseus did what he could to fend off the monsters, firing bolts of lightning from his fingers, but his pain disturbed his focus and he had used most of his mana easing the agony from his knee.

"Creating the Khaous is nothing to me," Beatrice shouted over the bestial sounds of the monsters. "I could create hundreds, thousands, millions. Wave after wave of them will crash upon you until you fall. There is only one way to end this, Pearl."

The Khaous moved out of the way to form a path between Pearl and Beatrice, and waited to see what would happen. Beatrice spread her arms, inviting Pearl to attack her. Pearl looked back at Theseus, who nodded at the lantern hanging from her belt. She nodded back and took a step towards Beatrice. As soon as Pearl walked away from Theseus and the Ghost Boy, the Khaous lunged on top of them, predators fighting over a small scrap of food.

"No," Pearl screamed. A burst of light evaporated the Khaous around Theseus and the Ghost Boy, who stood at the center of the burst. His armor, still damaged, had repaired itself enough to function.

"Go," the Ghost Boy commanded her, as he punched away a Khaous jumping at him. Pearl smiled and charged at Beatrice, raising Ragenoz Rako, but reaching for her lantern. Beatrice laughed and pointed at Pearl, a ray of black light shooting from her fingertip and knocking the lantern out of Pearl's hand. Pearl shouted a desperate plea and reached out to catch it, but it disappeared in the swarm of Khaous around Theseus and the Ghost Boy.

"Now, now," Beatrice wagged her finger. She summoned her crooked axe into her hand. "You know what they say about playing with fire."

"Damn you," Pearl cursed Beatrice. "You said no more games."

"I wasn't going to make it easy for you," Beatrice taunted. "Existence is a struggle between what was and what is. Would be successors fighting their predecessors for the right to live on. Rest assure, this ends here."

Pearl charged again, swinging Ragenoz Rako out and cutting through the Khaous lining the path to Beatrice. The runes on the sword soaked in the Chaos energy and burned with divine radiance. Pearl grabbed the bastard sword with both hands and leapt into the air at Beatrice, who pulled back her axe and waited for Pearl to fall. They slashed out at the same time, and their blades rung with a melancholy tone as they clashed, neither yielding to the other.

Then Ragenoz Rako chipped into the axe's blade. The entire axe broke apart into Chaos energy and the sudden influx overwhelmed her. Ragenoz Rako exploded with divine fire, which swept out in every direction and reduced the Khaous within the chamber to a field of ash. The inferno wrapped around Beatrice like a blanket, as though her body resisted it. She looked at the flames consuming her and ran her fingers through it. She stared at Pearl and her wicked smile cracked across her face.

"Thank you, Pearl," Beatrice giggled, and then laughed, and then cackled with mad glee. Her last mad laugh echoed out as the fire covered her and devoured her. Then, silence. Pearl looked around, waiting for something to take hold of her. But nothing happened. Just her, Theseus, and the Ghost Boy. The lantern with the Fire of God still intact.

"We did it," Pearl whispered to herself to make it real.

A cloud of shadows formed into the shape of Beatrice before her. Even though it didn't have any facial features, Pearl knew it smiled at her. Then the shadow let out an unearthly scream, a scream from an ancient, dark, long forgotten place, and rushed at Pearl, colliding into her and pushing its way through her skin to invade her body. Pearl thrashed about to throw off the darkness, but its grasp on her tightened and its weight forced her down to her knees. She only knew she had blacked out when she awoke in the Ghost Boy's cold, armored arms as he carried her to Theseus. When the Boy set Pearl down, Theseus pushed himself onto his one knee and looked down at her.

"Pearl," he shouted, as though to someone miles away. She flinched at his voice, then held up a hand to stop him.

"Theseus, there's not much time." Her vision went dark, then returned in between heartbeats. Theseus still hovered over her, lantern in hand.

"Here it is." Somehow, she had told him to get the lantern.

"Good," she told him. "Now you need to use it on me. You need to burn out the Black Heart."

"But, Pearl," Theseus questioned. "The Flame will—"

Pearl grabbed at her chest, her body's instinctual attempt at ripping out the darkness. She glared at Theseus and growled, "I know. Just do it."

Then everything went dark and silent.

Chapter 19

A strong wind woke Pearl, blowing right over her and whistling through the spaces between her arms and her head as she tried to shield her face. Certain the wind would knock her back down if she stood, she resigned to lay face down on the ground and try to resume sleeping. But her Forewarn kept her awake, bursts of noise in her head like the incessant barking of a frightened dog. She tried to ignore it, but when it didn't stop, she opened her eyes and pushed herself to her hands and knees. She leaned forward to keep her balance as the wind roared in her ears and tried to force her back down. At first, she thought she had gone blind, seeing no ground beneath her, until she noticed her feet and hands. The landscape was barren darkness without a horizon as sky and earth melded together. She took a step forward, wary if the ground continued in front of her, and sighed when her foot landed on something.

"Theseus," she called out. "Ghost Boy." Her shouts didn't travel far as the roaring wind drowned out her words as they left her mouth. She tried again and again, but only the wind answered her. She alone resided in this place.

"Oof," she grunted as a burst of air punched her in the stomach and knocked her onto her bottom. The wind swept down and kicked her in the chest, rolling her backwards head over heels. She managed to stretch out and lay down on her side, but the wind kept rolling her around. The occasional gust would lift her off the ground and an invisible force would knock her back down. She stood again and what felt like a punch to the back of her head made her fall forward to her knees.

"Alone," a voice echoed out from all around her. With that word, something threw Pearl backwards into the air. She looked for the ground to land on her feet, but with no way to judge her height off the ground, she crashed onto it. "Give up."

"I'm not alone," she growled as she stood up again and faced the windstorm. "And never."

Someone screamed, but Pearl saw no one else. She touched her mouth, found it open, and realized the screaming came from her. The voice returned, this time whispering in her ear, each word echoing within her. "There's no use in fighting. Just lie down and let it all end."

The voice belonged to her, just like the screaming. Yet she hadn't screamed or spoken. Before she could process the possibility of this, a weight dropped on her shoulders and forced her to her knees. As she struggled against the weight, something in her chest threatened to rip it open.

"Stay down. Sleep." Something knocked her knees out from under her. She tried to stand up, but a weight held her down on her back. Maybe she didn't want to get up. The darkness seeded her thoughts with her doubts, invasive ideas that she struggle to discern from her own. If she went back to sleep, she wouldn't have to worry about the weight upon her. She could be at ease.

"No," she whispered to herself. The idea of resisting filled her and speaking it breathed life into it. She pushed herself back to her hands and knees.

"No. You want to stay down," the voice, her voice, another's voice, whispered and screamed at the same time. The weight on her back increased, but she got one foot beneath her and then another. The winds returned, crashing into her, roaring like a demon, yet she stood tall and strong.

"I will stand," she defied the voice.

"You will suffer," the voice shrieked and growled. The wind stopped and silence fell over the dark world. Something approached with the ringing of shattering glass from far to her right, but she saw nothing. Then a piercing shriek cut and smashed into her, throwing her onto the ground. Her entire body ripped apart and a pain greater than any she thought possible coursed through her. In her desperate flailing, she grabbed at her hair and threw her body around, doing anything she could to distract her from the pain. Pearl looked down to see her body splitting apart into different pieces.

First her heart and veins ripped free from her body, followed by her muscles, then her skeleton, then her innards, and last, the systems of her body she didn't know existed, each fragment of her being hovering above her in tiers. She saw herself existing as components of a whole, and on each of these layers, black liquid oozed and spread. It squirmed within her, and wherever the darkness touched pained her the most. She fought it mentally, but nothing helped, and the darkness spread through her body unchecked.

"Help," Pearl breathed out through gritted teeth. "Help...someone...anyone..."

"Anyone?" An all too familiar voice asked, and with a finger snap, the pain ceased and the wind died completely. Pearl's components merged into her body without any physical sensation, but knowing the darkness remained within sent a shiver down her spine. A cold sweat covered her body and she just laid on the ground taking deep, comforting breaths. Approaching footsteps reverberated through the ground, but Pearl ignored them, staring straight up into the ebon sky. "If it's any consolation, this isn't the worst you've ever looked."

She tilted her head back to see Lucifer standing over her, his devilish smile across his face. Despite the torture and strain her body had just endured, Pearl scurried to her feet and faced him. Her hands shot down to her sides, but she discovered her weapons no longer hung on her belt. She raised her fists and shifted into a combat stance, the shift of weight almost throwing her off balance and threatening to drop her to the floor. "Where are we? What have you done with my things?"

"Me? What have I done?" Lucifer laughed as he looked around. "I've done nothing, save answer your plea for assistance. I've come to help you escape this predicament of yours, and it would appear I'm the only aid available."

"Where are we?" Pearl demanded. Lucifer stepped towards her, but stopped when she shifted away. He approached slower, treating her like a frightened and cornered animal, until he stood right in front of her.

"These are the confines of your mind," Lucifer gestured with a sweep of his arm. "I imagine it is a much more inhabitable, not to mention fuller, place when you're not being possessed by a Chaos Artifact."

"My mind?" Pearl repeated, looking around for any proof. Then she looked down at her body. "How am I in my mind? Why do I look like this?"

"This isn't your physical body," Lucifer explained. "Your physical body is without and currently around this place. The 'you' I'm conversing with is your mind's version of you, an avatar of the entirety of your mind's contents."

"But…if this is my mind, shouldn't I be…everywhere in here?" Pearl waved her arms out in every direction.

"Isolation, protection," Lucifer suggested. "The Black Heart is corrupting your body. Your mind withdrew itself into a more concentrated state, this avatar, to protect itself from being invaded, and the Black Heart filled the void left behind. Or perhaps the Black Heart forced your mind into a more singular state to contain you while it infects the rest of your body."

"It did try to pacify me," Pearl recalled. She mulled over everything he had said, one thing not making sense. "Why are you protecting me?"

291

Lucifer smiled. "A vested interest. You have to understand: the Black Heart will possess you completely. This is one fight you cannot win, at least not by yourself."

"And you can save me?" Pearl asked, skeptical. He gave her a gentle, devious smile and with flick of his hand, produced a large, black, leather-bound tome. The leather shone like the gold embroidery decorating the book and the three golden buckles keeping the book shut.

"I can save you," he assured her, his pride bleeding into his words. "Just sign my book, fulfill the promise made to me years ago, and I will stop the Black Heart from taking over your body."

"How do you know it will work?" Pearl questioned, her voice harsh. Lucifer suffered the slight with a smile and held out his hand.

"Child, if I couldn't keep my end of the deal, then 'making a deal with the devil' wouldn't be such a tempting proposition," he gloated. Then his smile faded, and concern settled over his face. "There is no other way, Pearl. Neither Theseus nor the little boy can save you now. You may fear me and what it means to sign my book, but remember what the Black Heart does. I will give you purpose, and make you a soldier for my cause, a threat only to my enemies. The

Black Heart will leave nothing of you left as it uses you to eradicate all that was, is, and will be."

Images of what Beatrice had become flashed through Pearl's head and, despite her best judgment, she considered the Devil's hand. Her body, or at least this avatar of her mind, grew hot, like the sun frying her on a windless, cloudless day. Sweat poured off her, drenching her clothes, if such a thing was possible in this mindscape.

"Time is not a commodity for you mortals to waste, and yours is running dry faster than most, Pearl. Do we have a deal?"

A new fear bloomed in Pearl. Not the obvious one she expected in these circumstances, but the fear of reuniting with her mother and brother as Lucifer promised. She never knew her mother, her memories of her included a few vague, time-distorted images and her mother's lullaby. As for her brother, her father had declared him stillborn, so Pearl had never seen him. They were blood, more so than anyone she had ever met, but they were also strangers to her. Would they accept her as family, or shun her as a pariah? What if they didn't love, or even like, her? What would they say? What would she say?

Her vision clouded and her head swirled. Her tongue stuck to every part of her dry mouth. A star burned within her, feeding itself on her core. Running out of time, she had to make a decision. Either choice damned her, but the Black Heart's powers seemed permanent while a deal could break. She reached out for Lucifer's hand, but missed, her arm heavy for some reason. She stared at his hand and it shifted from in front of her to a mile away. She took her time as she reached out again. She took hold of his hands, his fingers frigid against her burning skin.

"Deal," she mumbled, illness threatening to empty her stomach, if she even had one. Strange forces warred within her. With all of her will, she gave Lucifer's hand a strong shake, but he didn't release. Instead, he squeezed her hand even tighter.

"Deal," he echoed, a sharp toothed smile spreading across his face. He turned her hand over, and she screamed as an invisible knife carved a sigil into the back of her hand. It started with an inverted triangle, the lines of which extended beyond the bottom point, cutting through the side of a 'V' shape before curling up and inward. Two lines from the triangle's upper corners formed an 'X' in the center of the triangle, then passed through the slanted sides of the triangle before coming to a stop just beyond. What little blood the carved sigil spilled turned to steam as soon as it left her flesh. Once completed, the sigil glowed and burned hot, then faded into her soul without cooling. It burned like a brand within her,

294

and realized she had borne the Mark this whole time. Another fire erupted in her head, bright yellow, orange, and red flames as opposed to the Mark's dark crimson and infernal blaze, and she yanked her hand from Lucifer's grip to grab at her skull. Lucifer screamed as well, stumbling away with his right hand buried in the fold of his body.

"You little bitch," he hissed. "Did you think you could double cross _me_, the Deceiver?!?"

"What are you talking about?" Pearl opened her mouth to ask, but instead, she screeched out, dropping to her knees and hugging her body to hold it together.

"You're mine now," Lucifer stabbed his injured hand, blackened and charred by Pearl's touch, at her. "Come to me, my Condemned. Come and suffer."

Something in Pearl yearned, no, needed to obey his orders, but she resisted it. The war within Pearl paused for the moment, but strange and powerful mana mixed within her. Her body fluctuated between weak enough to shatter under a slight breeze and mighty enough to shape the Earth with a thought.

"I said, come," Lucifer commanded, the fingers of his charred hand cracking as they curled into a fist. She didn't move. He marched over to her and lifted her off the ground by her neck, holding her in the air for only a second before dropping her to the ground, his good hand scorched and sizzling now. He glared at her, his body shaking with rage. "You little bastard. You think you could destroy me by hiding the Fire of God within you…"

His voice trailed off as he watched her squirm in agony. He chuckled, then laughed at her, despite his own pain. "You didn't know the Fire of God was within you, did you? It appear as though someone else was trying to help you after all. A shame it's going to kill you. But when it does, I'll be back to collect what is now mine by contract."

His last words echoed in the darkness as he faded away from this place. With Lucifer gone, nothing shielded her from the Black Heart and the winds in her mind returned as a fierce tempest, lifting her off the ground and slamming her back down. A bright light came to life behind her and when she stood to face it, the light remained behind her. Flames blossomed around her, surrounding her just as the Fire of God had surrounded Beatrice, though they didn't burn. Even over the glow of the fire, Pearl could see the light shining behind her. The ground beneath her fell away, and the fire and the light fell with her as she floated like a leaf downward.

The flames around her flared away as she landed on a new surface and she found herself in a hall made of cracked diamonds. Shards of diamond hung in the air next to the holes they came from and didn't move when Pearl touched them. As she stared into one of the shards, she saw the Grey King approaching. A sword entered the image and thrust out at the Grey King. Confused, Pearl looked into another shard and saw Theseus pointing to a deer some distance away. A bow rose into view, an arrow shot out, and the deer fell. The hand holding the bow belonged to her. Each shard contained one of her memories. As she walked down the hall, she heard the roaring of fire, the crackling of lightning, and a deep tone she felt more than heard over the hollow echoing of her footsteps. She followed the sounds to their source, walking down the cracked hallway for hours without getting any closer to the end.

Just as Pearl wished to reach the end, the walls and ceiling shattered and crumbled away, bringing the end of the hallway to her. In the sphere shaped cavern beyond, a space rivaling the labyrinth's chamber beneath the Black Hill, hundreds, if not thousands, of openings to other hallways honeycombed the walls, ceiling, and floor. Two wide holes, at the top and bottom of the cavern, stretched up and down out of sight and without end. An orb of white light hovered at the cavern's core and served as the link connecting interlocking rings of fire, black mist, and crimson blood. The ring of blood stretched, then snapped back onto its connection to the other two rings. The fire roared like a whipped beast, the black mist crackled with purple lightning, and the blood bellowed with the haunting bass of the buried ruins of Hell. Pearl ached within and without, as though the collision had struck her. The force of the blow reverberated out in all directions and cracked the walls. Large chunks of diamond launched off into the air, only to freeze a second later and hang in time, unable to return to their spots on the wall. Pearl screamed as a rock the size of her head shot up from the floor in front of her.

"Your soul," a voice within the white light answered her question before she could ask and Pearl gasped when she saw the speaker. Another Pearl, dressed in white rags and sitting cross legged in meditation hovered within the orb of light. She smiled as she spoke to Pearl. "The center is damaged. The self is splintered."

"Why?" She grabbed one of the diamond chunks and tried to push it back into its hole. "I should be whole, centered. Haven't I faced enough? Haven't I proven myself? I fought the Black Heart for justice, and not for the vengeance I sought. George

Mallory may not be my father, but calling him so doesn't disturb me. Neither does not knowing who my real father is. I've accepted these truths." She stared at the ring of blood around the orb. "The deal with the Devil…he promised me my mother and a brother I didn't know I had…is that what burdens my soul? I didn't do it for them, I did it for me. I did it because there was no choice."

"The center is damaged. The self is splintered," the other Pearl repeated. Pearl shoved down on the shard as hard as she could, but it wouldn't budge. She stepped back and considered it. The shard appeared physical, but none of this existed in a physical form, but in a metaphysical state. She placed a hand on the shard and focused on placing it back in the hole it belonged in. The shard glowed and a memory came to Pearl: Duncan making fun of her and her making fun of him in return. She couldn't recall what either of them said, but it didn't matter. After all this time, after all that had transpired since then, it seemed petty. Not even a year had passed, and her childish behaviors then embarrassed her.

"I'm sorry," she apologized to the Duncan she remembered. "I'm sorry you died, and I'm sorry I didn't understand your fear and your hate. I wasn't smart enough then to know they were one in the same, and I'm sorry for not trying. I will do whatever

I can to make your death mean something. I will never forget why I fight Chaos."

The shard stopped glowing and dropped back into the hole it had come from. The cracks around the shard sealed up, leaving no trace of a break. Pearl smiled. "There. Not so broken anymore."

A chime rung out from both Pearls at the same time and reverberated throughout the chamber. All of the broken shards glowed and returned to the holes they had shattered from, sealing the entire chamber whole again. Yet the other Pearl still announced, "The center is damaged. The self is splintered."

"What's still broken?" The ring of fire expanded, then collapsed down on the Pearl connecting the rings. The resulting wave of energy failed to crack the walls, the floor, or the ceiling and the ring of fire returned to its normal size to resume its struggle with the other rings. As they warred to break one another, the rings pulled on the ball of light around the other Pearl. Pearl studied her other self's content face, then touched her own face and thought about what Lucifer had told her. She was a mere representation of her inner self, a metaphysical in her own mind. This other Pearl...who was she?

It hurt Pearl's head just thinking about it, then thinking about how her head could hurt if she was in her head made it only worst. Strange logic held domain in this place, so Pearl talked herself through it. "All of this is within me. I am me, within me. Or really, I'm a version of me capable of existing within myself. An observer, like those probes the Brotherhood used to explore the Black Hill. So, if I'm capable of exploring my inner self this way, there must be an inner self to explore. Which is all of this. And you…" Pearl pointed at the Pearl in the orb. "You're my core. The center of my being. My soul. And these rings must be the Artifacts trying to consume you…me…us. The center is damaged. The self is splintered."

She blinked and when she opened her eyes, she found herself in the place of the other Pearl within the ball of light. The rings pulled on Pearl, and while it didn't hurt, the sensation annoyed Pearl. She stood up and grabbed at the air within the ball of light, using her authority over this mind-space to take hold of the rings. The rings resisted her mental grip on them, but she held fast.

"This is my mind, my body, my soul," she grunted as she willed her hands towards one another. The rings fought against her, but despite their efforts, they drew closer to Pearl. Energy sparked from one ring to another and then at Pearl, protected by the orb. The chamber went dark as she brought her hands together, the ball around her the only source of light, which glowed with golden light as the rings melted into it. A golden spark hovered in her hand and as she stared at it in awe, Pearl noticed her held breath. As she exhaled, a single ring expanded out from the orb around her, a ring made of one part fire, one part black mist, and one part blood. It spun around her like the crawl of the planets. The golden spark in her hand drifted into her chest, and power, more power than she could conceive, flowed through her. Her body vibrated at frequencies known only to the divine, the damned, and the ancient.

Something beyond beckoned to her, a familiar and kind presence requesting an audience with her. She focused on the presence, as if staring at a spot on a map. Her mind needed to reach higher, but her thoughts held it within her.

So she cleared her mind and drifted away.

Chapter 20

Watchful stars dotting the black tapestry of night replaced the blinding light fading away in Pearl's mind. Pearl watched them in return as she laid on her back and the green, frail, and fake grass beneath her prickled her skin. A familiar song drifted through the air, its lullaby melody stirring Pearl's memories, but the strange lyrics spoiling any recollection. Sitting up, she found herself in front of a large house made of black stone, its window closed off with rusty bars. She didn't see any doors, but the house's interior didn't interest her.

The music came from around the left side of the house and she followed it, seeking its source. Turning the corner, Pearl walked between the black stone house and the wooden house painted her favorite shade of dark blue. The blue house awoke a memory, and Pearl realized she had seen these houses and more before. She ran to the front of the houses and before her laid the village she had seen in her dreams.

The houses looked identical in structure and almost fake, each made of a different material, such as the one made of metal sheets and the one made of woven leaves. They crowded around the village road, a single piece of black stone embedded into the ground lined with a trail of gray stone. Smaller paths reached out from the main trail to the front of each house. Just as she did in her dreams, Pearl walked along the side of the blue house, following the music to the front door. She reached out for the golden doorknob, hesitated, and then knocked on the door. When no response came, she opened the door.

"Hello?" she called into the house. No one answered, so she entered the house, closing the door behind her. The music played in the room to her left, a pink room with two large and wide cream-colored cushioned seats, one pushed against the far wall and one pushed up to the large window on the left wall. The window looked out on the other houses around the black stone road, but thin sheets of flimsy cloth obscured the view. Two glass shelves tucked in the corners held a variety of empty frames for small canvas. A tall, metallic silver stick with a glass bowl on top stood atop a silver circular base in the corner to Pearl's right.

Further along the right wall, an opening led to an empty room. Even this room felt empty despite its furnishing and, in the emptiness, the music played clear. A man crooned a melancholy lullaby with instruments playing softly behind him. Hearing the lyrics now, Pearl recognized the song, though most of the words varied. Pearl searched the room, but couldn't find the man singing. The music grew louder as she drew closer to a brown, wooden box sitting in the corner of the room. Four grooves cut into the face of the box and covered with thin cloth glowed with a soft, yellow light. Two small black wheels dotted the lower part of the box's face over a row of square buttons, giving the box's face the appearance of an actual face. The man's voice came out of the box, shaking the cloth covering the grooves with every word.

"How?" Pearl asked the box.

"It's a radio." Pearl whipped around and reached for her still missing sword. A woman had entered the room behind Pearl, and stood with her hands in the pockets of her black leather jacket, unconcerned about Pearl's battle ready stance. The woman's physical similarities unnerved Pearl, and she took a moment to study her. Despite standing a few inches taller and having a decade and so on Pearl, the woman shared Pearl's dark brown hair, fair skin, and slim figure. The jacket she wore over a gray hooded shirt ended just above the belt of her dark blue pants, from which hung a bastard sword with a black hilt in a black scabbard decorated with gold. The woman's eyes shined with violet light as she studied Pearl with a nurturing smile. She didn't recognize the woman, not even from her dreams, but knew this woman would do her no harm.

Then a thought came to Pearl, making her heart skip a beat and her palms sweat. "Are you...are you Judith? Are you my mother?"

"Oh my. I had forgotten..." the woman blushed. "I'm sorry, no. I'm afraid I'm not your mother. My name is Beatrice."

"Beatrice?" Pearl growled, though the woman looked nothing like Theseus's sister.

"No, not *that* Beatrice," Beatrice chuckled, but her laughter felt as empty as the room, carved out by something within her. "Gods, I hope I'm nothing like her. Well, not like the her you fought. Before that, she was a lovely child, or so I've been told. Gods, I'm rambling. Is this really how it sounded? I'm sorry. I must admit, you have me a bit flustered. I've been trying to reach you for some time and now here you are."

"Reach me?" Pearl repeated. "What for? How? Where are we?"

"So many questions," Beatrice cheered with a squeal of joy. "So many wonders you've yet to discover. Where should we start? Well, I've been meditating, sending my mind back to contact you mentally in the past. Making the call was the easy part, but getting you to pick up the phone proved challenging. You see, the further back in time the connection stretches, the more receptive you, Pearl, have to be for it to reach you. It also makes the message easier to intercept, which you've no doubt witnessed."

"That's why all of this was in my dreams," Pearl exclaimed, taking another look around the room. "The times my mind is most receptive is when I'm sleeping or meditating. Is this a dream right now?"

"Somewhat," Beatrice smiled. "You're not physically standing there. I'm projecting your mind into my reality, so while you can touch and move things in here, it's all really my doing."

"Everything is so clear," Pearl ran her hand over the floral design on the cloth of the cushioned seats. "So real. How is this possible? Nothing has ever been this clear in any of my other dreams."

"That's because, at this moment in your time, you are the most mentally receptive you'll ever be," Beatrice explained. She looked at the glass disk strapped to her wrist, and grimaced. She spoke faster. "You forced the three God Artifacts within you to form a united Artifact in your soul, sending a surge of energy through your body and mind, basically turning your mind into a large receiver dish—no, you don't have those yet...Ah. This will explain it. I'm whispering from far away and the surge is making your ears large enough to hear me."

"Oh," Pearl responded, her mind trying to comprehend all of Beatrice's words, understanding the core of the message. In the silence that fell between her and Beatrice, Pearl heard the song begin again. "What is this song? It sounds just like my—"

"Mother's lullaby?" Beatrice finished with a smirk. "It's not, though I'm beginning to think she heard part of it when my message reached her while you were still in the womb. The song is called 'Sleep Warm,' performed by Frank Sinatra. It won't be written for many years in your time. Over 200 years in fact."

"200 years?" Pearl shouted, unsure of what she just heard. Her body shook with fear, as though she stood on the edge of an invisible precipice. "Where are we?"

"See for yourself," Beatrice gestured to the window. Pearl hesitated, waiting for Beatrice to say or do something else, but the woman smiled and pointed at the window. Pearl pushed through the long, thin curtains covering the window and looked out onto the houses and the grass and the black stone road and the starry night's sky and the sun and the…

"What is that?" Pearl pointed to a large blue celestial body in the sky along with the Sun. "It looks like…there was a picture like that in Theseus's library—" The curtains ran into her neck as Beatrice pulled a string attached to the rail the curtains hung from, causing them to part. Pearl moved out of the way and the curtains bunched to the sides of the window, uncovering the view.

"Sorry. Forgot that you don't know about retractable curtains," Beatrice apologized. She went to Pearl's side, looked out the window with her, and pointed to the blue planet. "That's Earth."

"Earth," Pearl gasped. She looked down at her feet as though the ground beneath her would disappear. "Then where the hell is this?"

"The Moon." Beatrice's smile wavered as the radio crackled and another man's cold, rigid voice replaced the music.

"Attention," the man commanded. "All personnel. Evacuate the blast site immediately. I repeat. All personnel. Evacuate the blast site immediately. This is your final warning. Testing will begin in ten minutes. If in need of assistance, activate emergency locator now. Once more. All personnel. Evacuate the blast site immediately. Command, out."

"What is he talking about?" Pearl asked as the song resumed playing from its interruption. "What's happening?"

Beatrice didn't hear her. Her vacant eyes stared at the Earth above them. "A day will come for you, Pearl. It has already passed me, but you may be able to stop it yet."

"Now what are *you* talking about?" Pearl demanded in frustration.

"Mankind was evolving," Beatrice explained, her voice sober and filled with a haunting calm. "Humanity has been evolving slowly for thousands of years, but the true results of these changes couldn't be seen until...god, when was that? It feels like I've been trying to clean up this mess forever."

A tear rolled down Beatrice's cheek. She lifted a finger to catch it and looked at it as though she didn't know where it had come from. She continued, "It was foolish to believe so, but we thought the changes had reached their apex with Homo maximus, but we were wrong. I...I was wrong. In the end, Homo maximus became just another stepping stone, but at the time, it shook humanity to its core. Their genetic successors had sprung forth, and mankind feared for their survival. By the time the Ascended arose, the fear had turned to unwavering hatred."

"Who?" Pearl couldn't piece together the puzzle of Beatrice's warning, the final image impossible to know.

"Some misused their powers, but that's not an excuse to hate a whole people. They may have been more than human, but they didn't deserve to suffer, god damn it." Beatrice fell to her knees and punched the ground. Pearl could feel her inner pain, but, lacking context, it meant nothing. "Promise me you won't see them as monsters. Promise me you won't make the same mistakes that I've made. You must protect them. Or no one will."

"Please, why are you telling me this?" Pearl asked, countering Beatrice's hysterics with a calm voice. She knelt next to the crying woman, wrapped an arm around her, and held her tight. "What happened? Who are you, Beatrice?"

"Detonation in five minutes," the commanding man's voice announced from the box.

"I made a mistake." Beatrice shook her head as she lifted it from her hands "A terrible mistake. So many suffered for it. Years of hiding in the shadows as the planet's guardian, only to be ripped into the light when I became its greatest monster. So many hated me, but what's worse is I hated me. I had, I've always had, the power to stop it from happening, and

311

I failed. This power…is useless in my hands. I—I—I…"

Beatrice stood up and looked at the Earth. "By now, not only have I become immortal, but also invulnerable. Nothing can hurt me. A bullet to the skull vaporizes before it can reach my brain. Blades slide off my flesh without shedding any blood. Ropes snap, poisons fail. I have found no release, until today. They're going to test a quantum bomb here, and it just might be the only thing that can kill me."

She looked back at Pearl. Tears filled her eyes, but the light of hope glowed within her pupils as she smiled at Pearl. "The trials of your life still lie ahead of you, but you'll be ready for them. I know you will. Trust yourself to do the right thing, no matter how challenging, and always follow your own path."

Pearl opened her mouth to say something, but Beatrice raised a finger to her lips, silencing Pearl.

"Detonation in three minutes." Silence persisted for a few seconds after the announcement, and then the song began anew.

"I thought it was funny," Beatrice admitted as she swayed to the music. "That they would choose this of all songs, but apparently someone at mission control thought Frank Sinatra would be appropriate for the testing of a bomb. A lullaby for a mechanism of death, the ultimate sleep. How oddly fitting."

Pearl sat down and listened to every word Beatrice said, drawn to this strange woman. "But having listened to this song so many times, I've come to realize it is more than lullaby. It's a good bye, and a lamentation. Like a mother putting her child to sleep, before leaving the child's life forever. There's pain in these lyrics the two of us can empathize with."

Nobody spoke for the rest of the song. Beatrice performed a melancholy swaying as Pearl sat on the floor and watched her. As the song reached its end, the world disappeared in a flash of light, save for Beatrice, who looked into Pearl's eyes and gave her a reassuring smile, before breaking apart into a cloud of specks. The ground below Pearl fell away and Pearl fell with it. She didn't scream, despite not knowing where she would land. As she descended, she listened to the last notes of the lullaby.

Applause faded to black silence.

Chapter 21

Pearl awoke to find herself within another dream, so she forced her eyes open again, only to enter another dream. Waking over and over again, she ascended the levels of her dreaming, traversing the dreams of a thousand slumbers. Every layer she breached brought more life to her body. Her muscles exploded against the steel casing her skin had hardened into, yet her skin never felt softer and her body never felt lighter. A mighty, unstoppable wave of mana surged through her, the greatest magics danced at her fingertips. Her thoughts…if only others could understand the speed of thoughts has no limits and as they race towards infinity, thoughts transmute into energy and matter. The metaphysical becomes physical. It…Pearl's grip on reality slipped away as the machinations of her mind worked faster and harder, fueled by the energies of the Artifacts.

The tree hollow, she remembered, and imagined herself sitting with it, the influences of the Artifacts bombarding the tree from all sides. She centered her

mind and brought the Artifacts to heel before she lost
herself to them. As the hot ore of her new powers
cooled, reality pieced back together. Her body laid
upon cold, rugged stone. Her lungs breathed dry,
dead air. The dark of the tomb surrounded her, yet
there was movement nearby. The orange light from
the Ghost Boy's helm jumped into sight just above her
face, blinding Pearl. The aching all over her body
confirmed the dreaming had ended, and she had
returned to the labyrinth. The Ghost Boy knelt over
her, waving his hand in front of her face, and when
Pearl propped herself into a sitting position, he threw
his hands up in celebration. He moved to embrace
her, but a small *bing*ing sound within his helm
stopped him. He leapt back and raised his fists, but
didn't shoot, waiting for Pearl to do or say something.

"Don't worry," Pearl assured him. "It's me."

He didn't lower his guard. Pearl needed
something more. Something he would understand.

"The center is whole. I have bound the three
into one," Pearl explained, the words coming to her
faster than she expected, her thinking clearer than
ever. This gave the Ghost Boy pause and he lowered
his arms, though he remained armored. Pearl
elaborated, describing the fusion of the three Artifacts
and how her will held them in check. She stopped her
tale short of her meeting Beatrice, for that

conversation felt more intimate, a secret Beatrice entrusted her with and one Pearl intended to keep. At the story's end, a plane of orange light extending from the Ghost Boy's helm swept up and down Pearl's body. After the third scan, the light faded. The Ghost Boy stood still for a moment, then his armor clicked and clacked into its armlet, anklet, circlet, and belt forms. The knight had vanished and the boy had returned, running to her and hugging her with the unspoken promise of never letting go.

"Where is Theseus?" If anyone could make sense of what she had experience, he could. The Ghost Boy released her, his face grim as he pointed behind her. Pearl turned, but saw nothing. Then, her eyes made out a dark figure laying in the shadows several yards from where she had laid. She approached, her breathing catching in her throat when she found a charred black body with a lantern locked in a death grip. She released her breath and tears clouded her vision. Staring at Theseus's corpse, Pearl choked on her sorrow and gasped for air through her sobs. Losing her father once had hurt enough, and this felt like she had lost him again.

Angry at the world for cheating her once more, she punched the ground. Even though she pulled her punch as it struck the ground, the blow shook the entire chamber and forced the earth beneath her to

316

crater until it was deeper than she was tall. When she stepped to climb out of the crater, her feet lifted off the ground and she drifted up without trying. The Artifacts within her grew excited, an annoyance no more bothersome than a mosquito bite, but demanding caution nonetheless. She landed next to Theseus and returned to her sorrow.

"After all we've gone through, all he's gone through, and he's dead," she sobbed to the world. Could she have done something to save him? The weight of the question pained her, the lack of answer even more so. She blamed herself. She blamed the Black Heart. She blamed everything, until there was nothing left to blame. Yet Theseus was still dead. "He saved my life, and didn't even know."

Pearl stared at her hands and more mana than she had ever controlled pooled into each of them. So much power...she could bring him back. Theseus had told her never to raise the dead without their permission and hadn't taught her the basics of necromancy, but with the Artifacts, she could do anything. Reality bent to her will. "I need you, Theseus. I need someone. After my father...you were there. Now you're gone and I'm alone, when I need your help the most."

"Tsuneni hikari ga sonzai shimasu." Pearl looked up at the sound of Theseus's voice. The blackened corpse lay silent, but his words came from behind her. Armor covered the Ghost Boy's left arm and above the palm of his hand hovered an image of Theseus kneeling beside an unconscious Pearl, the Fire of God in his hand. The image spoke again, "There will always be light."

With that last prayer, Theseus pushed the Flame into Pearl's chest. It resisted, as though caught on something within Pearl, but with all of his weight on it, Theseus pushed the Flame all the way into Pearl's body. Theseus sighed when Pearl didn't burst into flames and smiled. He opened his mouth to say something, but fires erupting out of Pearl's body consumed him and the image disappeared. After a second's wait, the image reappeared, restarting with Theseus speaking. "Tsuneni hikari ga sonzai shimasu."

The Ghost Boy closed his hand and the image disappeared for good. Pearl wiped away the last tear on her face and a smile spread across her face. Theseus wouldn't want to come back like this, if at all. And to bring him back against his will would go beyond disrespectful and dishonorable. The mana in her hands flowed back into her body. "Thank you, Ghost Boy. Could you gather Theseus's things? His body won't survive the journey home, so we'll have to bury him here. Don't think he would mind that. He would probably approve in fact. One last spit in the face of the Khaous."

The Ghost Boy nodded, ran off, returning soon after with Theseus's hat and two swords. She considered taking Akuma no Satsugai-Sha with her but she laid it next to Theseus, laying the longsword Caliburnus Major on his opposite side. The two of them took a step away from Theseus, and the Ghost Boy watched Pearl work. With a point of her finger, Pearl pulled the ground under Theseus up as a rectangular altar until it reached waist height, the task no more challenging than pulling a loose string from cloth.

Around the altar, Pearl manipulated the stone to form a four side pyramid, sealing Theseus within. Then, on each face of the pyramid, Pearl inscribed an epitaph. In the months while training with him, Theseus had never mentioned his date of birth, and without a date of birth, the date of his death seemed morose, so she included neither. Knowing only a fraction of Theseus's life, Pearl buried two men: the Theseus she knew and the stranger she would never discover. So she wrote the truths she knew, and prayed it did enough to honor him.

THERE WILL ALWAYS BE LIGHT
HERE LIES THESEUS AEKER
PROUD MEMBER OF
THE BROTHERHOOD OF
THE STOLEN FLAME.
WARRIOR. MAGUS. PROTECTOR.
SMITH. TINKER. TEACHER.
FRIEND. BROTHER. FATHER.

Underneath all of this, she drew the symbol of his attunement, a fist grasping a bolt of lightning, within the simple flame insignia of the Brotherhood. The little she could do for him shamed her, after all he had done for her.

"I love you." Few tears fell now, but her heart ached as though someone had ripped it from her chest. The Ghost Boy's fingers skimmed hers and they locked together. She smiled at him and he smiled back, his smile full of holes where baby teeth had fallen out and adult teeth had yet to grow. Pearl chuckled and squeezed his hand.

"Let's leave this place." She pointed at the corner of the chamber, energy crackling over her body to her finger and electrifying the air. A pea sized orb of pure mana formed at the tip of her extended finger. Pearl imagined her hand as a pistol and pulled its 'trigger,' firing a massive stream of energy, as wide as she was tall. The blast pierced through the walls of the labyrinth and then the walls of the cavern. Dust clouds filled the beam's path and Pearl cleared it away with a simple wave of her hand, revealing a circular tunnel climbing up through the series of tunnels above and leading outside. Natural light flooded into the cavern, taking the place of the false light illuminating the labyrinth which had disappeared with Beatrice's demise. Hand in hand, they left.

Bright stars shone in the night sky, celebrating Pearl and the Ghost Boy's return to the surface. The tunnel brought them to the middle of the forest, though they spied the Black Hill through the trees. The cold, crisp air filled Pearl's lungs, refreshing her body. Despite all the changes to her body, the wind still stung her face, reassuring Pearl of her humanity.

"Hold on." She stopped the Ghost Boy from walking off without her. She looked back at the tunnel and clapped her hands together. As she pulled her hands apart, a ball of Chaos energy formed and grew to the size of an apple. She grabbed it and threw it down the hole. It flew down the tunnel without touching any of the walls or the floor or the ceiling. Pearl led the Ghost Boy to the clearing around the Black Hill just in time to watch the Hill collapse, piece by piece, into the hollow earth beneath it, as the small void Pearl created devoured stone and soil. The lake sunk into the crater and filled in the cracks of the debris. With time, the hole would fill again and the lake would truly return, larger and deeper than ever. Buried under the rubble and submerged in a lake, Theseus would lie in peace in his tomb. Pearl looked up to the sky and, hoping he could hear her, told Theseus, "It's done. We did it."

*   *   *

When they reached the clearing surrounding Lightholme, they found the house still intact and ready for its master's return. Theseus's golems had ceased their patrol of the forest's edge and stood in silence to honor their fallen creator, or so Pearl wanted to believe. She knew Theseus's will had animated the golems, and without it, they would spend the rest of their existence where they stood when Theseus died. Time and the elements would grind away at them, yet they would remain there as long as the gems powering them remained intact. As much as Pearl respected Theseus and desired not to tamper with his creations, she pitied the golems and wouldn't allow them to waste their lives as statues. She closed her eyes and imagined being able to see the full structure of the spells surrounding the golems, like removing a clock's face to better see the gears.

322

She opened her eyes, and gazed upon the gems within the closest golem. The unseen tethers and connections of magic, a crystalline construct linking the golems, became visible to her. Components of the spells animating the golems and giving them purpose had been broken, receivers for Theseus's presence severed by his death. Pearl focused on and reshaped this part of the spell, eliminating the need for an external entity, so the golems animated each other. All four shook with life anew and, without any display of gratitude towards unsurprised Pearl, resumed their patrols. When Pearl reached the front door, she realized the Ghost Boy had stopped following her and waited just within the golems' marching path. "Do you not want to come inside?"

The Ghost Boy shrugged.

"Are you going back to the other Ghost People?" She asked. He shrugged again, looking at the bands on his body, then the forest, then the stars above him, and then back at Pearl. He searched for purpose, and Pearl had just the thing for him. A plan had brewed in her head since leaving the Black Hill and she would need his help. "Listen, Ghost Boy, there is something I have to do. Something that will leave me vulnerable and unable to protect myself. Until I wake up, will you stay with me as my protector? Will you be my knight in shining armor?"

He nodded with a smile, and followed her into the house. Nothing had changed since they'd left, unsurprising after two days. After giving the Ghost Boy a shortened version of the tour she had received, Pearl left him in her bedroom. The trying events of the day had exhausted his young body and he fell asleep before Pearl closed the door behind her. She tucked him into her bed and kissed him on his forehead, then made her way to the study.

Without a fire in the corner hearth, an invasive cold dominated the large room. The books on the shelves regarded Pearl as a stranger and the high ceiling tried to crush Pearl with its overwhelming height. Lightholme's upkeep fell to her, yet it remained Theseus's to Pearl. She sat in Theseus's chair at Theseus's desk, feeling like an intruder the whole time, and thought about Theseus and George Mallory. *What would they think of me now? Would they be proud?*

She pushed these questions out of her head before she dwelt on them too long, making room for the future plans preoccupying her mind. If the future Beatrice's warning bore any truth, Pearl would need to prepare for the coming of Homo maximus, 'the greatest man,' as it translated, the Fire of God feeding her knowledge of the dead language. With no idea how far in the future this would occur, she formulated a plan to occupy herself in the centuries that laid ahead.

Any activity that before would have strained her mind, body, or magic excited the Artifacts within her and threatened to destabilize their union. To keep them unified, she would need to do more than suppressing their influence with her; she would need to take control of them. She crossed her legs in the chair and prepared to enter a deep meditative trance, turning all of her attention inward to focus on gaining total dominance over the Artifacts. She expected this feat to take years until completion, putting her that much closer to the future of which Beatrice warned.

She pointed at the fireplace and snapped her fingers. The logs sitting within caught ablaze and almost at once, a wave of warmth crept across the room. Pearl took one last look around at the library, finding it more welcoming of her presence in the light. Settling into Theseus's chair and closing her eyes, Pearl found herself humming. Listening to the tune, she smiled and sang her mother's lullaby to put herself to sleep.

Good night, sleep tight.
Until the morning's light.
Rest your head on the pillow.
Your warm, comfy pillow.
Close your eyes.

325

So close your eyes tonight.
Good night. Sleep tight.
Now dream only of light.
Sweet dreams of joy, my dear.
Close your eyes now. I love you.
And always here for you.
Good night, sleep tight, sleep warm.

Epilogue

In her dreams, she was a bright moon, watching a strange planet from on high. Or at least a part of her became the moon. Before that, she had become the entirety of existence until she shattered and scattered on the celestial winds.

But the 'how' lacked importance. She would become a moon, watching over a planet like her own. She would bear witness as events unfolded beneath her. It started with so much promise, but a new generation burdened by old wounds searched for some way to prove they could exceed the expectations weighing upon them. And forbidden fruit tastes the sweetest, especially when laced with promises.

Everything soured and rotted black. A poison infected the whole tree, one fruit at a time. An old narrative spoiled. A twisted fairytale. A dark fantasy.

And she said, "The path was chosen of free will. Let time judge its worth."

THE END of "The Lamplighter"

Book 0 of *The Lamplighter Saga*

Part of *The Infinitum Cycle*

Pearl will return in Book 1 of The Lamplighter Saga:

"The Awakening"

Made in the USA
Middletown, DE
10 April 2019